I0763593

Till We are Ghost's

By: Holly Price

Till We Are Ghost's

Self-Published in 2025 by Holly Price

Cover design by: Holly Price

Edited and Formatted by: Samantha AdamsMcCord

ISBN: 979-8-9998460-9-9

Printed in USA

First Edition: September 2025

Table of Contents

DEDICATION PAGE

I want this page to signify those who have come into my life during this journey. I want those people to be recognized as the amazing people they are and for the positive impact that have had in helping me on my book adventure. I have done so many amazing things so far and with the help of my new friends I can accomplish so much more.

Thank you so much to this person for helping me out with everything. Samantha Adams McCord you're amazing. I appreciate everything you do for me. You're the best, best friend a person could ask for. You have helped me grow in ways I didn't think I could grow. It's thanks to you that I now have more confidence in writing my books. You give me your honest reactions when I read you a sneak peak of the book and it just brings so much joy to my heart knowing you truly love what I wrote.

Chapter One The Blossom of a Forbidden Love

The air in the Blackwood College library hung heavy with the scent of aged paper and forgotten dreams. Dust motes danced in the slivers of light piercing the gloom, illuminating the towering shelves packed with leather-bound volumes and forgotten times. It was a place of hushed whispers and stolen glances, a sanctuary for introspective souls seeking solace in the written word. Elara, lost in the labyrinthine corridors of a gothic novel, barely registered the presence of another student until a soft sigh broke the silence.

Lyra. That was the name that whispered itself into Elara's mind, a name as dark and alluring as the poetry she often found herself reciting under her breath. Lyra sat a few feet away, her head bent low over a book, her auburn hair cascading around her shoulders like a fiery waterfall. Elara, drawn by an inexplicable pull, found herself stealing furtive glances, captivated by the curve of Lyra's neck, the delicate grace of her fingers tracing the worn pages. There was an intensity about her, a brooding stillness that mirrored Elara's own inner turmoil.

Their eyes met across the vast expanse of the library's silent expanse. It wasn't a long gaze, just a fleeting collision of glances, but it sent a jolt of electricity through Elara. It was as though a hidden current had connected them, bridging the distance between two solitary souls. Lyra's gaze held a hint of apprehension, a shy uncertainty that resonated with Elara's own hesitant nature. A faint blush crept onto Lyra's cheeks, a fleeting rose blooming against the pale skin of her face. Elara felt her own heart quicken, a flutter of anticipation stirring within her.

Over the next few weeks, their encounters became more frequent, almost as if orchestrated by a silent, unseen hand. They'd find themselves gravitating towards the same quiet corners of the library, drawn together by an unseen magnetic force. Their conversations started with shared observations about the books they were reading, the dark poetry of Edgar Allan Poe, the brooding romances of the Brontë sisters, their words weaving a tapestry of shared passions and unspoken desires. They discovered a common love for gothic literature, a shared fascination with the shadowy world of mystery and suspense.

It was a bond built on shared secrets, whispered confidences exchanged in hushed tones, their voices barely audible above the soft rustle of turning pages.

One day, Elara found Lyra sketching in a worn notebook, the charcoal lines capturing the ethereal beauty of a moonlit graveyard. The image was haunting, capturing a mood that resonated deep within Elara's soul. They started sharing their artistic endeavors, their creations echoing the darkness and intensity of their growing bond. Lyra's drawings were intricate and detailed, her strokes bold and dramatic, portraying a world where beauty and darkness danced in an eternal waltz. Elara, in turn, shared her poetry, words that danced between light and shadow, reflecting the turmoil of emotions brewing within her heart.

Their friendship blossomed in secret corners, amidst the quiet hum of the library, a haven from the prying eyes of the outside world. Stolen moments turned into quiet conversations, lingering touches morphing into shy embraces.

They'd find secluded spots in the college gardens, their laughter mingling with the rustling of leaves, the perfume of wildflowers carried on the gentle breeze. In the dimly lit cafe near campus, their hushed confessions became increasingly intimate, revealing the vulnerability beneath the layers of their carefully constructed personas. Their bond grew stronger, deepening into something more profound, a connection that defied description, transcending the boundaries of friendship.

The library, their first meeting place, transformed into a symbol of their shared intimacy, a stage for their romance. The towering shelves, once a barrier between solitary souls, now became silent witnesses to their evolving relationship, each book a silent guardian of their growing love. The hushed whispers of the library became the soundtrack to their hidden romance, a constant hum of unspoken desires and budding passions. The scent of aged paper and forgotten dreams now carried the fragrance of their stolen kisses, their lingering touches, the quiet intensity of their shared moments.

The darkness that once held them captive now enveloped them in a world of their own making, a space where their love could flourish, hidden from the judging eyes of the world.

The unspoken tension between them crackled with barely contained passion. Their fingers would brush accidentally, sending shivers down their spines. A simple smile could electrify the air, making the world around them fade into a blur of insignificance. They understood each other without words, sensing unspoken emotions with an uncanny accuracy. Their shared love for the macabre, for stories that explored the darker aspects of human nature, was the foundation of their unconventional bond, a shared fascination that transcended simple interest. It was a language spoken in glances, in shared silences, in the knowing smiles that passed between them. It was a silent agreement, a pact formed in the shadows of the library, a promise of something more profound than mere friendship.

One evening, under the silver glow of a full moon, amidst the tranquil serenity of a secluded meadow, their unspoken feelings finally spilled forth. Words tumbled out, raw and honest, mirroring the intensity of their connection. Their confession was not a grand declaration, but a quiet unveiling of souls, a sharing of vulnerabilities that exposed the depth of their affection. Tears welled in their eyes, blurring the breathtaking landscape around them, each tear a testament to the profound emotional intensity of this pivotal moment. The stars seemed to bear witness to their love, their silent sentinels guarding the fragility of their newfound happiness.

The world outside their secluded meadow faded, replaced by the intimate landscape of their shared emotions. It was a world where fear and insecurities existed, but were overshadowed by the overwhelming joy of their mutual confession, a world where their love was no longer a whispered secret, but a vibrant bloom unfolding in the moonlight, a testament to their courage to embrace their unconventional connection.

It was the beginning, a fragile start to a passionate love story, a testament to the power of shared darkness and the unyielding strength of their nascent affection. The forbidden nature of their love only served to intensify the emotional current running between them, a constant reminder of the risks they were taking in embracing their shared feelings, a shared risk they were both willing to take.

The hushed intimacy of the Blackwood College library, once their sanctuary, felt increasingly confining. The weight of their unspoken desires pressed heavily upon them, a silent tension that thrummed between them with each shared glance, each accidental brush of hands. They needed a space beyond the watchful eyes of the library's silent patrons, a place where their burgeoning feelings could breathe freely, away from the suffocating pressure of secrecy.

One crisp autumn evening, they found themselves drawn to the sprawling park bordering the college grounds. The air was cool, carrying the scent of damp earth and decaying leaves.

The moon hung high in the sky, casting long, ethereal shadows that danced across the manicured lawns. They walked in companionable silence, the rustle of leaves beneath their feet the only sound accompanying their shared journey. The moonlit park, bathed in silvery light, felt like a secret garden, a private sanctuary where their whispered secrets wouldn't be carried on the wind.

It was there, beneath the ancient oak tree whose branches stretched towards the heavens like gnarled fingers, that their first real touch occurred. Elara, reaching for a fallen leaf, brushed her fingers against Lyra's. The contact sent a jolt of electricity through their bodies, a silent confirmation of the unspoken feelings that simmered beneath the surface of their friendship. They lingered there, hands clasped unknowingly, the moon their silent witness. The silence was not awkward or uncomfortable, but charged with unspoken emotions, a symphony of yearning and anticipation. It was a moment pregnant with unspoken promises, a silent understanding that transcended words.

Their stolen moments blossomed into a series of clandestine meetings. The dimly lit corner booth of a cozy café near campus became their haven, a place where their hushed conversations stretched late into the night. The café, with its low lighting and hushed ambiance, provided the perfect backdrop for the unfolding of their affections. They shared stories, dreams, fears, each confession drawing them closer, weaving a tapestry of shared intimacy. Their laughter mingled with the clinking of coffee cups, their silences filled with an unspoken language of understanding. The warm glow of the café's interior provided a contrast to the darker aspects of their shared fascination, a gentle counterpoint to the shadowed world they explored in their literature.

These were not grand declarations of love; they were quiet moments of shared vulnerability, soft confessions exchanged in hushed tones. It was in these quiet spaces, away from the judging eyes of the world, that their love bloomed, fragile and tender, yet powerful and unwavering in its intensity. Each meeting was a carefully constructed secret, a delicate dance around the edges of their forbidden desires.

They moved with a tentative grace, acutely aware of the risks they were taking, the potential consequences that loomed on the horizon.

But the risk was a necessary one. The intensity of their affection was undeniable, a fierce current that flowed between them, connecting them on a level that transcended words and actions. Their eyes, filled with a profound understanding, met across café tables, whispered promises exchanged in quiet corners, stolen kisses in the soft darkness of moonlit nights. It was a love born in shadow, nurtured in secret, a testament to the enduring power of the human heart to find connection even in the most unexpected of places.

The internal conflict raged within them, a constant tug-of-war between the intoxicating joy of their burgeoning love and the crushing weight of societal expectations. Elara, haunted by the possibility of rejection, wrestled with her fears, her heart pounding against her ribs like a trapped bird. Lyra, equally tormented, struggled to reconcile her desires with the ingrained prejudices of the world around her.

Their love was a forbidden fruit, sweet and alluring, yet dangerous and potentially devastating.

Their anxieties manifested in subtle ways. Elara found herself becoming more withdrawn, lost in her own thoughts, her usually vibrant spirit dimmed by the weight of her secret. Lyra, on the other hand, became increasingly erratic, her emotions fluctuating wildly between ecstatic joy and crippling fear. These internal struggles cast a shadow over their shared moments, adding an undercurrent of tension to their interactions. The lightness and spontaneity that characterized their early encounters were sometimes replaced by moments of hesitation and uncertainty. The stolen kisses became tinged with an awareness of the potential consequences, the whispered confessions laced with a hint of trepidation.

Yet, despite the fear and the internal conflict, their love continued to flourish. Their shared moments, however fraught with apprehension, were imbued with an intense beauty, a poignant tenderness that underscored the precarious nature of their relationship.

They found solace in each other's arms, a refuge from the storm raging within them. Their love was a beacon of hope in a world that threatened to tear them apart.

One evening, nestled in a secluded corner of the café, Elara confessed her deepest fear: the fear of losing Lyra. The words tumbled out, raw and unguarded, exposing the vulnerability that lay beneath her carefully constructed façade. Tears streamed down her face, a silent testament to the depth of her love. Lyra, her own eyes brimming with tears, held Elara close, offering the comfort and reassurance that only true love can provide. In that moment of shared vulnerability, their love transcended the fears and anxieties that had threatened to overwhelm them.

They embraced the forbidden nature of their love, acknowledging the risks and challenges ahead, but choosing to embrace the beauty and intensity of their shared feelings. Their love was not a secret to be hidden away; it was a flame to be nurtured, a precious thing to be cherished.

It was a love that defied convention, a testament to the human spirit's capacity to find joy and connection even in the face of adversity. The intensity of their feelings intensified with each passing day, their love a vibrant bloom pushing against the confines of societal expectations, a powerful testament to the undeniable strength of their forbidden connection. The world outside their private sanctuary might not understand, might even condemn, but their love, fragile and beautiful, existed in its own right, a testament to the enduring power of their shared affection.

The whispers in the library, the stolen glances across crowded hallways, the quiet conversations in dimly lit cafés - all these were stepping stones on their journey towards a love that was both dangerous and exquisite, a testament to the undeniable pull of their connection, a love that defied the constraints of the world around them. The unspoken tension, the clandestine meetings, the hushed confessions - each moment woven into the rich tapestry of their unfolding affection, a love story as intricate and beautiful as the gothic literature they both adored.

Their love was a rebellious act, a testament to the unwavering strength of their bond, a story yet to be fully written, a story that only time would tell. The journey, however perilous, was one they were both willing to embark on, hand in hand, their love a beacon guiding them through the darkness.

The late afternoon sun cast long shadows across the meadow, painting the wildflowers in hues of gold and crimson. A gentle breeze rustled through the tall grasses, carrying with it the sweet scent of honeysuckle and wild roses. Elara and Lyra lay nestled amongst the blossoms, a vibrant tapestry of color surrounding them. The air hummed with the buzz of bees and the chirping of crickets, a symphony of nature's orchestra playing softly in the background. It was a scene plucked from a fairytale, a perfect setting for the unfolding of a love that defied the ordinary.

Silence settled between them, a comfortable silence filled with unspoken understanding. The earlier anxieties, the internal struggles, seemed to fade into the background, replaced by a sense of peace and tranquility.

The weight of their shared secret, the fear of discovery, still lingered, a subtle undercurrent beneath the surface of their newfound serenity. But for now, in this idyllic haven, it was a weight they could bear, a burden lightened by the overwhelming joy that flooded their hearts.

Elara, her fingers tracing the delicate petals of a wild poppy, broke the silence. Her voice, barely a whisper, carried on the gentle breeze. "Lyra," she began, her gaze fixed on the wildflowers, avoiding Lyra's eyes. The simple utterance of Lyra's name held a depth of emotion, a silent acknowledgment of the journey they had undertaken, the unspoken feelings that had finally found their voice.

Lyra reached out, her hand gently covering Elara's. The contact sent a familiar jolt of electricity through their bodies, a silent confirmation of the bond that tied them together. "Yes, Elara?" she responded, her voice soft and tender, mirroring the gentleness of her touch.

Elara finally met Lyra's gaze, her eyes filled with a mixture of love, fear, and overwhelming vulnerability.

"I... I think I love you," she confessed, the words tumbling out in a rush, a torrent of emotions released after weeks of suppressed feelings. The confession hung in the air, delicate and fragile, yet imbued with a raw honesty that left no room for doubt.

The words hung between them, heavy with unspoken emotions. Lyra's breath hitched in her throat. She had anticipated this moment, dreamt of it, yet the reality of hearing Elara's confession, witnessing the raw emotion in her eyes, left her speechless. Tears welled up in her eyes, a silent testament to the depth of her own feelings.

Lyra leaned in, her lips brushing against Elara's ear. "I love you too, Elara," she whispered, the words a soft murmur against Elara's skin. It was a confession born not of spoken words alone, but of shared glances, stolen moments, and a silent understanding that had grown between them. It was a love forged in secrecy, nurtured in shadow, and now blossoming under the warm embrace of the afternoon sun.

The confession wasn't a grand, dramatic declaration, but a quiet, intimate acknowledgment of the profound love that had bloomed between them. It was a love that was fragile, vulnerable, yet powerful and unwavering in its intensity. It was a love that defied convention, challenged societal norms, and celebrated the unique bond they shared.

They embraced, their bodies intertwining amongst the wildflowers. The world around them faded away, leaving only the intense intimacy of their shared moment. It was a moment of pure, unadulterated joy, a testament to the enduring power of love to conquer fear and insecurity.

As they lay embraced, their emotions ebbed and flowed, a mixture of overwhelming joy, tender vulnerability, and a lingering apprehension about the future. The idyllic setting, the beauty of the natural world surrounding them, enhanced their emotional intimacy, creating a sanctuary where their love could flourish, free from the judgmental eyes of the world.

The meadow became their haven, a place where they could be themselves, free from pretense and societal expectations. They spent hours there, sharing stories, dreams, fears, and confessions. Each whispered word, each shared glance, deepened their connection, strengthening their bond. The meadow became a symbol of their love, a testament to their unwavering commitment to one another.

Their fears and insecurities, though present, felt less overwhelming. The act of confessing their love had brought them closer, erasing the subtle barriers that had previously separated them. They held each other, finding solace and comfort in each other's arms. The fear of rejection, of societal condemnation, still lingered, but it was overshadowed by the powerful force of their shared affection.

The sun began to dip below the horizon, casting long shadows across the meadow. The air grew cooler, carrying with it the scent of approaching twilight. As the sky transformed into a masterpiece of fiery oranges and deep purples, they knew it was time to return.

But the memory of their declaration of love, the raw emotion and profound intimacy they shared, would forever be etched into their hearts. The meadow, their secret sanctuary, held a piece of their souls, a constant reminder of their forbidden love. They left hand in hand, their steps light, their hearts filled with a love that was both fragile and enduring, a testament to the enduring strength of their shared bond. Their love story had just begun. The journey ahead would undoubtedly be challenging, fraught with obstacles, but they would face them together, their love a beacon of hope guiding them through the darkness.

Their love was a whispered secret, a forbidden bloom, blooming fiercely and beautifully against all odds, a declaration of love made in the heart of a wildflower meadow, forever etched in the tapestry of their lives.
The crisp white sheets of the hospital bed felt stark against Lyra's skin, a jarring contrast to the soft grasses of the meadow where their love had blossomed just days before. The air, thick with the sterile scent of antiseptic, was a world away from the sweet perfume of wildflowers. The silence, once a comfortable haven, now pressed down on them, heavy and suffocating.

The doctor's words, delivered with a detached professionalism that felt utterly devoid of empathy, echoed in Elara's mind, a cruel counterpoint to the joyful melody of their recent confession.

Lyra lay still, her eyes fixed on the ceiling, the vibrant color of her life seemingly leached away, replaced by a pallid pallor that mirrored the stark whiteness of her surroundings. Her breaths came shallow and uneven, each inhale a fragile gasp, each exhale a whisper of a life slipping away. The vibrant energy that had pulsed through her just days ago, the light in her eyes that had captivated Elara, had dimmed, replaced by a weary stillness. Elara's heart ached, a physical pain that mirrored the emotional devastation that threatened to consume her.

She reached out, her hand gently covering Lyra's, the familiar comfort of their touch a lifeline in this sea of despair. Lyra's hand, usually warm and alive, was cold, clammy, a stark reminder of the fragility of her life.

Elara's fingers tightened, a silent plea for strength, for hope, for anything that could stave off the encroaching darkness. But the cold reality of the diagnosis hung between them, an insurmountable chasm separating their idyllic world from the harsh realities of illness and mortality.

The news had struck Elara like a physical blow, an unexpected punch that knocked the wind from her lungs. Initially, disbelief had been her dominant emotion. It couldn't be true. Lyra, vibrant, passionate, full of life, couldn't be facing such a devastating prognosis. The doctor's clinical explanation, the medical jargon, washed over her, failing to penetrate the wall of denial she had built around her heart.

But the denial couldn't last. The stark reality of Lyra's weakening condition, the chilling certainty in the doctor's eyes, gradually chipped away at her defenses. The image of Lyra's pallid face, the exhaustion etched into her features, the way her breaths came in short, shallow gasps, shattered the fragile façade of disbelief.

The acceptance of her fate, slow and agonizing, was a journey through despair.

Tears streamed down Elara's face, hot and relentless, mirroring the storm raging inside her. The pain was a visceral, gut-wrenching agony, a combination of grief, fear, and the crushing weight of helplessness. She wanted to scream, to rage against the unfairness of it all, but the only sound that escaped her lips were choked sobs, muffled by her trembling hands.

Lyra's eyes, clouded with pain and weariness, met hers. There was no anger, no resentment, only a deep, abiding love that transcended the limitations of their earthly existence. In that gaze, Elara saw a reflection of her own despair, but also a quiet strength, a resilience that surprised and comforted her. It was a strength born not of denial, but of acceptance, a quiet understanding of mortality.

Lyra reached up, her touch feather-light, and traced a tear from Elara's cheek. "Don't cry, my love," she whispered, her voice barely audible, yet laced with an unexpected calmness. The strength in her voice, so fragile yet unwavering, stunned Elara. "We have time," Lyra continued, her eyes searching Elara's. "We have each other."

The words, simple yet profound, resonated within Elara, a beacon of hope in the encroaching darkness. "Time," she repeated, her voice hoarse with emotion. "How much time?"

Lyra hesitated, her gaze dropping to their intertwined hands. The silence that followed was heavy, laden with unspoken anxieties and the bitter knowledge of their limited time. The question hung unanswered, yet its implication weighed heavily upon them.

The sterile environment of the hospital room felt acutely oppressive, amplifying the despair and amplifying the fragility of Lyra's condition. Each ticking second seemed to echo their limited time, a constant reminder of the relentless march of time towards an inevitable end.

The once joyful simplicity of their love was now shadowed by the grim reality of death's inevitable approach.

Elara clung to Lyra, her body trembling, finding solace in the familiar comfort of their embrace. The fear, the pain, the overwhelming sense of loss, felt insurmountable. Yet, in Lyra's unwavering gaze, in the quiet strength of her words, Elara found a spark of resilience, a determination to cherish the remaining moments, to celebrate their love, however fleeting.

The days that followed were a blur of medical procedures, consultations, and the slow, agonizing decline of Lyra's health. Each day brought a new challenge, a new symptom, a new reminder of the inevitability of her fate. Yet, amidst the despair, there was a quiet, unwavering love that blossomed even in the shadow of death.

They spent their time in the small hospital room, sharing stories, reminiscing about their shared moments in the meadow, and whispering promises of eternal love that transcended the boundaries of life and death.

The meadow, once a symbol of their blossoming love, became a memory, a bittersweet reminder of their fleeting happiness. But the love that bloomed there, strong and defiant, refused to be extinguished, even as Lyra's life ebbed away. The sun-drenched meadow became a ghost in their minds, a vibrant and heartbreaking memory that existed in contrast to the sterile confines of the hospital room.

This stark contrast, the exquisite beauty of the memories versus the harsh clinical reality, only served to make their time together that much more precious, a testament to the impermanence of life, and the endurance of love. It was a love story told not in the gentle rustle of wildflowers and the song of the meadow, but in the sterile scent of antiseptic and the rhythmic beep of heart monitors, a testament to the enduring power of love in the face of mortality.

The stolen moments became monuments to the intensity of their shared love, each whispered word, each shared glance, a precious gem in the tapestry of their fading time.

It was a love that bloomed under the shadow of illness, a love defiant in the face of death, a love story written in the harsh realities of a hospital room, but forever etched in their hearts.

The rhythmic beep of the heart monitor became the soundtrack to their lives, a relentless percussion accompanying the slow, agonizing decline. Lyra's breaths grew shallower, her skin more translucent, her once vibrant eyes now clouded with a weary exhaustion. The meadow, once a vibrant tapestry of color and life, existed now only in their memories, a haunting reminder of a happiness that felt impossibly distant. The sterile scent of antiseptic, the harsh glare of the fluorescent lights, the constant hum of the hospital – these had become the new landscape of their love story, a stark and unrelenting backdrop to their dwindling time.

Elara's hands, perpetually cold from the chill of the hospital, never left Lyra's side. She traced the delicate veins on Lyra's wrists, her fingers lingering on the fading warmth of her skin, as if trying to imprint the memory of its touch onto her very being.

The once playful banter, the shared laughter that had filled their days, were now replaced by a heavy silence, broken only by the occasional whispered words of comfort, of love, of promises whispered into the suffocating silence of the hospital room. Sleep became a luxury they could rarely afford. Elara would often sit by Lyra's bedside, watching her breathe, her heart aching with each shallow gasp. The nights were the worst – the silence amplifying the fear that gnawed at her soul, the darkness mirroring the encroaching void that threatened to consume them both. She would hold Lyra close, whispering stories of their life together, trying to etch their memories into the fabric of their shared existence, as if to somehow make them eternal.

The nurses, initially detached and professional, began to soften, witnessing the unwavering devotion in Elara's eyes, the unspoken love that filled the small hospital room. They would offer words of comfort, a gentle touch, acknowledging the extraordinary bond between these two women, a bond that transcended the boundaries of mortality. Their compassion, though small, offered a flicker of warmth in the chilling reality of Lyra's fading life.

Lyra's pain intensified, her body wracked with discomfort. The medications dulled the edge, but couldn't extinguish the fire of suffering that consumed her. Elara would hold her, whispering soothing words, her touch a constant source of comfort in the relentless storm of Lyra's pain. She would read to her, her voice a soft melody against the backdrop of the mechanical beeping, reciting poetry, sharing stories, anything to distract Lyra from the relentless ache that consumed her. The simple act of reading became an offering, a testament to her enduring love.

One day, Lyra awoke with a clarity that surprised them both. The fog of pain momentarily lifted, revealing a radiant spark in her eyes, a sudden burst of energy that felt almost miraculous. She asked Elara to sing. Elara, her voice trembling, began to sing a simple melody, a song they had both loved, a song that spoke of love's enduring strength. Lyra's eyes closed, a small smile playing on her lips, a profound sense of peace replacing the pain. In that moment, surrounded by the sterile atmosphere of the hospital, they found a fragile peace, a shared moment of clarity amidst the overwhelming despair.

The fleeting moments of peace were few and far between. The decline continued, relentless and unforgiving. Each day brought a new challenge, a new symptom, a new wave of grief washing over them both. Elara found herself increasingly exhausted, the emotional toll of witnessing Lyra's suffering taking its toll. Yet, she persevered, fueled by an unwavering devotion, an intense love that defied the limitations of their circumstances.

The days blurred into weeks. Visits from friends and family became less frequent, replaced by the quiet solitude of their shared grief. Elara barely left Lyra's side. She slept in a chair beside the bed, her body aching, her mind consumed by a relentless fear. She fought back the tears, the overwhelming sense of helplessness, keeping her anguish hidden, her facade of strength a shield against the despair that threatened to overwhelm her. She would speak to Lyra, whispering words of love, sharing memories, her voice a lifeline in the encroaching darkness.

Lyra's decline was not a simple fading away; it was a brutal dance with death, a series of small victories and crushing defeats. There were moments of lucidity, punctuated by periods of agonizing pain and disorientation. Each lucid moment became a precious gem, an opportunity to reaffirm their love, to share precious memories, to whisper promises of a future they might not share. Each shared glance, each tender touch, held the weight of a lifetime of love, a poignant reminder of their fleeting time together.

As Lyra's strength ebbed, Elara's resolve grew stronger. She refused to give in to despair. She found solace in their shared memories, in the strength of their unwavering love. The meadow, though distant, remained a beacon of hope, a symbol of their enduring connection. The memories of wildflowers and sunlight provided a stark contrast to their bleak reality, but instead of intensifying the pain, it underscored the beauty and preciousness of their love story. It reminded her of the strength of their bond, a strength capable of carrying them through the darkest moments.

The image of the meadow, vivid and poignant, fueled her determination to honor their love, to cherish every remaining moment with the ferocity of a love that knew no bounds.

The last days were a blur of intense emotion. Lyra's breaths became ragged, her body frail, her spirit fading. Elara held her close, whispering words of love, her heart breaking with each passing moment. The sterile scent of the hospital room seemed to intensify, the rhythmic beep of the heart monitor a relentless countdown to an inevitable end. Yet, amidst the overwhelming grief, there was a profound sense of peace, a quiet understanding that their love, however short-lived, had been a testament to the enduring power of the human heart.

In Lyra's final moments, Elara held her hand, her tears falling silently onto the bedsheets, a testament to the immensity of her grief. Lyra's last breath was a whisper, a soft sigh that escaped her lips, leaving Elara enveloped in a profound silence, a silence heavy with the weight of loss, yet strangely peaceful, as if a part of her had flown away with Lyra, leaving behind only the enduring echo of a love that transcended the limitations of life and death.

The sterile environment of the hospital room felt empty, the silence amplifying the absence that left an unbearable ache in her heart. Yet, amidst the pain, a small spark of resilience flickered; the memory of their love, vibrant and strong, a testament to a love story written in the face of mortality, a love story etched in her heart, forever. The meadow would forever be a bittersweet memory, a symbol of their forbidden love and its tragically beautiful end.

Chapter Two The Crushing Weight of Grief

The rhythmic beeping ceased. It wasn't a dramatic silence, not a sudden, sharp cut, but a gentle fading, like the last embers of a dying fire. The air in the room, thick with the scent of antiseptic and the lingering sweetness of Lyra's favorite lavender lotion, seemed to hold its breath. Elara didn't move. Her hand, still clasped tightly in Lyra's, felt the chilling absence of warmth, the final relinquishing of life's fragile hold. The world around her dissolved into a blurry, indistinct haze, the harsh fluorescent lights blurring into an unforgiving glare. Time itself seemed to fracture, collapsing into an agonizing present where only the crushing weight of grief existed.

It wasn't immediate, this cataclysmic wave of sorrow. First, there was a numbness, a blankness that felt both terrifying and strangely comforting. A denial that refused to acknowledge the reality staring her in the face. Lyra's stillness was deceptive, a cruel mimicry of sleep. Any moment, Elara thought, her chest heaving with each choked breath, she would stir, her eyes would open, and the terrible silence would be replaced by the familiar rhythm of her breathing. She would speak, her voice a soft melody that would dispel this agonizing nightmare.

But the silence persisted, a suffocating blanket that wrapped around Elara, stealing her breath, constricting her chest. The denial crumbled, replaced by a surge of anger, a violent, irrational fury directed at the indifferent universe that had dared to steal her love. She clenched her fists, her knuckles white, her silent scream trapped within the confines of her aching heart. Why her? Why Lyra? The question echoed in the sterile silence, a painful refrain that played on repeat, a maddening torment that offered no solace, no explanation.

Then came the tears, a relentless torrent that washed over her, leaving her weak and trembling. They were not tears of simple sadness, but of a grief so profound, so all-consuming, that it threatened to obliterate her very being. Each tear was a testament to the immensity of her loss, a physical manifestation of the void Lyra's absence had left behind. The tears flowed, relentless and unceasing, a release of pent-up emotion that had been held captive by the relentless fear of the preceding weeks.

The nurses entered the room, their faces etched with a mixture of sympathy and professional detachment. They spoke in hushed tones, offering condolences that seemed hollow and inadequate in the face of her overwhelming pain. Their gentle touches, meant to comfort, felt intrusive, their words empty platitudes that failed to reach the depths of her despair. Elara barely registered their presence, lost in the labyrinth of her grief.

She remained frozen, her gaze fixed on Lyra's still form, her heart shattering into a million pieces.

The next few days were a blur of rituals – the hushed whispers of condolences, the impersonal efficiency of the funeral arrangements, the sympathetic yet distant faces of friends and family. Elara moved through it all in a trance, a ghost inhabiting a body ravaged by sorrow. The world continued its relentless march, oblivious to the chasm that had opened up in her life, a gaping void that threatened to consume her entirely. She felt detached, as if watching her life unfold from a distance, a spectator in her own tragedy.

The meadow, once a place of vibrant life and shared joy, became a haunted memory, a symbol of what had been stolen from her. The wildflowers, once bright and cheerful, now seemed muted, their colors dulled by the shadow of grief. The sunlight, once a source of warmth and comfort, now felt harsh and unforgiving. Everything was different, tainted by the bitter knowledge of Lyra's absence.

Sleep offered no escape. Nightmares plagued her, visions of Lyra fading away, her laughter dissolving into silence, her touch becoming increasingly distant. Each morning, she would wake up to an unbearable emptiness, a sense of profound desolation that clung to her like a second skin. The world felt muted, the colors drained, the sounds muted. Even the sounds of birdsong, once a source of comfort, now grated on her ears, a constant reminder of the vibrant world she could no longer fully appreciate.

The days turned into weeks, the weeks into months. The raw, agonizing pain gradually subsided, replaced by a chronic, aching emptiness. It wasn't the same, this newer grief. It wasn't the piercing stab of a freshly inflicted wound, but the dull ache of a deep-seated scar, a constant reminder of the irrevocable loss. The world continued, but Elara found herself increasingly isolated, adrift in a sea of grief. The vibrant tapestry of life had become a monochrome existence, devoid of joy, devoid of color.

The once-familiar comfort of their shared home now felt like a mausoleum, each object a stark reminder of Lyra's absence. The shared laughter, the whispered secrets, the intimate moments once filled with warmth and affection, became ghostly echoes, haunting memories of a life lived, a love now tragically lost. The scent of Lyra's favorite perfume, a once-comforting fragrance, became a relentless torment, a constant, sharp reminder of an irreplaceable presence now absent from her life.

Slowly, painstakingly, Elara began to rebuild her life, but it was a different life, a life forever marked by Lyra's absence. It was a life infused with a profound sadness, a constant undercurrent of sorrow, but also a life where she carried the memory of their love, like a precious, fragile flame, a testament to the enduring power of a love that knew no boundaries, a love that even death could not extinguish. It was a life filled with bittersweet memories, a life she had to navigate with a mixture of grief and enduring love.

The meadow, once a symbol of their forbidden love, was now a poignant reminder of their story, a bittersweet memory engraved into the tapestry of her heart, a story that, although ending tragically, would endure through time. The absence would forever be felt, but so would the love, a love that transcended death, a love that had been eternally etched in her heart.The apartment felt cavernous, the silence a physical entity pressing down on Elara. Lyra's absence was palpable, a gaping hole in the fabric of the space they had once shared. Each object - the worn armchair where they'd spent countless evenings lost in conversation, the half-finished painting on the easel, Lyra's scattered books, each holding a silent story of their shared life - was a cruel reminder of what she had lost. The scent of lavender, once a comforting aroma, now clung to the air like a phantom, a mournful ghost of Lyra's presence. It was a cruel mockery, a constant, aching reminder of the void that had been ripped into her world.

Days bled into nights, marked only by the relentless cycle of sleeplessness and the gnawing emptiness that refused to release its hold. Food became a tasteless chore, swallowed without pleasure, a mere function to maintain the barest minimum of physical existence. The city outside, usually a vibrant tapestry of life, now appeared grey and muted, reflecting the bleakness within her.

The bustling streets, the cheerful chatter, the vibrant colors of the market stalls – all seemed distant and unreal, belonging to a world she could no longer access. She existed in a parallel universe, a monochrome existence devoid of joy and light.

Elara's routine became a monotonous ritual. She would wake, dress in the same grey clothes, day after day, and sit by the window, staring at the city below, a passive observer of a world that no longer held any meaning for her. The hours stretched before her, empty and relentless. The television blared indifferently in the background, its mindless chatter a hollow echo in the vast emptiness of her apartment. She didn't engage, didn't try to connect, merely allowed the noise to fill the suffocating silence that clawed at her from within.

Attempts at connection felt futile, a shallow imitation of the genuine intimacy she had once shared with Lyra. Friends and family reached out, their kindness a well-intentioned gesture that failed to penetrate the impenetrable wall of grief that had enveloped her.

Their words of comfort, once reassuring, now sounded hollow, their presence intrusive, a constant reminder of the life she had lost. She retreated further into herself, isolating herself from the world, convinced that her pain was too profound, too personal to be understood or shared. Their sympathy only served to amplify her isolation, to underscore her solitude, the stark, chilling reality of her solitary existence.

The simple act of leaving the apartment felt like a monumental task. Each step out into the city was a struggle, a relentless battle against the crushing weight of her sorrow. The city, once a source of inspiration and adventure, now felt like a hostile entity, a cold, indifferent landscape that offered no refuge, no solace, no escape from the relentless torment that consumed her. The faces of strangers seemed blurred and indistinct, each interaction a pointless and meaningless exchange that served only to heighten her sense of disconnect. The constant hum of the city, the cacophony of noise, served only to amplify her profound isolation, accentuating the chasm between her and the world outside.

Sleep, when it came, was a torment. Nightmares plagued her, vivid and disturbing visions that played out the last moments of Lyra's life, replaying the agonizing details, re-experiencing the terror, the pain, the finality of her loss. She would wake in a cold sweat, her heart pounding, her body trembling, the memory of Lyra's fading breaths clinging to her, a painful echo in the quiet of the night. Even the brief moments of respite offered by sleep were tainted by sorrow, by the relentless, inescapable weight of her grief.

The lack of sleep intensified her despair. Dark circles formed under her eyes, deepening the hollows of her face, giving her a gaunt and haunted appearance. Her reflection in the mirror was a stranger to her, a pale imitation of the vibrant, joyful woman she once was. The mirror held only a reflection of her own grief, a testament to the devastating loss that had consumed her entirely.

The thought of therapy, of seeking professional help, felt impossible. The very idea of articulating her pain, of confessing the depth of her despair to a stranger, seemed like a betrayal of Lyra's memory.

To share her grief would be to acknowledge its existence, to give it form and substance, a process she felt completely unable to undergo. The pain felt too raw, too personal, too devastating to share with another soul.

The days stretched into weeks, the weeks into months, each passing moment an excruciating testament to her unrelenting sorrow. The once-vibrant tapestry of her life had been reduced to a monochrome existence. The vibrant colors of her existence had faded to a bleak grey, mirroring the emptiness that now consumed her, replacing the joy and laughter once so central to her being. Every aspect of her life, once filled with warmth, laughter, and love, now bore the chilling imprint of Lyra's absence, a stark and unforgettable reminder of her profound and devastating loss.

Elara found herself clinging to rituals, to habits, to anything that would offer even a momentary distraction from the all-consuming emptiness that threatened to engulf her. The simple act of making coffee each morning, the repetitive movements of washing dishes, the mechanical act of showering—these mundane tasks were her only anchors in the stormy sea of her grief.

One day, she stumbled upon Lyra's journal, tucked away in a forgotten corner of their bedroom. Its pages lay untouched, silent witnesses to a love story tragically cut short. As Elara ran her fingers over the worn cover, she felt a pang of longing so intense it made her gasp. Each entry, penned in Lyra's familiar handwriting, was a painful yet precious reminder of the vibrant love they had shared, a love that even death couldn't diminish.

She opened the journal and began to read, allowing herself to immerse in the words that flowed from Lyra's heart, words that spoke of dreams, aspirations, of a love that defied logic and expectation, words that spoke of a bond that stretched beyond time and space, words that reflected a love that transcended everything.

Slowly, carefully, she began to relive the moments, the adventures, the profound connection that had defined their relationship.

Through Lyra's words, Elara began to remember the joy they had shared, the laughter they had exchanged, the quiet moments of intimacy that formed the bedrock of their love story. It was a painful, heart-wrenching process, but it was also a process of healing, a gradual acceptance of the irreplaceable nature of their loss. Each entry in the journal was a precious shard of memory, a reminder of the unbreakable bond they had shared, a testament to a love that even death couldn't erase.

As she turned the pages of the journal, reading Lyra's words, Elara began a slow, gradual descent into the depths of her memory. There, in the recesses of her mind, she found an assortment of moments, sights, smells, sounds that painted a vivid image of her life with Lyra. These were not just memories, but living, breathing parts of her that had been stifled by her grief. Gradually, Elara found herself able to retrace her steps, to relive her emotions, to engage with the essence of her feelings.

The images were vivid, the emotions potent, and she felt the depth of her connection with Lyra more strongly than ever.

Her solitude, her isolation, her depression – these were the tools of her grief, but they were also the gateways to the eventual acceptance of what she had lost and what she still had to live for. It was a long and torturous process, marked by moments of intense pain, of unbearable loneliness, and yet punctuated by the quiet moments of acceptance, of healing, and of reconciliation with her grief. It was a testament to the enduring power of love, a love that transcended death, a love that had etched itself deeply into the fabric of her very being.

The scent of woodsmoke and roasted chestnuts, a scent that always clung to Lyra's woolen scarf, suddenly filled Elara's senses, conjuring a vivid image of a crisp autumn evening. They were huddled together, laughing, on a park bench, watching children chase fallen leaves. Lyra's hair, the color of burnt cinnamon, was tumbling around her shoulders, catching the last rays of the setting sun.

Elara could almost feel the warmth of Lyra's hand nestled in hers, the comforting weight of her body pressed against hers. The memory was so intense, so real, that she could almost taste the sweetness of the chestnuts they shared. But the sweetness quickly turned to ash in her mouth, the warmth of the memory dissolving into the icy chill of her current reality. The vibrant colors of the autumn scene faded, leaving behind only the stark, grey emptiness of her apartment.

A wave of nausea washed over her, the bittersweet nostalgia morphing into a sharp, agonizing pang of loss. She closed her eyes, trying to hold onto the fading image, to recapture the warmth of Lyra's presence, but the memory slipped away like sand through her fingers, leaving behind only the hollow ache in her chest. The laughter, the warmth, the shared intimacy – it all felt impossibly distant, a beautiful dream from a life that no longer existed.

Another memory surfaced – the sound of Lyra's laughter echoing through their tiny kitchen as they attempted to bake a disastrous chocolate cake. Flour dusted their clothes, their faces smeared with chocolate, their eyes shining with mischievous glee. The kitchen, usually a source of quiet domesticity, had become a battleground of playful chaos, their laughter filling the cramped space. The aroma of burnt sugar and chocolate, a testament to their culinary ineptitude, hung heavy in the air, a poignant reminder of their shared imperfections and their boundless love. But now, the joyful chaos felt like a cruel mockery, the aroma a painful reminder of a happiness she could never recapture.

Then came the memory of a silent sunrise on a remote beach. They were wrapped in each other's arms, watching the first rays of dawn paint the sky with hues of orange and pink. The air was filled with the salty tang of the sea, the gentle rhythm of the waves a soothing lullaby. Lyra's head rested on her shoulder, her breath warm against her neck. The stillness, the intimacy, the shared peace – it was a moment etched forever in Elara's memory, a precious jewel amidst the ruins of her grief.

But the beauty of the sunrise was overshadowed by the darkness of her present reality, the vibrant colours of the memory a stark contrast to the grey, monotonous landscape of her grief.

These memories, once sources of joy and comfort, now became weapons of self-torment. Each cherished moment was a painful reminder of what she had lost, a constant replay of the vibrant, joyful life that had been so cruelly snatched away. The intensity of these recollections only served to deepen the chasm of her sorrow, to underscore the unbearable weight of her loss. The happiness she once knew felt like a phantom limb, a constant, aching reminder of a life that was forever beyond her reach.

She spent hours poring over photographs, each image a bittersweet reminder of their shared life. Lyra's radiant smile, their arms intertwined, their laughter echoing silently in the stillness of her apartment – each photograph was a microcosm of their love story, a testament to the depth and intensity of their connection.

But the photographs also served as a constant reminder of the finality of Lyra's death, the irreparable breach in her life, the unfillable void in her heart. The vibrant colours of the past seemed to mock her present desolation, the happiness captured in each frame a stark contrast to the greyness that now dominated her world.

One picture in particular, haunted her. It showed them standing on a mountaintop, the wind whipping through their hair, their faces lit up with exhilaration. Lyra's eyes, bright with laughter, held a spark of wild, untamed joy. Elara remembered the feeling of the wind, the cold air biting at her skin, the breathtaking vista that stretched out before them. They had felt invincible then, their love an unbreakable shield against the storms of life. But the invincibility was an illusion, the shield had shattered, leaving Elara exposed to the harsh realities of grief, her own vulnerability laid bare.

The contrast between the vibrancy of their shared past and the bleakness of her present was unbearable. The mountaintop, once a symbol of their shared dreams and aspirations, now stood as a monument to her loss, a stark reminder of the joy she could never recapture. The photograph, once a source of happiness, became a constant source of pain, a testament to the devastating impact of Lyra's death.

Elara found herself revisiting these memories repeatedly, replaying them in her mind, dissecting them, searching for clues, for explanations, for some way to make sense of her loss. The intensity of her grief was a whirlwind, a maelstrom of emotions - pain, anger, despair, guilt, regret - all swirling together in a chaotic vortex that threatened to consume her entirely. Each memory was a new wound, each recollection a painful reminder of the irreplaceable nature of her loss.

Yet, amidst the pain, there was a glimmer of something else – a slow, gradual recognition that even in the depths of her despair, the love she shared with Lyra had not diminished. The memories, though painful, were also a testament to the depth and beauty of their relationship. They were a reminder of the joy they had experienced together, of the love that had bound them together, a love that even death could not erase. It was a subtle shift, a faint flicker of hope in the overwhelming darkness of her grief, a quiet affirmation of the enduring power of love in the face of death. It was a beginning, however tentative, on the long, arduous road to healing.

The flickering gaslight cast long, dancing shadows across the walls of her apartment, mimicking the frantic rhythm of her own heartbeat. Elara sat on the worn, wooden floor, clutching a chipped mug of lukewarm tea, its contents long forgotten. The silence was oppressive, a suffocating blanket woven from grief and despair. The memories, once a source of solace, now felt like relentless tormentors, each one a fresh stab to her already wounded heart. The photographs, the scents, the sounds – they were all sharp, agonizing reminders of Lyra's absence, a constant assault on her already fragile sanity.

She traced the outline of a faded photograph, her finger lingering on Lyra's smiling face. Lyra, vibrant and alive, a stark contrast to the greyness that had settled over Elara's world. The image felt like a cruel joke, a mocking reminder of the happiness she could never experience again. A wave of nausea washed over her, the familiar sting of grief tightening its grip around her chest. The air felt thick, heavy, as if the very room was suffocating her.

A cold, calculating voice, born from the depths of her despair, began to whisper insidious suggestions. It painted a picture of reunion, a release from the unbearable agony of her loss. It promised an end to the relentless pain, an escape from the crushing weight of grief.
It spoke of a place where Lyra was waiting, where the pain would cease, where they could be together once more, forever untouched by the cruel realities of this world.

The thought, initially repulsive, began to take root, its tendrils wrapping around her heart, squeezing the life out of her hope. It was a seductive whisper, a siren's call promising a haven from the storm. Logic, reason, even the faint glimmer of hope she had discovered, were drowned out by the deafening roar of her despair.

Elara's mind raced, dissecting the idea, examining it from every angle. She considered the practical aspects - the method, the timing, the aftermath. The gruesome details were strangely detached, clinically observed, as if she were a detached observer studying a scientific experiment, rather than the subject. The cold logic of her plan was frightening, the ease with which the details unfolded a stark testament to her utter desolation. She felt a chilling sense of calm, a disturbing serenity that bordered on numbness. The pain had become so acute, so overwhelming, that oblivion seemed preferable to its unrelenting torment.

The concept of suicide wasn't a spontaneous act of desperation; it was a meticulously planned escape, a carefully considered solution to a problem she couldn't solve. It was a rational, almost logical choice within the confines of her grief-stricken mind. She wasn't embracing death with reckless abandon; rather, she was succumbing to it as a gentle release, a welcoming embrace after months of brutal torment. This wasn't a cry for help, but a quiet surrender, an acceptance of defeat in the face of an enemy she couldn't conquer.

She thought about her family, her friends. The guilt, sharp and piercing, momentarily threatened to shatter the calm she had painstakingly constructed. Images of their faces flashed before her eyes – their worried expressions, their tear-stained cheeks, their desperate pleas. She imagined their grief, compounded by the knowledge that she had willingly chosen this path. The guilt was a heavy burden, but it was overshadowed by the overwhelming desire for reunion with Lyra.

The thought of Lyra's gentle touch, her warm embrace, her reassuring smile, became a powerful motivator. The imagined reunion fueled her decision, offering solace and a glimpse of the peace that had eluded her for so long. This wasn't an act of self-destruction, but a desperate attempt to reunite with the only person who truly understood her, the only person who could offer her comfort and solace. It was an act of love, albeit a misguided, tragically flawed one, born from the depths of her unbearable grief.

Her mind replayed countless memories – Lyra's laughter, her touch, the warmth of their shared moments. Each memory was a dagger, twisting in her heart, yet simultaneously a source of comfort, a reminder of the bond that transcended life and death. She clung to those memories, finding a strange solace in their painful beauty, a testament to the enduring power of their love. They were the fuel that drove her decision, the justification for her desperate attempt at reunion, her tragic quest to find peace in a world that had become irrevocably broken.

Hours passed, each one blurring into the next. The gaslight sputtered and died, plunging the room into darkness, a mirror of the void within her soul. She remained seated, motionless, a prisoner of her own mind, wrestling with the weight of her decision, the enormity of her choice. The rational part of her brain fought a losing battle against the overwhelming tide of despair, the quiet surrender to oblivion slowly eclipsing all other thoughts and emotions.

The darkness was complete, a stark contrast to the kaleidoscope of memories that continued to flood her thoughts. These memories weren't just painful reminders of what she had lost; they were also a map, guiding her toward her final decision, a path toward the only imagined solace - a reunion with Lyra, beyond the confines of this world, beyond the crushing weight of her grief.

This wasn't a rash decision, but a carefully considered choice, weighed against the unbearable weight of her sorrow. It was the culmination of months of agonizing pain, a desperate attempt to escape the relentless torment, to find peace in the arms of her beloved.

It was a choice made in the darkness, born from despair, fueled by love, and ultimately, a testament to the devastating power of grief. The decision was made, the plan set in motion, a final, tragic act of love and surrender. The gaslight, finally extinguished, left Elara in absolute darkness, a fitting reflection of the void that had consumed her. She sat, unmoving, the chill of the concrete seeping into her bones, a physical manifestation of the icy grip of despair. Yet, strangely, a calm had settled over her, an unnerving tranquility that was far removed from the tempest that had raged within her for months. This wasn't a cessation of pain, but rather its transformation into a dull, persistent ache, a constant hum beneath the surface of her numb acceptance.

The darkness was a comfort, a shroud protecting her from the intrusive memories that had relentlessly haunted her waking hours. But in the quiet, the echoes of those memories still persisted, not as sharp, piercing stabs, but as soft whispers, a melancholic soundtrack to her final preparations. She moved with a deliberate slowness, each action imbued with a quiet dignity, a poignant acceptance of her fate.

First, she rose, her limbs stiff from prolonged stillness, and went to the window. The city below was a blur of muted lights, a sea of indifference to her private tragedy. She traced the faint outline of the cityscape with a trembling finger, a fleeting moment of connection to the world she was leaving behind. But there was no regret, no lingering wish for a different outcome. Only a profound sadness, a heavy resignation that settled deep within her soul.

She returned to the center of the room, moving with a strange grace, a practiced elegance that belied the turmoil within. She began to systematically organize her belongings, a ritualistic act of closure. Each item was handled with care, a silent farewell to the objects that had witnessed her life with Lyra. A worn copy of their favorite poetry book, its pages dog-eared and marked with annotations in Lyra's familiar handwriting, was placed carefully on the mantelpiece. A collection of dried flowers, pressed and framed, a testament to their shared love for nature, was arranged precisely on the small table near the window.

Each action felt deliberate, almost ceremonial. It wasn't merely cleaning; it was an orchestration of farewells, a meticulous arrangement of memories, a testament to the careful consideration she had given to her final act. The apartment, usually a haven of chaos and comfort, was now meticulously organized, reflecting the order she was imposing on her final moments. The transformation was stark, the apartment mirroring the newfound calm that had taken hold within her. It was a testament to the control she was exercising over her own demise, a stark counterpoint to the uncontrollable grief that had consumed her for so long.

She selected a simple, dark dress from her wardrobe, the fabric soft against her skin, a stark contrast to the rough concrete floor she'd been sitting on. It was a dress Lyra had loved, a dress that held memories of laughter and shared dreams. Putting it on, she felt a strange sense of peace. It wasn't a morbid anticipation, but a quiet acceptance, a subtle affirmation of her decision.

She wrote a letter, not a desperate plea for help, but a quiet explanation, a tender farewell to those she was leaving behind. Her words flowed effortlessly, expressing her love, her sorrow, and her ultimate acceptance of the path she had chosen. The letter was a testament to her courage, a final act of care, a gift of closure for those who would grieve her loss. There were no accusations, no blame, just a quiet understanding, a tender acknowledgment of her profound love for Lyra, a love that had ultimately led her to this decision.

Her next actions were more difficult, tinged with a deeper sadness. She carefully gathered Lyra's belongings, the mementos of their life together. Lyra's favorite scarf, a soft, woolen creation, was wrapped gently around a small, framed photograph of them together. Her favorite book, its spine slightly worn from years of use, was placed next to the photograph. These items, symbols of their shared history, were now being prepared for a final journey, a journey beyond the boundaries of their earthly existence.

The final hours passed in a somber quietude. The apartment, transformed into a sanctuary of remembrance, reflected the serenity she had found within herself. It was a place of peace, a space free from the turmoil of grief, a stage set for her final act. There was no frantic energy, no last-minute regrets. Just a quiet acceptance of the inevitable, a serene resignation in the face of death.

She looked at her reflection in the mirror, her face pale but composed. There were no tears, no visible signs of emotional turmoil. Only a quiet stillness, a deep-seated tranquility that belied the depth of her sorrow. It wasn't an absence of feeling, but a transcendence of it, a conscious choice to find peace in the face of overwhelming despair. She had chosen her path, and she was proceeding with a quiet dignity, a deep respect for her own decision. This wasn't a surrender to despair, but a deliberate act of love, a tragic quest for reunion, a final farewell to a world that had become unbearably painful.

The cold seeped into her bones as she finished her preparations. It mirrored the icy grip of despair that had held her captive for so long. She'd braced herself for the chill, for the numbness that would soon accompany the finality of her choice. But strangely, the cold felt like a solace, a comfort in its stark indifference.
It was a detachment, a separation from the searing pain of grief, a gradual immersion into the peaceful stillness of the coming oblivion.

The silence was profound, broken only by the faint ticking of a clock, a relentless reminder of the time slipping away. Yet, she felt no urgency, no rush. She had surrendered to the inevitable, accepting her fate with a quiet dignity that defied her despair. The darkness embraced her, the silence swaddled her, and in that moment, she found a strange serenity, a quiet acceptance of her tragic destiny. It was a peaceful surrender, a quiet goodbye to a world that had shattered her heart, a final embrace of the darkness that promised reunion with the one she loved beyond measure.

Her final act, meticulously planned, was an act of love, a desperate attempt at reunion, a testament to the devastating power of grief and the seductive allure of oblivion. The stage was set; the curtain was about to fall.

Chapter Three Beyond the Veil

The chill intensified, a creeping frost that invaded not just her skin but her very being. It wasn't the physical cold of the apartment, but something deeper, something that seeped into her soul, a mirroring of the icy grip of despair that had held her captive for so long. Yet, paradoxically, this chilling embrace brought a sense of calm, a release from the searing pain that had consumed her. It was as if the cold was washing away the remnants of her grief, leaving behind a quiet emptiness, a space for something new to emerge.

Then, a change. It wasn't a sudden shift, but a gradual unfolding, like a slow sunrise breaking through a dense fog. The darkness that had surrounded her began to thin, to soften at the edges. It wasn't replaced by light, not in the way she understood light, but by something akin to luminescence, an inner glow that emanated from within her, a soft, ethereal radiance that dispelled the oppressive darkness.

She felt herself dissolving, not in a painful way, but in a way that felt almost like melting. Her body, once a vessel of intense sorrow, was becoming fluid, her physical form losing its rigidity, softening into something intangible. It was a strange sensation, liberating and unsettling all at once. She was untethered, unburdened by the weight of her physical existence.

The boundaries of her body blurred, dissolving into the surrounding darkness, which in turn was dissolving into something far more profound, more encompassing.

The sounds of the city faded, replaced by a symphony of whispers, a chorus of unseen voices humming a song of release and transformation. The whispers were not words in any language she knew, but vibrations, feelings, echoes of emotions that resonated deep within her soul. It was a comforting sound, a lullaby that soothed her anxieties, a hymn of acceptance and transition.

Her senses, dulled by grief, sharpened, becoming hyper-aware. The subtle shifts in the surrounding luminescence were now perceptible as a shimmering cascade of colors, impossible hues that defied earthly description. It was a visual feast, a kaleidoscopic display that danced and flowed around her, a testament to the limitless possibilities of this new realm.

The air, once cold and oppressive, was now filled with a gentle warmth, not the familiar heat of a fire or the sun, but a warmth that emanated from within her, from the very essence of her being. It was a comforting embrace, a gentle hand guiding her through the transition, a sense of nurturing energy that eased her fears.

Smells, too, were intensified. Not the familiar scents of her apartment, but ethereal fragrances, the scents of distant lands, of ancient forests, of blooming flowers that never existed on earth. It was a heady mixture, a symphony of aromas that evoked emotions far removed from her earthly experiences. The scents were infused with a profound sense of peace and serenity, a balm for her wounded soul.

Even the taste of the air changed. It wasn't a taste in the conventional sense, but a sensation, a perception, a feeling of exquisite sweetness, of pure energy, of life force that seemed to penetrate her being, filling her with an inexplicable joy. It was the taste of freedom, the taste of release, the taste of rebirth.

And then, there was touch. Not a physical touch, but a sensation of gentle pressure, of soft caresses, of loving embrace. She felt enveloped in a comforting presence, a nurturing energy that reassured her, that guided her, that loved her. It was a touch that transcended the physical, a touch that reached into her soul, mending her wounds, repairing her broken heart.

As she continued her journey, the world around her started shifting, morphing and changing. The colours intensified, the whispers evolved into a melodious chorus, the fragrances became even more intricate. It was a constant state of flux, a dynamic landscape that shifted and changed with her perception, a realm of infinite possibility where reality was fluid and malleable.

She sensed a presence, not a person exactly, but an essence, a consciousness that was both ancient and new, wise and compassionate. It emanated an aura of unconditional love, acceptance, and understanding. This presence offered her no words of comfort, no explanations or justifications. Instead, it simply held her, cradling her gently as she navigated this strange, new realm. It was a presence that validated her journey, her pain, her loss, and her choices.

Time, as she understood it, ceased to exist. There was no past, no future, only a timeless present, a moment of pure being, a state of complete immersion in this ethereal landscape. She was free from the constraints of time and space, unburdened by earthly limitations. The weight of her grief, the burden of her past, began to fade, replaced by an overwhelming sense of peace and contentment.

This new state was a paradox—a profound emptiness filled with indescribable richness. It was a void that resonated with infinite possibility, a silent symphony echoing with boundless energy and serene beauty. It wasn't the nothingness she had anticipated, but a plenitude that surpassed all earthly comprehension.

The transition wasn't an arrival at a destination but a metamorphosis, a profound and continuous shift of her very essence. She was becoming something new, something beyond her earthly comprehension. It was a journey into the unknown, yet it held no fear, only a sense of wondrous anticipation, a sense of homecoming.

The luminescence intensified, encompassing her completely, dissolving the last remnants of her physical form. She felt a surge of energy, a wave of pure joy, a sensation of complete liberation, of utter freedom. It was not merely the end of her life, but the beginning of something far more profound, more magnificent, more utterly beyond her previous comprehension.

Lyra. The name echoed in her mind, not as a memory but as a feeling, a vibrant presence that pulsed with warmth and love. She felt a connection, a resonance, a recognition that transcended the boundaries of life and death. Lyra wasn't lost, but waiting, her essence resonating with the vibrant energies that surrounded Elara in this new ethereal space. The reunion, so desperately sought in life, was finally within reach. The darkness that had once been a symbol of despair was now a gateway, an opening to a realm of infinite love and boundless possibility, a realm where she could finally be with Lyra, not in the limited form of her mortal existence, but in a union as boundless and eternal as the space around her.

And in that moment of absolute, ethereal peace, Elara finally understood: death wasn't an ending, but a transformation, a transition, a homecoming. The veil had parted, and she was home.The luminescence intensified, no longer a gentle glow but a radiant, incandescent light that enveloped Elara completely. It wasn't blinding, but rather a soothing warmth that permeated her being, dissolving the last vestiges of her physical form. She felt herself expanding, not in a physical sense, but in a way that transcended the limitations of her body. She was becoming boundless, limitless, a part of the very fabric of this ethereal realm.

The whispers, once a subtle hum, coalesced into a melodious chorus, a symphony of celestial voices that sang a song of peace and acceptance. The music was not merely sound, but a vibration that resonated deep within her soul, cleansing her of the lingering pain and sorrow. Each note was a balm, soothing her wounds, mending her broken heart. The melody shifted and changed, adapting to her emotional state, offering solace and comfort in its ethereal embrace.

The kaleidoscopic display of colors intensified, a breathtaking spectacle of impossible hues that shifted and flowed like a living, breathing artwork. There were shades of amethyst so deep they seemed to hold the secrets of the universe, and emeralds so vibrant they radiated an inner light. Scarlet and gold danced together in a breathtaking ballet, while sapphire and pearl created a mesmerizing blend of serenity and majesty. It was a visual feast that overwhelmed her senses, a testament to the boundless creativity of this otherworldly realm.

The fragrances, once subtle, now overwhelmed her, a heady mixture of intoxicating scents that evoked a myriad of emotions. There were the delicate perfumes of unknown flowers, sweet and intoxicating, that filled her with a sense of blissful serenity. Then came the earthy scents of ancient forests, rich and musky, that grounded her in the immensity of this new reality. And finally, there was a subtle hint of spice, a warmth that hinted at the infinite possibilities that lay ahead. Each scent was a story, a memory, a feeling, woven together to create a tapestry of olfactory sensations that both soothed and exhilarated her.

As Elara continued her journey through this ethereal landscape, she noticed the landscape itself began to change, morphing and shifting in response to her thoughts and emotions. Sometimes, she found herself surrounded by rolling hills of shimmering light, the grass a vibrant emerald that sparkled with an inner radiance.

At other times, she was enveloped by vast, star-studded skies, the constellations shifting and changing in a mesmerizing celestial dance. The landscape was fluid, dynamic, a mirror reflecting her inner world.

The sense of touch, too, was amplified. It wasn't the familiar touch of skin on skin, but a sensation of pure energy, a gentle caress that enveloped her in a loving embrace. It was a nurturing touch, a comforting presence that reassured her, guiding her through this unfamiliar landscape. She felt held, supported, cherished, and loved unconditionally. This wasn't merely a physical sensation but a deep spiritual connection, a feeling of belonging that transcended the limitations of the physical world.

She sensed a presence, but not a defined entity. It wasn't a person, or an angel, or a god, but something far more profound – a consciousness, an energy, a boundless love that permeated everything. This presence didn't speak, but it communicated. Its silence was more eloquent than words, conveying an understanding, an acceptance, a profound empathy that resonated deep within Elara's soul. It was a validation of her journey, her pain, her grief, her love for Lyra. It was a silent assurance that she was home.

Time, as she had known it, was meaningless here. There was no past, no future, only an eternal present. Each moment stretched and expanded, allowing her to fully immerse herself in the beauty and wonder of this ethereal realm. She was free from the constraints of the earthly world, unburdened by the weight of time, the burden of memories, the shackles of earthly limitations.

And then, she saw her.

Lyra.

Not as a ghost, or a specter, but as a vibrant, radiant being of pure energy, her essence glowing with an ethereal light that rivaled the brilliance of the surrounding landscape. Lyra was beautiful, not in the conventional sense, but in a way that transcended physical beauty, a beauty that emanated from her very being, a radiant expression of love and joy. She was everything Elara had longed for, everything she had lost, and now, everything she had found again.

There were no words exchanged, no explanations needed. Their reunion was a silent symphony, a merging of two souls that had been separated by the veil of death but reunited in this boundless expanse of love and light. It was a recognition, a connection that transcended the limitations of life and death, a bond that had been forged in life and now solidified in eternity.

The emptiness that had once consumed Elara was now filled with an indescribable richness, a plenitude of love and joy that surpassed any earthly experience.

Lyra moved towards her, and Elara felt a surge of pure joy, a feeling of completeness that she had never known before. It wasn't merely happiness, but a state of being, a blissful union of two souls, a merging of two spirits that had been inextricably linked since the beginning of time. The grief that had haunted her for so long finally released its hold, dissolving into the radiant light of this ethereal realm.

In this realm, there was no sorrow, no pain, only an eternal peace. The cold that had once gripped her heart was replaced by a warmth that radiated from the very core of her being, a love that was boundless, eternal, and unconditional. She was home. She was whole. She was with Lyra.

The ethereal landscape shifted around them, changing and morphing to reflect their joy, their love, their union. Sometimes, they were surrounded by a field of luminous flowers, their petals shimmering with an inner light that cast a spellbinding glow. Other times, they found themselves soaring through the star-studded skies, the constellations swirling around them in a dazzling display of cosmic beauty. The landscape was a reflection of their inner world, a testament to the boundless love that united them.

Their reunion wasn't a mere meeting, but a merging, a becoming one. They weren't two separate entities, but a single, unified consciousness, a radiant expression of love and light. They danced in the shimmering light, their laughter echoing through the ethereal landscape, a song of joy that resonated through eternity. This was their home, their sanctuary, a place of eternal peace and boundless love, a place where their journey together would never end. The veil had parted, and they were finally together, beyond the boundaries of life and death, in a realm where their love would forever flourish. This was their forever. This was home.

The luminous flowers surrounding them pulsed with a gentle rhythm, their petals unfurling and closing in a slow, hypnotic dance. Each bloom was a kaleidoscope of colors, shifting and changing with the subtle movements of the ethereal breeze. Amethyst, emerald, sapphire, ruby - hues beyond earthly comprehension - blended and swirled, creating a breathtaking spectacle that mirrored the kaleidoscope of emotions swirling within Elara's heart. She reached out a hand, her fingers brushing against a petal, and felt a surge of warmth, a comforting energy that flowed into her being, soothing the last vestiges of her earthly grief.

Lyra smiled, a radiant expression that lit up the entire landscape. It wasn't a simple smile, but a reflection of the profound connection they shared, a silent communication that transcended the need for words. Her eyes, pools of shimmering light, held a depth of understanding that resonated deep within Elara's soul. They were eyes that had witnessed loss, pain, and the agonizing separation of death, but now shone with a joy that was both overwhelming and profoundly comforting.

Elara moved closer, drawn to Lyra as a moth is drawn to a flame. She felt a pull, a magnetic force that drew their essences together, a silent affirmation of their enduring bond. There were no awkward silences, no hesitant approaches. Their reunion was a seamless continuation of their love, a testament to the strength of a connection that transcended the physical realm.

As Elara reached Lyra, she felt a wave of warmth wash over her, a feeling of homecoming so profound it brought tears to her eyes. These weren't tears of sorrow, but tears of relief, of joy, of complete and utter fulfillment. She had found her peace, her solace, her forever in Lyra's embrace.

The embrace itself was not merely physical; it was a merging of souls, a union of two beings who were now inextricably linked in a way that defied the limitations of life and death. It was a silent exchange of love, a comfort that seeped into the deepest recesses of their beings, healing the wounds that had been inflicted by loss and grief. In this embrace, there was no need for words, for explanations, or for apologies. Their silence spoke volumes, a symphony of unspoken emotions that resonated with a power greater than any spoken language.

Time, as Elara had known it, ceased to exist. There was only the present moment, an eternity spent in the loving embrace of the woman she had loved more than life itself. The weight of grief, the crushing burden of loss, melted away like ice in the sun. In Lyra's arms, Elara felt lighter, freer, more complete than she had ever imagined.

They stood amidst the luminous flowers, their bodies intertwined, their hearts beating as one. The flowers shimmered around them, their colors mirroring the emotions that surged between them - joy, relief, love, and an unwavering certainty that their journey together was far from over. The landscape itself seemed to celebrate their reunion, the stars above twinkling in approval, the gentle breeze whispering secrets of eternity.

Lyra's hand moved to Elara's face, her touch gentle yet powerful. It was a caress that spoke volumes, a silent assurance of love, of acceptance, of unwavering devotion.

Elara leaned into the touch, finding comfort in the warmth of Lyra's energy, a warmth that seeped into her very soul. It was a feeling of profound peace, a sense of homecoming that transcended earthly comprehension.

"I missed you," Elara whispered, her voice barely audible above the gentle hum of the ethereal landscape. The words were simple, yet they held the weight of a lifetime of unspoken emotions. They encapsulated the longing, the grief, the unwavering love that had sustained her through years of unbearable pain.

Lyra's response was a smile, a gentle squeeze of Elara's hand. It was a smile that communicated everything Elara needed to hear – reassurance, forgiveness, unwavering love. It was a smile that banished the lingering shadows of doubt and fear, replacing them with a radiant light of hope and joy.

They walked hand-in-hand through the field of luminous flowers, their laughter echoing through the ethereal landscape. Their laughter was not merely sound, but a manifestation of their joy, a celebration of their reunion, a testament to the enduring power of their love. The flowers swayed around them, their petals shimmering in response to their mirth, their colors deepening and intensifying, reflecting the depth of their happiness.

As they strolled, Elara noticed details she hadn't perceived before. Tiny creatures, like luminous fireflies, danced among the flowers, their light adding to the enchanting spectacle. The scent of the flowers was intoxicating, a heady blend of perfumes that evoked a myriad of emotions – serenity, peace, joy, and an overwhelming sense of belonging. The air was filled with a gentle hum, a celestial symphony that resonated deep within their hearts, a comforting melody that spoke of eternity.

They stopped by a crystal-clear stream, its waters reflecting the brilliant colors of the surrounding flowers. The stream seemed to flow with an ethereal luminescence, its waters shimmering with an inner light. Elara and Lyra knelt beside the stream, their reflections shimmering back at them from the surface. They looked at each other, their eyes locked in a silent exchange of love that transcended words.

"It's beautiful, isn't it?" Elara whispered, her voice filled with awe.

Lyra nodded, her eyes glistening with tears of joy. "More beautiful than I ever imagined," she replied, her voice echoing the same wonder.

They continued their walk, their hands clasped tightly together. They talked, not about the earthly realm they had left behind, but about their future, their forever. They shared memories, not of loss and pain, but of joy and love.

They planned adventures, not in the mundane world of reality, but in this ethereal realm of eternal peace.

As twilight descended, the landscape transformed, the luminous flowers giving way to a breathtaking expanse of stars. They lay down in a clearing, nestled amongst the flowers, their bodies intertwined, gazing up at the celestial display. The stars twinkled above them, forming constellations that shimmered with an ethereal light. It was a sight beyond earthly comprehension, a testament to the boundless beauty of this otherworldly realm.

They spoke little, their silence filled with a profound understanding. They held each other close, finding comfort in the warmth of each other's embrace. This was their home, their sanctuary, a place where their love would forever flourish, a place where their journey together would never end. The veil had been lifted, the chasm bridged. They were whole. They were together. Their love, once threatened by the cold hand of death, now bloomed eternally in this radiant paradise. This was their forever, their beginning, their home. And in that eternal embrace, Elara finally understood - true love didn't end with death; it simply transcended it.The luminous flowers, their colours a constant, shifting symphony of impossible hues, swayed gently in an unseen breeze. The air hummed with a low, resonant thrum, a comforting vibration that seemed to penetrate Elara's very being. There was no harsh sunlight here, only a soft, diffused light that bathed the landscape in an ethereal glow.

Time, as she had known it, felt fluid, untethered to the rigid constraints of seconds, minutes, hours. It was an eternity, yet it was also the present moment, pure and unburdened.

Lyra's hand rested on Elara's, their fingers intertwined, a physical manifestation of the unbreakable bond that stretched beyond the veil of death. They walked in silence for a long while, their steps slow and measured, each footfall cushioned by the soft earth. The silence wasn't empty, though; it was filled with the quiet murmur of their shared understanding, a comforting blanket woven from years of unspoken emotions, now finally released into the open. It was a silence that whispered promises of eternity.

Elara felt a deep, pervasive sense of peace settle over her, a calm she hadn't experienced since before Lyra's passing. The crushing weight of grief, the agonizing ache of loss, had gradually receded, replaced by a profound sense of acceptance. This wasn't a forced acceptance, born of resignation; it was a gentle understanding, a quiet acknowledgment of the natural ebb and flow of life and death. She had grieved, deeply and intensely, but now, in Lyra's arms, surrounded by this breathtaking, otherworldly beauty, she felt whole. Complete.

They paused by a crystal cascade, the water tumbling over smooth, luminous stones. The water was impossibly clear, revealing the bed of the stream in dazzling detail. The light refracted through the water, creating shimmering rainbows that danced on the surface, mirroring the kaleidoscope of emotions that still swirled within Elara, now softened by a gentle understanding.

Lyra smiled, a soft, tender smile that reached her eyes, making them sparkle like distant stars. It was a smile that spoke of forgiveness, of understanding, of a love that defied the limitations of mortality.

"It's... different, isn't it?" Elara whispered, her voice barely a breath against the gentle hum of the landscape. The words felt inadequate, clumsy, unable to fully capture the immensity of her experience.

Lyra nodded, her gaze fixed on the dancing rainbows. "Different," she agreed, her voice soft as the falling water. "But... better. More real, somehow."

Elara felt a tear trace a path down her cheek, but it wasn't a tear of sorrow. It was a tear of release, a single drop of emotion that washed away the last vestiges of her earthly pain. She wasn't afraid anymore. The fear of loss, the fear of separation, the fear of death itself, had been replaced by a quiet acceptance, a calm understanding of the natural order of things.

They sat together by the cascading water, their hands clasped tightly. They didn't speak much, their conversation flowing more through unspoken understanding than articulated words. The setting provided a constant backdrop of tranquil beauty, reinforcing their shared serenity. It was a comforting constant in their newly discovered world.

The sun, or whatever celestial body illuminated this realm, seemed to move slowly, casting long, ethereal shadows that danced with the light. As the light shifted, the colours of the flowers changed subtly, creating a moving tapestry of impossible hues. The scene was both timeless and fleeting, a constant reminder of the ephemeral nature of everything, yet simultaneously providing a sense of unending permanence.

Lyra leaned her head against Elara's shoulder, her breath warm against Elara's skin. The physical warmth was comforting, a tangible reminder of their connection, a reassuring touchstone in this surreal landscape. It grounded her, anchoring her in this new, beautiful reality. The feeling was unlike anything she had ever known; it was an acceptance of her own mortality woven seamlessly into the fabric of an everlasting love.

They explored the landscape, hand in hand, their footsteps barely disturbing the soft earth. They encountered creatures of light, ethereal beings that shimmered and danced in the air, their movements graceful and fluid.

The creatures seemed curious, but not intrusive, observing them with a silent respect. It was as if the very essence of this realm understood and honored their connection.

The flowers, with their ever-changing colours, seemed to reflect their mood, shifting in tone from radiant joy to a gentler serenity, mirroring the ongoing emotional landscape of their reunion. Sometimes, a deeper hue of amethyst or sapphire would briefly appear, reflecting a moment of lingering sadness or a memory of earthly pain, but those moments were brief, quickly fading into the dominant colours of peace and acceptance.

They discovered hidden glades, bathed in the soft glow of luminescent fungi, each mushroom a tiny beacon of light. They wandered through fields of shimmering grass, each blade radiating a gentle warmth. It was a world of sensory delights, designed to soothe and heal, to nurture and comfort.

As the light began to fade, they found a clearing overlooking a vast expanse of stars, each one shimmering with an intense, vibrant light. The stars seemed to stretch on forever, a testament to the infinite nature of existence. The feeling of mortality they had carried from the earthly realm seemed to diminish as they gazed into the vastness of space. They were part of something immense, a larger, more enduring whole.

They lay down amongst the flowers, their bodies intertwined, their hearts beating in unison. They felt no hunger, no thirst, no physical needs. They existed purely in the present moment, in the unwavering strength of their love, in the quiet peace of their newfound reality.

In the heart of this ethereal paradise, amidst the luminous flowers and the endless stars, Elara and Lyra found not just solace, but a profound acceptance of their reality. It wasn't an erasure of their past, nor a denial of their loss, but rather a peaceful integration of their grief into the vast tapestry of their unending love. They were together, forever bound by a love that death could not touch. This was their peace. This was their home. This was their beginning, again.

The stars above them pulsed with a gentle rhythm, mirroring the steady beat of their hearts. Lying amidst the luminous flora, Elara felt a profound sense of contentment wash over her, a feeling so complete it bordered on the overwhelming. The weight of the world, the crushing burden of grief that had shadowed her for so long, had vanished completely. It wasn't a forgetting, not exactly; the memories of Lyra's life, vibrant and full of laughter and light, remained, but they were now woven into the fabric of their present reality, transformed from sharp edges of pain into soft threads of cherished memory.

Lyra's hand, cool and smooth yet somehow radiating a comforting warmth, rested lightly on her own. Their fingers laced together, a silent promise whispered between them, a testament to the unbreakable bond that transcended the veil of death. She could feel Lyra's breath on her skin, a gentle caress that spoke volumes of affection, and the rhythmic rise and fall of her chest, a silent echo of their shared life, a rhythm that would continue forever.

The air hummed with a gentle energy, a harmonious vibration that resonated deep within Elara's soul. It was a symphony of peace, a comforting lullaby that soothed the deepest recesses of her being. The flowers around them shimmered and shifted, their colours a mesmerizing dance of vibrant hues, mirroring the ever-changing emotions that still flickered within her—a lingering sadness, a bittersweet ache for the life they could have had, a profound gratitude for the life they shared, and an overwhelming joy for the eternity they would spend together.

Elara traced the delicate curves of Lyra's cheekbone, her fingers lingering on the soft skin. She remembered the feel of Lyra's touch, the way her hand would find hers in times of trouble, the comforting weight of her head on her shoulder during moments of quiet contemplation. Those memories, once sharp and agonizing, were now bathed in a soft, golden light, reminders of their shared journey, imbued with a tenderness that time could not diminish.

They remained in silent communion for a long time, their bodies intertwined, their souls entwined even more deeply. The silence was not empty; it was filled with the unspoken language of love, a profound understanding that transcended words. It was a silence that echoed with the gentle murmur of their shared history, with the unspoken promises of their future. A future that stretched out before them, infinite and unbound by the constraints of time and space.

As the first rays of dawn, or whatever celestial phenomenon illuminated this realm, touched the horizon, casting a gentle, ethereal glow across the landscape, Elara felt a surge of emotion. It wasn't sadness or regret, but a profound sense of awe and wonder. She had journeyed beyond the veil of death, into a realm of unimaginable beauty, and in doing so, she had found not only her lost love, but a deeper understanding of life, loss, and the enduring power of love itself.

She looked into Lyra's eyes, eyes that held the vastness of the cosmos, the depth of an ocean, and the gentle warmth of a hearth fire. They were eyes that reflected an eternity of love, a love that transcended the boundaries of life and death. In those eyes, Elara saw not just her beloved, but the mirror of her own soul, a soul forever linked to Lyra's.

Lyra smiled, a serene smile that touched her heart, a smile that held the promise of endless happiness, a smile that spoke of an eternal bond that no force could ever break.

It was a smile that transcended time, a smile that held the weight of a lifetime of love, a smile that reflected their shared journey, their shared grief, and their shared joy. The smile of a love that had conquered death itself.

The flowers around them pulsed with a radiant energy, their colours shifting and swirling, mirroring the emotions that flowed between them – joy, peace, contentment, a lingering whisper of sadness, yet ultimately, an overwhelming sense of complete and utter happiness. They were surrounded by a tapestry of beauty, a testament to the enduring power of love, a landscape that reflected the depth and complexity of their relationship.

This was their sanctuary, their haven, a place where their love could bloom eternally, untouched by the harsh realities of the earthly realm. Here, time held no sway; their love was a constant, an unwavering beacon in the vast expanse of eternity. The world around them, with its ethereal light and shifting colours, was a reflection of their love story, a testament to the enduring power of the human spirit, a celebration of their unwavering connection.

They stood, hand in hand, gazing out at the breathtaking vista.

The stars above twinkled, as if in celebration of their reunion, a silent testament to the enduring power of their love, a chorus of celestial voices singing their eternal song. There was a profound sense of peace, a feeling of completion that permeated their being, a quiet understanding of their journey together, their love story woven into the very fabric of existence.

Elara and Lyra, forever bound by an eternal love, stood at the edge of eternity, their hearts beating as one, their souls intertwined in a dance that transcended time and space. This was their home, their haven, their eternal sanctuary, a place where their love would bloom forever, a testament to the enduring power of the human spirit and the unbreakable bonds of true love.
This was their beginning, again. And it would last forever. Their love story, etched into the fabric of eternity, was a testament to the power of love that knew no bounds, a love that defied death, a love that would endure forever. This was their eternal love, and it was perfect. It was complete. It was theirs.

Chapter Four Echoes of the Past

The scent of woodsmoke and damp earth clung to Elara's memory, a phantom smell that transported her back to a blustery autumn afternoon. She was ten, small and shivering, huddled against the rough bark of an ancient oak, its branches gnarled like arthritic fingers reaching for the bruised sky. She'd been lost, utterly and terrifyingly lost, in the sprawling woods behind her grandmother's house, a labyrinth of shadows and whispering leaves. Tears had frozen on her cheeks, blurring the already fading light.

Then, a small voice, hesitant and reedy, had broken the silence. "Are you alright?"

Elara, startled, looked up. A girl, no older than herself, stood before her, her face framed by a cascade of fiery red hair that seemed to catch the last embers of the dying sun. Her eyes, the colour of warm honey, held a surprising calmness, a quiet strength that belied her petite frame. This was Lyra.

Lyra hadn't hesitated. She'd led Elara back to the edge of the woods, her hand small but firm in Elara's, her quiet chatter a lifeline in the growing darkness. She'd known the woods like the back of her hand, navigating the treacherous paths with an uncanny ease, her knowledge a quiet comfort in Elara's mounting fear. They'd shared a stale gingerbread biscuit, its sweetness a tiny victory against the growing despair. That shared biscuit, crumbly and slightly burnt, became a symbol of their burgeoning friendship, a testament to their shared vulnerability and their unexpected connection.

Over the next few years, their friendship blossomed, nurtured by shared secrets and whispered confidences. They were an unlikely pair: Elara, quiet and contemplative, drawn to the solitude of books and the company of her own thoughts; and Lyra, vibrant and impulsive, a whirlwind of energy and infectious laughter. Yet, their differences were not a barrier, but a bridge. Elara found herself drawn to Lyra's fierce spirit, her unwavering loyalty, her ability to find joy in the simplest things.

Lyra, in turn, found solace in Elara's calm presence, her unwavering support, her ability to see beyond the surface, to understand the quiet depths of Lyra's often turbulent emotions.

Their shared experiences were the threads that wove their bond tighter and tighter. They built elaborate treehouses, their laughter echoing through the branches, their imaginations transforming the mundane into the magical. They spent countless hours lost in the world of books, sharing favorite passages and debating the merits of various authors. They'd spend summer afternoons by the river, their toes submerged in the cool water, weaving fantastical stories and sharing dreams as bold and bright as the summer sky.

One summer, they discovered a hidden cove, a secret sanctuary nestled amongst the rocks and tangled vines. It was their place, a refuge from the pressures of growing up, a space where they could simply be themselves, free from judgment and expectation. There, amongst the whispering reeds and the murmur of the river, they shared their deepest fears and their wildest dreams.

They talked of love and loss, of heartbreak and hope, of their ambitions and aspirations. The cove became a witness to their burgeoning womanhood, a silent observer to the evolution of their friendship into something deeper, something more profound.

There were quieter moments too, moments of shared understanding that transcended words. They understood each other's silences, those moments of introspection where words seemed inadequate. They knew when the other needed space, when a comforting hand on a shoulder was all that was needed, when a shared silence was more powerful than any explanation. These unspoken moments, woven into the tapestry of their memories, were perhaps the most precious of all.

Lyra's laughter echoed in Elara's mind, a sound as vibrant and life-affirming as the summer sun. She remembered the time they'd snuck into the town carnival, their hearts pounding with a mixture of excitement and apprehension. The smell of popcorn and cotton candy still lingered in her memory, a bittersweet reminder of youthful exuberance.

They'd won a stuffed panda bear, its fur soft and comforting, a prize that symbolized their shared adventures and their enduring friendship. The panda still sat on Elara's bed, a silent testament to the joy and recklessness of their youth.

Then there was the time they'd gotten hopelessly lost in a corn maze, their initial panic melting into laughter as they stumbled through the towering stalks, their faces covered in cobwebs and mud. Elara remembered the feeling of Lyra's hand in hers, a lifeline in the confusing labyrinth. They had emerged hours later, dishevelled and laughing, their clothes torn, their spirits unbroken. It was a reminder of their resilience, their shared capacity to navigate life's uncertainties together.

There was a poignant beauty in their memories, a bittersweet ache that reminded Elara of the preciousness of what she'd lost. Lyra's absence was a gaping hole in her life, a silence that echoed in every room, a void that no amount of time could fill.

Yet, in these memories, Elara found solace, a connection to the life they'd shared, a reminder of the strength of their bond, a testament to the love that had bloomed in the most unexpected of places, a love that death couldn't extinguish.

The image of Lyra, standing before her in the autumn woods, all those years ago, her red hair like a beacon in the fading light, burned bright in Elara's mind. That image, like a kaleidoscope, spun into a thousand other memories. The scent of woodsmoke and damp earth, the feel of Lyra's hand in hers, the shared warmth of the gingerbread biscuit, the laughter echoing through the branches of their treehouse, the whispering reeds of their secret cove, the smell of popcorn and cotton candy at the carnival, the confusion and laughter in the corn maze—all these fragmented moments coalesced into a vivid portrait of their friendship, a testament to the depth and richness of their connection, a bittersweet symphony of joy and loss. It was a love story, in a way, though not the one she'd initially envisioned.

A love story woven into the fabric of their shared past, a tapestry rich with detail, with color, with the bittersweet echo of laughter and loss. A love story that would continue to echo through her memories, a love story forever etched into her heart.

Even in this ethereal realm, amidst the luminous flora and the gentle energy that surrounded them, Elara could feel the weight of Lyra's absence. It wasn't a painful absence, not exactly. It was more like a faint echo, a gentle reverberation of a life that had been, a reminder of the profound impact Lyra had made on her life. The memories weren't just happy recollections; they were complex, multi-faceted, a tapestry woven with threads of joy and sorrow, of laughter and tears, of shared dreams and unspoken fears. The full spectrum of their relationship—its light and its shadow—was present in these memories, a testament to their authentic connection.

It was not simply a remembering; it was a reliving, a re-experiencing of emotions that were both intensely personal and deeply shared. The warmth of Lyra's hand, the comforting sound of her voice, the unspoken understanding that passed between them—these were not mere recollections, but sensations that resonated through Elara's being, drawing her back to moments of joy, of vulnerability, of shared experience that defined their friendship.

The grief hadn't vanished completely; it had simply been transformed. It was now interwoven with the happiness, the joy, the love, creating a tapestry of complex emotions that felt both profoundly sad and profoundly beautiful. It was a grief that allowed Elara to appreciate even more deeply the beauty of the life they had shared, the impact of Lyra's presence in her life, and the enduring power of their connection. And in this acceptance, in this embrace of the full spectrum of their shared past, Elara found a peace that was both profound and deeply satisfying.

It was a peace that transcended the boundaries of life and death, a peace that was only possible because of the enduring power of their friendship, a friendship that had blossomed in the most unexpected of places, and one that, even in death, continued to bloom. This was a love story, a friendship story, a story of shared memories, and one that would continue, forever, in the quiet corners of Elara's heart.

The memory flickered, a half-remembered dream at first, then sharpening into vivid detail. It was a late spring afternoon, the air thick with the scent of honeysuckle and damp earth. They were in their secret cove, the sun dappling through the leaves, casting dancing shadows on the water. The river murmured a gentle lullaby, a soothing counterpoint to the frantic beat of Elara's heart.

Lyra was there, radiant in the sunlight, her red hair a fiery halo around her face. Her eyes, usually sparkling with mischief, were soft, pools of honey reflecting the golden light. There was a stillness about her, a quiet intensity that Elara had never seen before. It was a vulnerability that mirrored her own, a shared unspoken truth hanging heavy in the air between them.

The air crackled with an unspoken energy, a silent conversation that needed no words. Their gazes locked, a silent acknowledgment of the unspoken feelings that had been simmering beneath the surface of their friendship for years. It wasn't just the shared memories, the laughter, the secrets; it was something deeper, something more profound, a connection that transcended the boundaries of friendship.

Elara remembered the hesitancy, the delicate dance of their approaching hands, fingers brushing lightly before intertwining. The touch sent a jolt of electricity through her, a feeling both exhilarating and terrifying. It was a confirmation, a silent affirmation of the feelings that had been growing within her, a recognition of the undeniable chemistry that had always existed between them, a chemistry that had been carefully masked, subtly nurtured, until it finally erupted in this moment of raw, unfiltered emotion.

Lyra's hand cupped Elara's cheek, her touch feather-light, yet imbued with an intensity that stole Elara's breath. Elara leaned into the touch, closing her eyes, surrendering to the moment.

The warmth of Lyra's hand radiated through her, chasing away the chill that had unexpectedly settled in her bones. It was a comforting warmth, a familiar comfort, yet charged with a new and unfamiliar voltage.

And then, the kiss.

It wasn't a passionate, fiery kiss. It was gentle, hesitant, a tentative exploration of uncharted territory. It was a kiss born of shared vulnerability, a tender exploration of emotions that had been unspoken, carefully guarded, yet undeniably present. It was a kiss that whispered of secrets shared and unspoken desires. It was a kiss that spoke volumes without uttering a single word.

Lyra's lips were soft, her touch tentative, as if afraid to break the fragile spell that had been woven between them. It was a kiss that promised more than it delivered, a taste of something deeper, something more profound, a promise of a future that was both thrilling and terrifying. The taste of her lips was like honey and sunshine, sweet and intoxicating, a taste that lingered long after the kiss had ended.

The silence that followed was not awkward or uncomfortable. It was a charged silence, pregnant with unspoken emotions. It was a silence that allowed them to absorb the impact of the moment, to process the profound shift that had just occurred in their relationship. Their hands remained clasped, a physical connection anchoring them to the reality of the moment. The world around them seemed to fade, the sounds of the river, the rustling of the leaves, reduced to a gentle hum. Their world became a private sanctuary, a space inhabited only by the two of them, enclosed by the silent understanding that had passed between them.

The memory of the kiss, years later, wasn't just a recollection of a physical act; it was a reliving of a moment of profound emotional intimacy. It was the memory of vulnerability laid bare, a shared silence broken by a hesitant touch, a gentle exploration of unspoken emotions. It was a memory imbued with a raw honesty that transcended words, a moment of connection so profound it had altered the trajectory of their lives.

Elara remembered the lingering warmth on her cheek, the way Lyra's breath hitched as their lips parted. The scent of honeysuckle and damp earth, infused with the subtle fragrance of Lyra's perfume, filled her senses, transporting her back to that idyllic moment. It was a moment etched into her memory, forever intertwined with the tapestry of their shared experiences.

The kiss had been a turning point, a silent acknowledgment of a love that had been growing unseen, unspoken, for years. It had been a love that transcended the limitations of friendship, a love that blossomed in the fertile soil of shared experiences, whispered secrets, and unspoken understandings. It was a love that had defied societal expectations, a love that was both tender and fierce, a love that was both profoundly intimate and deeply comforting.

It wasn't a love story that unfolded with dramatic declarations or grand gestures. It was a love story whispered in shared silences, in stolen glances, in the quiet comfort of shared memories.

It was a love story woven into the fabric of their everyday lives, a love story found not in romantic novels, but in the ordinary moments of their extraordinary friendship.

The kiss had transformed their friendship. It didn't erase the years of shared laughter, whispered secrets, and comforting silences; instead, it deepened those elements, adding a layer of profound intimacy and understanding. They were still themselves, Elara the quiet observer, Lyra the vibrant whirlwind, but now there was an additional dimension to their bond, a connection that pulsed beneath the surface, a silent affirmation of a love that was both fragile and incredibly strong.

The memories of that afternoon by the river continued to haunt Elara in the ethereal realm. It wasn't just the kiss itself that resonated; it was the entire context, the feeling of utter connection, the shared vulnerability, the hushed intimacy of their secret cove, the gentle murmur of the river, the dappled sunlight filtering through the leaves.

All these elements combined to create a powerful sensory memory, a bittersweet symphony of emotions that both filled her with joy and pierced her with the sharp sting of loss.

Even in this otherworldly space, Elara could still feel the ghost of Lyra's touch, the lingering warmth of her hand on her cheek. It was a tangible sensation, a phantom memory that brought both immense joy and excruciating pain. The grief hadn't disappeared; it was woven into the very fabric of the memory, intertwined with the happiness, the joy, the intoxicating sweetness of the kiss.

The pain of Lyra's absence was a constant companion, a mournful echo that resonated in the quiet moments. Yet, within that pain, there was a profound gratitude, an appreciation for the beauty and intensity of their love, for the unique bond they had shared. It was a bittersweet symphony of joy and sorrow, a testament to the powerful and enduring nature of their connection.

The love story they had shared wasn't merely a memory; it was a living, breathing entity, forever etched into Elara's soul, forever shaping her understanding of love, loss, and the enduring power of human connection.

The scent of honeysuckle and damp earth, once a trigger for grief, now brought a complex mix of emotions; a flood of memories, a rush of happiness and a deep well of sorrow, a poignant reminder of the love that had blossomed in their secret cove. The kiss remained a symbol of that love, a testament to the intensity of their connection, a silent promise that their love, even in death, would forever echo in the quiet chambers of Elara's heart. It was a love story etched not in words, but in the shared memories of two souls bound by an undeniable and unwavering affection, a love that transcended the boundaries of life and death itself. Elara found herself drifting further back, past the kiss, past the secret cove, to a time before the shadow of illness had fallen across their lives. She saw them, younger, their laughter echoing in the sun-drenched fields behind Lyra's family home. They were sprawled on a blanket, surrounded by wildflowers, their faces tilted up towards the endless blue expanse of the sky.

They were making plans, grand and audacious plans that held the weight of a lifetime of dreams.

Lyra, ever the visionary, spoke of opening an art gallery, a space where her vibrant paintings could fill the world with color and light. She described it with such fervent passion, her eyes blazing with an intensity that mirrored the fiery hues in her hair. It wouldn't be just any gallery, she declared, but a haven, a place where artists could thrive, a sanctuary of creativity where kindred spirits could connect. She'd even sketched out blueprints on the back of a napkin, a whirlwind of bold strokes and impossible angles that somehow perfectly captured the essence of her vision.

Elara, the quieter of the two, imagined a life spent writing, her words weaving stories that would resonate with others, giving voice to the unspoken emotions that dwelled within their hearts. She dreamt of a cozy cabin nestled in a secluded wood, a sanctuary where she could lose herself in the rhythm of her typewriter, the rhythmic clack-clack-clack a comforting counterpoint to the rustling of leaves.

She pictured a place where she could write without interruption, the only sounds were the whispering wind and the quiet patter of rain on the roof. Lyra would come to visit, of course, bringing laughter and her vibrant energy, her presence a constant source of inspiration and support.

They planned journeys together, far-flung adventures to exotic lands, a lifetime spent discovering the hidden wonders of the world. They imagined themselves trekking through lush rainforests, scaling snow-capped mountains, exploring ancient ruins, their laughter echoing in the canyons, their footprints leaving a trail of joy across the globe. They'd create a travel blog, Elara chronicling their escapades with her insightful prose, while Lyra captured the essence of each place through her paintings. They would share their adventures with the world, hoping to inspire others to embark on their own journeys of self-discovery.

Their plans weren't just abstract hopes; they were carefully considered, meticulously crafted details. They knew precisely which countries they wanted to visit, which museums they craved to explore, which ancient cities they yearned to wander through. They'd spent countless hours poring over maps, travel guides, and art books, poring over images of ancient temples and bustling marketplaces, each image fueling their dreams with fresh enthusiasm.

Elara remembered the late nights they'd spent huddled together, their heads bent over a stack of books, their fingers tracing the contours of faraway lands, their voices hushed as they shared their visions for the future. They'd discussed the small details, the everyday moments that would fill their lives, the quiet joys they hoped to savor. They envisioned cozy evenings spent by a fireplace, sipping warm cocoa, lost in conversation or engrossed in a good book. They talked about adopting a stray dog, a scruffy mutt who would become their loyal companion, their adventures forever imprinted in their shared memories.

They even talked about having children, a family built on a foundation of mutual love, support, and shared experiences. They'd imagined their child growing up surrounded by art, filled with stories, surrounded by the echoes of their shared laughter and their endless dreams. They'd envisioned their child walking in their footsteps, inheriting their zest for life and their passion for adventure. They imagined a child who embodied the best of them both, a child who would illuminate the world with their unique talents.

Lyra would be the vibrant, free-spirited parent, fostering creativity and imagination, while Elara would provide the steady, grounding presence, offering comfort and support. They'd support each other through thick and thin, always prioritizing their child's wellbeing. They saw themselves as a team, their combined strengths creating a nurturing and supportive family unit. They imagined themselves growing old together, their hair streaked with silver, their laughter lines etched deep into their faces, their hearts forever intertwined.

The vividness of these shared dreams intensified the agony of their loss. Each detail was a dagger twisting in Elara's heart. The vibrant colors of Lyra's imagined gallery seemed to mock the emptiness of her now-silent studio, the cozy cabin a stark contrast to the hollow emptiness of Elara's own solitary existence. The bustling marketplaces and ancient ruins seemed to amplify the silence and stillness of her own world, a world suddenly devoid of Lyra's infectious energy and boundless enthusiasm.

The pain was a relentless companion, a shadow that clung to her, refusing to let go. It was a pain that resonated through every fiber of her being, a constant reminder of what had been lost, of the future that would never be. Yet, even in the depths of her despair, Elara clung to the memory of those shared dreams, those carefully constructed plans that spoke of a life filled with joy, laughter, and endless possibilities. It was a testament to the depth of their connection, a reminder that even in death, their love lived on, an eternal flame flickering in the shadows of her heart. Those dreams, once a source of immense joy, now served as a poignant reminder of the preciousness of life, and the enduring power of love.

They were a legacy, a testament to the unbreakable bond between two souls, forever intertwined in the tapestry of memory.

And in the quiet moments, when the pain was less acute, Elara found solace in the bittersweet echo of their shared aspirations. They weren't just dreams; they were a roadmap, a guide that pointed towards the life they were meant to live. They were a legacy that she would carry forward, a reminder of the love that had blossomed between them, a love that transcended the boundaries of life and death, a love that would forever resonate in the chambers of her heart, forever guiding her path. The memories, once a source of unending grief, now represented a path forward, a testament to the enduring power of love, loss, and the enduring strength of the human spirit. They were a beacon, illuminating her way through the darkness, a reminder that even in the face of unimaginable loss, hope still remained.

Even in the ethereal realm, Elara felt a responsibility to honor those dreams, to ensure that Lyra's vision would live on. She felt a responsibility to continue writing, to create the stories that would resonate with others, to share the magic of their shared dreams. She resolved to find a way to honor Lyra's passion for art, to find a way to give life to the gallery that once existed only in their shared imagination. She'd use her words to paint a picture of the world they had dreamed of, a world filled with vibrant colors, heartfelt stories, and endless adventures. It would be a tribute, a lasting monument to their love, a testament to the enduring power of their bond. In doing so, she would keep Lyra's spirit alive, her legacy forever etched in the pages of her stories, forever resonating in the hearts of those who read them. The dreams they once shared would become a tangible reality, a living testament to the unbreakable bond of love that transcended the confines of life itself.

The sun dipped below the horizon, painting the sky in hues of bruised purple and fiery orange, a stark contrast to the sterile white of Lyra's hospital room.

The air hung heavy with the unspoken, a suffocating blanket woven from fear and denial. We sat on either side of her bed, the rhythmic beeping of the heart monitor a relentless percussion to our strained silence. Lyra, her face pale and drawn, looked smaller than I remembered, her vibrant spirit seemingly dimmed by the relentless assault of the disease.

It had started subtly, a persistent cough, a nagging fatigue. We'd dismissed it initially, attributing it to overwork, stress, the relentless pursuit of our dreams. But the cough worsened, the fatigue deepened, and the vibrant fire in Lyra's eyes began to flicker, replaced by a weary acceptance. The diagnosis had been swift, brutal, a death sentence delivered with clinical detachment. The doctor's words still echoed in my ears: "aggressive," "incurable," "limited time." Those words, so coldly precise, had shattered the fragile foundation of our carefully constructed future.

The difficult conversations began then, hesitant at first, then increasingly raw and honest as the weight of our impending reality settled upon us.

We talked about the unfinished paintings stacked in her studio, the canvases teeming with vibrant colors, promising masterpieces left incomplete. We discussed the travel blog that would remain unwritten, the exotic landscapes still unexplored, the adventures left unlived. Each conversation felt like chipping away at a precious statue, each word a chisel that chipped away at the beautiful edifice of our dreams.

I remember one particularly harrowing evening. The sterile scent of antiseptic clung to the air, a constant reminder of our grim reality. Lyra, her hand clasped tightly in mine, spoke of her fears, her voice barely a whisper. She talked about her unfinished business, her regrets, the things she wished she'd done differently. She feared leaving me behind, her voice laced with a heartbreaking vulnerability. She spoke of the pain of leaving behind a life unfulfilled, of dreams unachieved, of a future that would never be.

"I'm scared, Elara," she whispered, her voice catching in her throat. "Scared of the unknown. Scared of leaving you alone. Scared of... of not seeing our dreams come true."

Tears streamed down my face, blurring the already indistinct lines of the hospital room. “We’ll face it together,” I managed, my voice choked with emotion. “We’ll figure it out. We always do.” It was a hollow promise, a desperate attempt to conjure a strength I didn’t possess, a desperate attempt to stave off the encroaching darkness.

But even as I spoke, I knew the futility of my words. We couldn't figure it out. There was no solution, no magic spell to undo the damage, no cure to reverse the relentless march of the disease. We could only face it, together, holding onto each other as the world crumbled around us.

We talked about practical matters, the mundane details that loomed large in the shadow of our impending loss. We discussed the disposition of her artwork, the unfinished manuscripts I'd been working on, the financial burdens we'd leave behind. These were conversations we should have had years down the road, amidst the comfortable familiarity of our cozy cabin, not here, in this stark, sterile environment, with the shadow of death hanging over us like a shroud.

But even amid the practicalities, the raw emotion spilled over. There were moments of bitter laughter, the dark humor born out of sheer desperation. There were moments of silent tears, shared grief silently acknowledged in the space between us. There were moments of intense, searing intimacy, a closeness forged in the crucible of our shared sorrow. We spoke of our life together, the memories we would carry, the legacy we would leave behind. These conversations were not merely conversations about logistics or practicality; they were a testament to the depth of our connection, the intensity of our love.

One conversation stands out, etched in my memory with a painful clarity. It was a quiet afternoon, the sun casting long shadows across the room, illuminating the dust motes dancing in the air. Lyra was unusually quiet, her eyes fixed on the distant horizon, a faraway look in her eyes. I knew she was contemplating her mortality, the inevitable end. I held my breath, waiting for her to speak, to break the fragile silence.

When she did, her words were as unexpected as they were heartbreaking. She spoke of her regrets, not the grand regrets of unfulfilled ambitions, but the small, quiet regrets of everyday life. She regretted the harsh words she'd spoken in anger, the moments of impatience, the missed opportunities to express her love. She regretted not telling her family how much she loved them, not spending more time with them, not making more memories to cherish.

Her words struck a chord deep within me. I, too, had regrets, the unspoken words, the missed chances, the moments that slipped through my fingers like grains of sand. We confessed our unspoken anxieties, the things we'd wished we had done differently, the things we'd silently regretted. These confessions, raw and honest, stripped bare our vulnerabilities, exposing the tender core of our love.

The unspoken words hung in the air, a symphony of regrets and unspoken truths. We spoke of the life we'd built together, the shared dreams that now lay shattered before us.

We revisited the idyllic landscapes of our dreams, the vibrant colors of Lyra's paintings, the cozy comfort of our imagined cabin. We spoke of the life that would never be. Each word was a knife, twisting in the wounds of our hearts, yet each word served as a testament to the enduring power of our love. It was a love born in shared dreams, nurtured in shared experiences, and tested in the crucible of unimaginable loss.

In the end, the silence between us was more profound than any words could ever express. It was a silence filled with unspoken love, unyielding grief, and the enduring legacy of a bond that transcended life itself. The silence was punctuated only by the rhythmic beep of the heart monitor, a relentless countdown, a constant reminder of the time we had left. But even as the clock ticked down, even as darkness crept closer, our love remained, a beacon of light in the face of overwhelming despair. And in the heart of that darkness, in the face of our profound loss, those difficult conversations became a testament to the enduring strength of our love, a legacy etched in the annals of our memories, a love that would forever resonate in the chambers of my heart.

The final sunset bled across the hospital room, casting long shadows that danced with the dust motes, mimicking the fragile dance of life itself. Lyra's breathing, once a steady rhythm, had become shallow, a whisper against the insistent beep of the heart monitor. Her hand, still clasped in mine, was cold, the skin paper-thin, almost translucent. But her eyes, oh, her eyes still held that familiar spark, a stubborn refusal to succumb to the encroaching darkness.

We didn't speak for a long time. Silence had become our language, a shared understanding that transcended words. It was a silence pregnant with unspoken emotions—a symphony of grief, love, and acceptance. I leaned closer, my cheek resting against her hair, inhaling the faint scent of lavender and something else... something indefinably *her*. The scent of a life lived fully, a life that was now fading.

She stirred slightly, her eyelids fluttering open. A weak smile played on her lips, a ghost of the radiant smile that had once lit up my world. "Remember that time," she whispered, her voice barely audible, "in the Tuscan hills? The sun was setting just like this... the cypress trees silhouetted against the fiery sky..."

The memory flooded back, vivid and sharp: the warmth of the Tuscan sun on our skin, the scent of rosemary and olive trees, the gentle breeze whispering through the fields of sunflowers. We were young then, carefree, our future stretching before us like an endless canvas. We had laughed, dreamt, and planned, our lives intertwined, our hearts beating as one. Now, the memory felt like a cruel taunt, a stark reminder of what was lost.

"I remember," I choked out, tears blurring my vision. "Every detail." I traced the delicate lines of her face, each wrinkle a testament to a life lived, a life I was about to lose.

She squeezed my hand, her grip surprisingly strong for someone so frail. "Don't be sad, Elara," she whispered, her voice laced with a weariness that belied her inner strength. "We had a good run, didn't we?"

A good run? It felt like a lifetime compressed into a few short years, a whirlwind of laughter, tears, shared dreams, and now, this devastating farewell. "More than a good run," I managed, my voice breaking. "A lifetime. The best lifetime."

She closed her eyes, her breath growing shallower with each passing moment. I continued to hold her hand, my fingers interlaced with hers, feeling the faint rhythm of her pulse, a pulse that was slowly fading. The rhythmic beep of the monitor was our grim metronome, marking the passage of our final moments.

I told her stories then, snippets of our life together, recalling funny anecdotes, shared adventures, moments of pure joy. I painted vivid pictures with words, hoping to somehow capture the essence of our love, to etch it permanently into the fabric of our memories. I spoke of the little things—the way she used to hum while she painted, the way her eyes crinkled when she laughed, the comforting weight of her head resting on my shoulder. Each memory was a precious jewel, a treasure I was holding tightly, afraid to let go.

She listened patiently, her eyes closed, a peaceful expression settling on her face. Occasionally, a faint sigh escaped her lips, a soft sound that pierced my heart. I knew she was drifting, her spirit slowly detaching from her mortal coil.

Yet, even as she slipped away, I felt her presence, her love, an unwavering connection that transcended the physical realm.

As the light faded, the room filled with a profound sense of stillness, a quiet that was both comforting and terrifying. The beeping of the monitor became the soundtrack to our farewell, a steady drumbeat against the silence. I whispered promises of remembrance, of keeping her memory alive, of carrying her spirit within my heart. I vowed to live a life worthy of her love, a life filled with purpose and meaning.

In the twilight of her life, as her spirit prepared to take flight, she reached out and touched my face, her touch feather-light, yet impossibly strong. A single tear traced a path down my cheek, a tear of grief, yes, but also a tear of gratitude. Gratitude for the time we'd shared, for the love we had known, for the memories we would forever cherish.

Her breathing grew even shallower, becoming little more than a ghost of a breath. The beep of the monitor faltered, sputtered, and then... silence.

The silence was absolute, broken only by the ragged gasps of my own grief. The world around me seemed to dim, the vibrant colors of the sunset replaced by a grayscale of sorrow.

But in the midst of my despair, I felt a profound sense of peace. Lyra was gone, yes, but her love remained, a vibrant tapestry woven into the fabric of my being. Her memory would live on, not just in the paintings she'd left behind, but in every sunrise, every sunset, every memory that we had created together. And in those memories, in that enduring love, I found the strength to carry on, to live a life worthy of the love we had shared, a love that had defied even death itself. The echoes of her laughter, her whispers, her love, would forever reverberate in the chambers of my heart, a testament to a love story that transcended time and mortality. The final moments were not an ending but a transformation, a transition into a different kind of love, a love that existed beyond the boundaries of life and death.

Her absence was a profound ache, but her presence, in the memories we shared, the love we had created, remained a beacon of light, guiding me through the darkness. The world may have lost its vibrant colours, but the colours of our memories would forever shine brightly within me.

Chapter Five The Afterlife Unveiled

The silence wasn't the deafening kind, the kind that presses against your eardrums and screams of absence. It was a different silence, a quietude so profound it felt like a physical presence, a vast, encompassing emptiness that held within it a strange, unsettling peace. It wasn't the absence of sound; it was the absence of... everything else. The sharp edges of grief had been softened, smoothed over by an unseen hand, replaced by a gentle numbness. I was aware of my body – or rather, the lack of the familiar weight of it. There was lightness, a floating sensation, as if I were suspended in a boundless, inky ocean.

My senses, normally vibrant and alive, were muted, yet simultaneously heightened. Colors existed, but they lacked their usual intensity, washed out like faded watercolors. Sounds drifted in and out, ethereal whispers that lacked definition, like distant echoes in a cavernous space. The scent of lavender, so intimately associated with Lyra, was still there, but it was fainter, more elusive, a phantom perfume clinging to the edges of my awareness. Taste and touch were almost nonexistent, replaced by a strange, pervasive feeling of... nothing. Yet, within that nothing, there was something else - a sense of being, of existence, of a consciousness detached from the physical world.

Panic, a cold, clammy hand, reached for me, threatening to pull me under the waves of this unfamiliar reality. But it didn't last. Instead, it was replaced by a growing sense of curiosity, a strange detachment from the overwhelming grief that had consumed me moments before. This wasn't the oblivion I had feared; it was... different. It was a transition, a metamorphosis of being. It was... peaceful.

Slowly, gradually, my awareness expanded. The inky blackness began to recede, replaced by subtle shifts in light and shadow, delicate gradients of color that shimmered and pulsed like a living aurora borealis. There were forms, but they weren't sharply defined; they were fluid, ethereal, shifting like a heat haze on a summer's day. I wasn't sure if I was seeing them or sensing them; the boundaries between sight, sound, and feeling blurred into a seamless tapestry of experience.

And then I saw her.

Lyra.

Not the frail, weakened woman lying on the hospital bed, but a radiant, vibrant being of pure light. She was translucent, almost shimmering, yet undeniably her. Her eyes, those incredible eyes that held so much love and light, shone with an intensity that made my heart ache with a mixture of joy and longing. She smiled, a smile so beautiful, so full of grace and compassion, that it brought tears to my eyes – tears that, surprisingly, didn't fall. They existed, I felt them, but they didn't have a physical form.

She approached me, moving with a fluidity that defied gravity, her form gently rippling like water. There was no sound to her movement, no touch, yet her presence enveloped me, a warm embrace of pure energy. "Elara," she whispered, her voice not an audible sound, but a direct resonance within my mind, a feeling rather than a sound. It was both comforting and unsettling, like a dream that felt too real.

“Lyra,” I responded, the word forming not in my throat, but somehow within my very being. The sound was a sensation, a vibration in the ethereal space between us.

She didn't answer verbally. She didn't need to. Her presence communicated everything: love, acceptance, peace. She showed me, not told me, the nature of this new reality. It wasn’t a place, not in the traditional sense. It was a state of being, a realm of pure consciousness, unbounded by space or time. Memories flickered around us, not as static images, but as living, breathing experiences. We relived moments from our life together – the Tuscan sunset, the laughter in the rain, the quiet moments of shared intimacy. They weren’t just memories; they were emotions, sensations, a kaleidoscope of shared experience that existed outside of the constraints of time.

I learned, slowly, that grief existed here too, but it was different. It wasn't a crushing weight, but a poignant echo, a lingering sweetness tinged with sadness. It was an acknowledgement of loss, but not a surrender to it. It was a part of the tapestry of our existence, woven into the fabric of our shared experiences.

The ethereal plane wasn't a monochrome afterlife, devoid of emotion. It was a place of vibrant sensations, though muted and subtle compared to the physical world. It was a place where emotions flowed freely, unburdened by the physical constraints of the body. It was a place of profound connection – not just with Lyra, but with everything. I felt the threads of connection extending outwards, linking me to every living thing, every thought, every memory ever created. It was an overwhelming, humbling experience.

It wasn’t a heaven or a hell, not in the traditional sense of the words. It was something beyond human comprehension, a realm of pure energy, pure consciousness, where the boundaries between life and death blurred and dissolved. It was the essence of existence distilled, refined, purified.

Days, weeks, months – or perhaps they were moments, eons, or nothing at all – passed in this altered state. Time here was fluid, malleable, without the rigid structure of the physical world. I began to understand the nature of our connection. It wasn't limited to the physical realm.

Our love, our shared experiences, existed outside of time and space, an eternal bond that transcended mortality. The pain of loss was still there, a gentle ache in the soul, but it was tempered by the overwhelming joy of our continued connection. Lyra was not gone; she was simply transformed.

As I adapted to this new reality, I discovered that it wasn't an end, but a beginning. The transition wasn't just a move from one state of being to another, it was a growth, a transformation. The restrictions of mortality were lifted, replaced by a boundless ocean of possibilities. It was the freedom to explore, to learn, to grow, unburdened by the limitations of the body. This new realm offered a clarity and understanding I never possessed before, a perspective that transcended the limitations of the physical world. I learned that death wasn't the end of our story; it was simply a transition to a different chapter, a different kind of love, a love that extended beyond the boundaries of time and space. And in that profound understanding, I found a peace that surpassed even the greatest joys of my earthly life.

The grief remained, a constant reminder of the life we'd shared, but it was tempered by the knowledge that our connection was forever, unbreakable, extending far beyond the confines of this life, and into the infinite expanse of eternity. The vibrant colours of life, though dimmed in this new realm, were replaced with a subtle, pervasive light – the light of our eternal love.
The initial shock of Lyra's presence began to fade, replaced by a growing awareness of other... things. They weren't exactly people, not in the way I understood the word. They were... energies, shimmering forms, some translucent, others vibrant with an inner light that pulsed with a life of its own. They drifted around me, their movements graceful, fluid, like leaves on a gentle breeze. There was no sense of urgency, no clamor, only a serene, almost silent movement.

One form approached, its light a soft, calming blue. It coalesced, taking on a semblance of human shape, though the edges remained blurred, indistinct. The being didn't speak, but images flooded my mind – a life lived on a remote island, surrounded by the crashing waves and the cries of seabirds, a life filled with quiet solitude and deep contemplation. I saw the face of an old woman, etched with the lines of time and wisdom, her eyes reflecting a lifetime of watching the sun rise and set over endless horizons. Then the image faded, replaced by a feeling – a sense of serene acceptance, of a life lived fully and without regret. The blue light pulsed gently, a silent farewell, before drifting away to join the others.

Another form, radiating a fiery orange, moved closer. This energy felt different – turbulent, passionate, filled with a restless energy. The images that poured into my mind were rapid, intense: a whirlwind of romance, adventure, loss, and desperate yearning. I saw a young man, vibrant and full of life, his eyes filled with a burning intensity, his life a kaleidoscope of vibrant experiences and passionate relationships, each ending in heartbreak. The feeling accompanying the images was a poignant mixture of regret and fierce longing, a desperate search for something elusive, an unending desire for connection. The orange light pulsed faster now, almost frantically, before dissipating into the ethereal landscape, leaving behind a lingering echo of unfulfilled potential.

Over time, I encountered countless others. A soft green light revealed a life dedicated to healing and nurturing, a quiet life filled with acts of kindness and compassion, leaving behind a legacy of love and gentle grace. A deep violet light showed a life lived in the pursuit of knowledge and understanding, a journey marked by intellectual curiosity and a tireless quest for truth, the final image a vast library bathed in the soft glow of moonlight. Each encounter was unique, each life a tapestry woven from joy and sorrow, success and failure, love and loss.

Their stories were not told in words, but in emotions, sensations, a vibrant symphony of experience. I learned that death didn't erase their experiences; it transformed them. The grief they carried wasn't a crushing weight, but a gentle melancholy, a bittersweet reminder of a life lived, a testament to the intensity of their feelings. Each soul carried its own unique burden, yet there was an underlying current of peace, a sense of acceptance that transcended the individual experiences.

One being, whose light was a shimmering silver, resonated deeply within me. The images that flooded my consciousness were less vivid than others, more fragmented, but the emotions were intense – a love both profound and devastating, a loss so profound it threatened to consume everything. I sensed a connection to this soul, a shared understanding of the profound pain of loss, the relentless ache of longing for a love that transcends mortality. This being didn't offer a life story, but an empathy so profound it felt like a shared experience, a silent acknowledgment of a grief that words cannot capture. The silver light pulsed slowly, steadily, like a heartbeat in the vast stillness.

As I spent more time in this realm, I began to notice patterns. The colors of the light seemed to correlate with the dominant emotions of the souls they embodied – red for intense passion, blue for serenity, yellow for joy, and so on. But these colors weren't fixed; they shifted and changed, reflecting the ebb and flow of their emotions, their experiences. There was no static state of being; everything was fluid, constantly in motion, a testament to the dynamic nature of existence itself.

There were also souls who existed as pure energy, without a defined form. Their presence was felt as a vibration, a resonance, a subtle shift in the ambient energy of this ethereal plane. They were the echoes of lives lived, their individual stories lost to time, yet their essence remained, woven into the fabric of this realm. They were a reminder of the vastness of existence, the countless lives lived and lost, the echoes of experience that permeate everything.

I began to understand that this wasn't simply an afterlife; it was a tapestry of existence, a boundless ocean of consciousness where every life, every experience, every emotion had its place. There was no judgment, no heaven or hell, only a profound interconnectedness, a symphony of experiences played out across the vast expanse of eternity. The souls I encountered weren't simply ghosts; they were fragments of a larger consciousness, each a unique note in a cosmic melody.

The initial fear I felt had long since vanished, replaced by a sense of wonder and awe. This wasn't the oblivion I had dreaded; it was a realm of profound beauty and unexpected peace. The pain of loss remained, a constant reminder of Lyra's absence in the physical world, but it was softened, tempered by the knowledge of our enduring connection. This realm wasn't an escape from grief; it was a transformation of it, a refinement, a distillation of the raw emotion into a poignant echo that resonated within the vastness of eternity. The grief was a part of me, as was the boundless joy of our continuing connection.

One night, or perhaps it was a day, or maybe neither - time had lost all meaning in this realm - I encountered a soul whose light shone with an almost unbearable intensity. It was a white light, pure and radiant, so bright it momentarily overwhelmed my senses. As I recovered, I saw, or perhaps felt, the totality of existence itself. All the souls I had encountered, all the lives they had lived, all the experiences they had shared - everything was connected, interconnected in a way I had never fathomed before. It was an overwhelming vision of unity, of the interconnectedness of all things, of the boundless nature of existence. It was a glimpse of the source, the origin, the ultimate reality that underlay everything I had experienced. The image faded, and the brilliant white light receded, leaving me with a profound sense of peace and understanding. I had seen the entirety of existence, and it was beautiful, terrifying, and utterly magnificent. And at the heart of it all, I felt Lyra's presence, a constant, reassuring beacon in the vast expanse of eternity. The light of our eternal love shone ever brighter in this new realm, a testament to the unbreakable bond that transcended death, time, and space. This was our new beginning.

The shimmering forms continued their silent dance, a ballet of souls unfolding before me. I had spent what felt like eons in this ethereal realm, and yet, time remained a fluid concept, a meaningless measure in this boundless expanse of being. The initial terror of death, the overwhelming grief of Lyra's loss, had begun to recede, replaced by a slow, tentative acceptance. It wasn't a sudden shift, not a dramatic revelation, but a gradual unfolding, a gentle easing into the reality of this existence beyond the veil.

It started with small things. The recognition that the vibrant colors of the souls weren't static, that they shifted and changed, mirroring the complexities of their lives. A fiery orange might dim to a soft amber, a deep violet lighten to a gentle lavender, reflecting a life's transition from passionate turmoil to tranquil reflection. I saw this not as a lessening of their being, but as an evolution, a continuous flow of experience, a testament to the dynamic nature of existence itself.

I began to observe the patterns of their movements. Certain souls clustered together, their lights intertwining, creating a shimmering tapestry of shared experiences. I saw families reunited, lovers embracing in silent communion, friends sharing laughter that echoed through the ethereal landscape. These were not the stiff, formal reunions I had imagined, but joyous, spontaneous interactions, a testament to the enduring power of human connection. It wasn't a heaven, not in the traditional sense; it was something more profound, more intimate, more deeply personal.

There were others who remained solitary, their lights shimmering independently, their energy radiating a sense of profound introspection. These were not lonely souls; they were individuals embracing their own unique journeys, finding peace in solitude, content in their own company. They were a reminder that acceptance of death wasn't about escaping oneself, but about embracing the totality of one's being, flaws and all.

My own journey towards acceptance was intertwined with my encounters. Each soul I met, each life I witnessed, contributed to my growing understanding of death and its implications. The initial fear gave way to curiosity, then fascination, then finally, a profound sense of peace. The grief for Lyra remained, a constant ache in my heart, but it was no longer a consuming force. It was a part of me, an integral element of my being, woven into the fabric of my soul. I had lost her in the physical world, but our connection, our love, endured, transcending the limitations of mortality.

I learned to distinguish the different qualities of grief. There was the raw, immediate pain of loss, the overwhelming sense of emptiness that had consumed me in the early days. Then there was the lingering sorrow, the quiet ache that reminded me of Lyra's absence, a bittersweet memory that evoked both joy and sorrow. And finally, there was a gentle melancholy, a soft sadness that felt less like a burden and more like a cherished memory, a testament to the depth and intensity of our love.

The transformation wasn't simply emotional; it was spiritual. I began to see life and death not as opposing forces, but as two sides of the same coin, integral parts of a larger, more expansive reality. Death wasn't an ending, but a transition, a passage to another realm, another state of being. The physical body might perish, but the essence of a person, the soul, endured.

And it wasn't just the souls of humans I encountered. I saw the spirits of animals, their lights shimmering with the same vibrant energy as the human souls.

A playful golden light represented a dog's unbounded joy, a majestic silver light reflected the wisdom of an old owl, a vibrant green light spoke of a cat's independent spirit. The interconnectedness extended beyond humanity, a vast web of life encompassing all sentient beings, a reflection of the holistic nature of existence.

The most profound change, however, was in my perception of time. In the physical world, time was linear, a constant march forward, relentless and unforgiving. In this realm, time was fluid, cyclical, almost nonexistent. There was no past, no present, no future; there was only the eternal now, an infinite expanse of being. This shift in perception liberated me from the constraints of linear thinking, allowing me to embrace the totality of my experience, both in life and in death.

The souls I encountered offered lessons in acceptance, not just of death, but of life itself. They showed me the beauty of imperfection, the strength in vulnerability, the enduring power of love. Their lives, both joyful and sorrowful, were a testament to the richness and complexity of human experience.

They taught me that life wasn't about avoiding pain or suffering, but about embracing the full spectrum of emotions, acknowledging the darkness as much as the light.

One day, or perhaps it was a night, I saw a soul whose light was a deep, rich indigo. As I approached, images flooded my consciousness - a life dedicated to artistic expression, a life filled with creativity and passion, a life marked by both triumph and profound disappointment. I saw the pain of rejection, the struggle for recognition, the yearning for connection. But I also saw the joy of creation, the exhilaration of pushing boundaries, the satisfaction of leaving a lasting legacy. The soul's light pulsed with a rhythm that mirrored the ebb and flow of its experiences, a perfect reflection of the complexities of a life lived to its fullest.

This soul taught me that the pain of loss, the sting of rejection, the bitterness of disappointment - these were not obstacles to be avoided, but integral parts of the human experience, essential ingredients in the recipe of a meaningful life.

They were not things to be feared or suppressed, but acknowledged, embraced, and integrated into the whole.

Through my encounters with these souls, I learned that acceptance of death wasn’t about forgetting or denying the pain of loss. It was about integrating that pain into the fabric of my being, transforming it into something meaningful, something that enriched my life rather than diminished it. It was about acknowledging the totality of my experience, embracing the light and the dark, the joy and the sorrow, the triumph and the defeat.

My grief for Lyra didn't disappear; it transformed. It became a gentler, more nuanced emotion, interwoven with the joy of our enduring connection. It was a testament to the intensity of our love, a reminder of the beauty and fragility of life. It became a source of strength, a wellspring of inspiration, a reminder to live each moment with passion and intention, knowing that life is precious and fleeting. This afterlife, this ethereal realm, wasn't an escape from grief, it was a crucible, a place where the raw pain of loss was refined, transformed, and ultimately, transcended.

It was a new beginning, a continuation of our journey, an eternal love story playing out in a realm beyond time and space. And in that, I found a profound and enduring peace. The shimmering forms around me continued their ethereal dance, but my focus shifted inward. The vastness of this afterlife, the countless souls swirling around me, faded into the background as I retreated into the sanctuary of my memories. Lyra. The name itself, a whisper on my lips, carried the weight of a thousand unspoken words, a lifetime of shared laughter and whispered secrets, of sun-drenched days and moonlit nights.

It began subtly, a flicker of an image, a scent on the wind – the intoxicating fragrance of her favorite lavender perfume, a ghost of her laughter echoing in the silent expanse. Then came the flood. Not a chaotic deluge, but a gentle, persistent tide, drawing me back to the shores of our past. I saw us, young and carefree, running barefoot on a beach, the sun warming our skin, the salty air filling our lungs. I felt the warmth of her hand in mine, the thrill of our first kiss, the shared exhilaration of discovering hidden coves and secret beaches.

These weren't just visual memories; they were sensory experiences, resurrected with astonishing clarity. I could feel the texture of her hair against my cheek, the softness of her skin under my fingertips. I could taste the salty tang of the sea air, the sweet tang of the wild strawberries we'd stolen from a nearby field.

These memories weren't merely snapshots of a life lived; they were portals, opening into a world of shared emotion. Each memory was a keystone, supporting the arch of our love story, each a testament to the depth of our bond. I saw us at our most vulnerable, our moments of shared pain and doubt, of anxieties and fears. But even these moments, shrouded in shadows as they were, held a certain beauty, a testament to the strength of our relationship, the unwavering support we offered each other during the storms. There was a profound understanding woven into the tapestry of our experiences, a silent recognition of our shared humanity, our flaws, our strengths, our vulnerabilities.

The weight of her loss, which had initially been a crushing burden, felt different now. It was still present, an ache in my chest, a constant reminder of her absence. But it wasn't the suffocating grief that had consumed me in the days following her death. This grief was softer, more nuanced. It was a constant companion, a part of me now, woven into the fabric of my being.

I revisited the day we met, a chance encounter in a bustling city square, our eyes locking across the crowded space. I could hear the rhythm of her laughter, the gentle cadence of her voice, the sweet melody of her words. I saw the shy smile that played on her lips as we began our conversation, the hesitant touches that gradually transformed into confident embraces. Each moment played out before me, not as a static memory, but as a vibrant and evolving narrative, imbued with emotional depth.

I remembered our first arguments, passionate and intense, the stormy clashes that tested the limits of our love. Yet, even these memories weren't simply painful. They were reminders of the fierce passion that ignited our relationship, the deep connection that allowed us to navigate the turbulent seas of our disagreements, to emerge stronger and more intertwined than before.

There were quieter moments as well, the shared silences, the comfortable companionship, the unspoken understanding that transcended words. I saw us curled up together on a rainy afternoon, reading books, the gentle patter of rain against the windowpane creating a soothing soundtrack to our quiet intimacy. I remembered the warmth of her presence, the comfort of her nearness, the unspoken bond that connected us on a deeper level than words could ever express.

Through these memories, I found healing. It wasn't a linear process, not a simple progression from sorrow to joy. It was a complex, multi-layered experience, a journey through a labyrinth of emotions. There were times when the grief would surge, overwhelming me with the raw pain of loss. But I learned to allow myself to feel these emotions, to embrace the sorrow without judgment, to acknowledge its power without succumbing to its tyranny.

The memories of Lyra weren't just about the past; they were about the present and the future. They were a testament to the enduring power of love, a reminder of the depth of our connection, a source of strength that carried me through the darkest of times. They showed me that our love wasn't confined to the boundaries of the physical world; it transcended mortality, echoing through the ethereal landscape of this afterlife.

I saw her in the gentle sway of the willow trees, in the iridescent shimmer of a dragonfly's wings, in the soft whisper of the wind through the leaves. I felt her presence in the warmth of the sun, in the cool caress of the moonlight, in the vibrant energy of the surrounding souls. It wasn't a hallucination, not a figment of my imagination. It was a recognition, a deep-seated knowing that her essence remained, interwoven with the very fabric of this realm.

This afterlife wasn't a desolate wasteland of souls; it was a kaleidoscope of experiences, a vast tapestry of memories, emotions, and connections. And within that tapestry, within the heart of this ethereal realm, I found Lyra again, not as a ghost or a specter, but as a constant source of inspiration, a guiding light, a beacon in the vast expanse of this afterlife. The ache remained, but it was now a gentle ache, a bittersweet memory that evoked both profound sadness and profound love.

It was in these memories that I found solace, not an escape from grief, but a sanctuary within the storm. It was in the revisiting of our shared moments, the re-experiencing of our love story, that I began to heal. The grief transformed, evolving from a crushing weight into a gentler, more manageable sorrow. It became a source of strength, an integral part of my being, a testament to the depth and intensity of our love. Lyra's absence was still palpable, a constant reminder of the preciousness of life, but I no longer felt lost or alone. I had found her, and myself, in the heart of the memories we had created together. And in that, I discovered a peace that was both profound and enduring, a peace that transcended the boundaries of life and death.

Our love story, once confined to the mortal realm, continued to unfold in this ethereal space, a testament to a connection that was stronger than death itself. And that, I realized, was the truest form of solace. A love that lived on, eternally.
The shimmering forms around me thinned, the ethereal music fading to a low hum. The initial chaos of arrival had settled into a strange, quietude. It wasn't emptiness, not exactly. More like a vast, echoing chamber where the whispers of countless lives mingled, a symphony of sorrow and joy, triumph and defeat. Yet, amidst this celestial cacophony, a singular clarity emerged - the realization that this afterlife wasn't a judgment, not a reward or punishment, but a continuation, a transformation.

My understanding of death, so rigidly defined by the limitations of my earthly existence, shattered like fragile glass. Death, I now saw, wasn't an ending, but a transition. A shedding of the physical form, a release from the constraints of the body, a journey into the boundless expanse of consciousness.

This wasn't the heaven or hell of religious dogma; it was something far more nuanced, far more complex. It was a reflection of the lives we lived, the choices we made, the loves we embraced, the losses we endured.

The souls around me weren't ghosts in the traditional sense; they weren't shadowy figures clinging to the mortal world. They were... vibrant. Energy. Light. Each soul glowed with an inner luminescence, a testament to the unique experiences of a life lived. Some shimmered with a radiant, almost blinding light, while others burned with a softer, gentler glow. Some were vibrant, pulsating with energy, while others were still, serene, radiating a profound sense of peace. I sensed no judgment, no hierarchy, just a vast spectrum of existence, a reflection of the diversity of human experience.

I wandered through this ethereal landscape, drawn by an invisible force, a silent invitation to explore the nature of this existence. I saw souls engaged in joyful reunions, their forms intertwining, their light mingling in a radiant embrace. I witnessed others grappling with unresolved issues, their light flickering, their energy struggling to find equilibrium. There were those who seemed lost, adrift in the vastness of this realm, their light dimmed, their energy scattered, lost in the echoes of their past.

The weight of Lyra's absence still tugged at my heart, a constant reminder of the void she left behind. But here, in this otherworldly realm, it felt different. It wasn't a gaping wound, but a scar, a testament to a love that had burned bright, a love that transcended the limitations of time and space. The pain remained, but it was softened, nuanced, woven into the fabric of my being. I understood, with a clarity that defied logic, that our connection didn't end with her death. It evolved, transformed, taking on a new dimension in this ethereal expanse.

I began to understand that the afterlife was less about a physical location and more about a state of being. It was a realm of consciousness, a reflection of the soul's journey. The souls I encountered weren't confined to a specific location; they existed in a fluid state, their essence shifting, evolving, adapting to the nature of their experience. Some seemed anchored to particular memories, replaying moments from their lives, reliving emotions with intense clarity. Others moved freely through the landscape, exploring, learning, evolving.

I spent days, weeks, perhaps even centuries in this otherworldly space, time having lost its linear progression. I watched souls evolve, heal, grow. I saw those who had been consumed by bitterness and anger gradually release their burdens, their light growing brighter, their energy more vibrant. I saw others who had lived in fear or shame find solace and acceptance, their energy shifting from a muted flicker to a radiant glow. This realm offered opportunities for growth, for healing, for reconciliation, a chance to confront unresolved issues, to find peace, to achieve a sense of completion.

The philosophical implications were profound. If this was the afterlife, then the meaning of life itself took on a new dimension. It wasn't about achieving worldly success or accumulating material possessions. It was about the connections we forged, the love we shared, the impact we made on the lives of others. It was about the journey, not the destination.

I began to understand the true nature of grief. It wasn't something to be overcome or suppressed. It was a testament to the depth of love, a reminder of the preciousness of life, an integral part of the human experience. Here, in this realm of ethereal energy, I felt no judgment for my grief, no pressure to move on. The pain was acknowledged, respected, integrated into the tapestry of my being. It was a part of my story, and like all stories, it had its shadows as well as its light. The darkness merely served to highlight the brilliance of the light.

My own light, once dimmed by the weight of Lyra's loss, began to glow brighter. I felt a sense of peace, a profound acceptance, a deep understanding of my place in the universe. This wasn't an escape from reality, but an expansion of it. It was a realization that the boundaries of life and death were far more permeable than I had ever imagined. The love I shared with Lyra, the memories we created, they weren't confined to the mortal realm. They existed here, too, woven into the fabric of this ethereal landscape.

The most striking aspect of this afterlife was the absence of judgment. There was no celestial court, no divine reckoning. Each soul seemed to find its own path, its own rhythm, its own pace. The energy of the realm itself seemed to support this process, offering guidance, comfort, and an opportunity for profound personal growth. It was a space for healing, for learning, for understanding.

I realized that the afterlife wasn't about a reward or punishment; it was about growth, transformation, and integration. It was about confronting unresolved issues, reconciling with oneself and others, and ultimately, finding peace. This understanding offered me a perspective that transcended the limited view I had held while alive. The concept of 'moving on' was irrelevant here. It was more about embracing the totality of one's existence, acknowledging both the light and the darkness, and finding a sense of wholeness.

And in this vast, ethereal space, I found Lyra not as a ghostly apparition but as a resonant energy, a subtle presence woven into the fabric of the afterlife. Her light, brighter and more vibrant than I'd ever imagined, danced among the countless others, a testament to a life lived fully, loved deeply, and mourned profoundly. Her absence didn't diminish, but it shifted, transforming from a raw wound into a soft, persistent ache, a reminder of a love that continued to illuminate my soul.

This afterlife, I concluded, was less a place and more a state of being, a continuation of consciousness, a reflection of the lives we lived, and a testament to the enduring power of love and connection.
It wasn't a destination, but a journey, a constant evolution, a never-ending exploration of the self and the universe. And in that journey, I found a peace that transcended death itself – a peace that was both profound and profoundly personal.

Chapter Six A Ghostly Existence

The initial shock of disembodiment slowly gave way to a strange sort of acceptance. It wasn't the serene, blissful transition I might have imagined from earthly tales. Instead, it was a chaotic symphony of sensations – a constant hum beneath the surface, a kaleidoscope of colours shifting and swirling around me like a living aurora borealis. The whispers of countless souls, a chorus of untold stories, washed over me in waves, sometimes gentle, sometimes overwhelming.

Initially, I found navigating this ethereal landscape disorienting. My perception of space and time warped, becoming fluid and almost intangible. Distances stretched and compressed, moments expanded and contracted, depending on the intensity of the emotions surrounding me. I could be standing in a garden of radiant light one moment, and the next, plunged into a swirling vortex of shadows and whispers, a maelstrom of unresolved grief and lingering regrets.

The sensory experience was unlike anything I had ever known. Touch was replaced by a sense of resonance, a vibrational connection with the energy of other souls. I could feel the joy radiating from those who had found peace, the lingering bitterness of those still wrestling with earthly attachments, and the deep, resonant sadness of those who had left behind unfinished business. Sight evolved into an awareness of light and energy, of vibrant hues and shadowy depths, each shade reflecting the emotional spectrum of the souls around me. Sound transformed into a multi-layered hum, a constant symphony of whispered conversations, echoing laughter, and melancholic sighs. Even the concept of taste and smell was altered, morphing into a kind of energetic essence, reflecting the vibrancy or stagnation of a soul's energy.

One of the most significant challenges was learning to manipulate my own energy. It was a slow, painstaking process, akin to learning to walk again after a debilitating injury. Initially, I drifted aimlessly, a leaf on a celestial wind, carried by the currents of energy surrounding me. I learned to focus my intent, to concentrate my energy, to gradually exert more control over my movements.

It was a delicate dance, a process of learning to inhabit this new form, this ethereal body of pure energy.

The most remarkable aspect was the ability to connect with other souls. Communication wasn't verbal in the traditional sense. Instead, it was a shared understanding, a direct transmission of thoughts and emotions. I could feel the pain and sorrow of those who had lost loved ones, the joy and contentment of those who had found peace, and the lingering anger and frustration of those who had unresolved conflicts.

I encountered many souls grappling with their mortality. Some clung fiercely to their earthly memories, replaying their lives on a continuous loop, unable to let go of regrets or unfinished business. Others were lost, adrift in the vastness of this realm, their energy flickering weakly, their spirits fragmented. I learned that the duration of one's time in this space was not fixed. Some souls lingered for centuries, while others seemed to pass through almost instantaneously, their energy fading into the ether.

Over time, I learned to recognize patterns in this ghostly existence. I discovered that those souls who found peace and resolution often radiated a calm, harmonious energy, their light strong and steady. They were able to connect with others, offering comfort and understanding. On the other hand, those consumed by negative emotions - anger, resentment, guilt - were often trapped in cycles of repetition, their energy fragmented and weak. Their light flickered, casting long shadows.

There were also those who seemed to be stuck in a state of transition. They weren't fully integrated into the spirit world, nor were they completely detached from the earthly realm. These souls often manifested as wispy, fragmented forms, their energy drifting and uncertain. Their experiences mirrored the unresolved issues they had carried with them from their earthly lives. The weight of their past held them captive, preventing them from finding peace and moving on.

I watched as some souls underwent a process of healing and transformation. Their initial pain and despair gradually gave way to acceptance, understanding, and finally, peace.

Their light grew brighter, their energy stronger, their forms becoming more defined and whole. The process was often slow and painful, marked by moments of intense emotional turmoil. But the potential for growth and healing was undeniable.

I eventually learned to navigate this ethereal plane with a newfound ease. I learned to recognize the subtle energies of the realm and communicate with other souls. I discovered that this world was not a static realm but a fluid, evolving landscape, constantly shifting and changing in response to the collective energies of those within it. The absence of physical constraints allowed for greater emotional freedom, but it was also a place where emotional intensity was amplified.

In this spectral realm, emotions were not masked or hidden. They were raw and powerful, both exhilarating and terrifying. Grief, loss, love, anger – all intensified beyond anything experienced in the physical world. But, paradoxically, this raw intensity opened doors to deep understanding, self-acceptance, and profound empathy.

The more I learned to navigate this emotional landscape, the clearer my own path became.

The absence of Lyra continued to weigh on me, but the nature of my grief was transformed. It was no longer a gaping wound, but a deep, resonant ache, woven into the fabric of my being. Her presence, though ethereal, was palpable. I felt it as a gentle warmth, a comforting energy that enveloped me like a soft light. She wasn't a ghost in the traditional sense, but a radiant energy, a persistent echo of our love, a reminder of a life lived fully, a connection that transcended the limitations of time and space. And in this spectral realm, where connections ran deeper than anything I'd ever known, I knew that our bond wasn't broken, but merely transformed. This wasn't an ending, but a continuation of a journey we were undertaking together, in a new and unexpected way. The memories we shared were not merely memories, but resonant energies that danced and intertwined with us in this new existence. This afterlife was a tapestry woven from threads of love, loss, and the enduring power of connection.

From my ethereal vantage point, the living world appeared as a vibrant, chaotic tapestry. I watched, unseen, unheard, yet acutely aware of the ebb and flow of human lives. The intensity of their emotions, once experienced firsthand, now struck me with a new kind of clarity, a detachment that allowed for a deeper understanding. It was like watching a play, a drama unfolding with characters caught in the throes of their own narratives.

I saw lovers embrace, their energy intertwining in a radiant glow, a testament to the potent force of connection. Their joy resonated with me, a warm current in the otherwise cool, ethereal atmosphere. Yet, even in their happiness, I detected a subtle undercurrent of vulnerability, a fragility that underscored the transient nature of earthly existence. Their laughter, once a familiar sound, now held a poignant echo, a reminder of the fleeting nature of moments.

I observed families gathered, their energies blending in a complex pattern. The intricate dance of familial love, with its inherent tensions and unspoken resentments, was laid bare. I saw the weight of expectation, the burden of unspoken words, and the quiet ache of unmet needs. The children's energy pulsed with a bright, untainted innocence, a stark contrast to the more complex, often muted energies of their parents. The children's radiant energy reminded me of the purity of life before the world's weight settles upon our shoulders.

Then there were the solitary figures, their energy dimmed and isolated, a testament to the loneliness that permeates even the most densely populated areas. Their spirits flickered like dying embers, their forms indistinct, almost transparent. Their isolation resonated with the quiet solitude of my own experience, a shared silence that transcended the boundaries between the living and the dead. Their quiet despair echoed my own quieter moments of loneliness in my disembodied state.

The city throbbed with a relentless energy, a frenzied rhythm of movement and interaction. The energy was intense, a complex symphony of desires, ambitions, and anxieties. I saw the ruthless pursuit of success, the desperate craving for connection, the quiet resignation to mundane routines. The relentless pursuit of material wealth struck me as a curious spectacle, a frantic dance around the ephemeral. The living seemed so preoccupied with their earthly pursuits, so engrossed in their own dramas, oblivious to the subtle energies that surrounded them, the silent chorus of departed souls.

I watched individuals struggling with their own internal battles, their energies tangled and conflicted. I saw the weight of regret etched into their very essence, the lingering shadows of past mistakes clinging to them like unwanted garments. Their struggles resonated deeply, a painful reminder of the battles I'd fought myself during my earthly existence, and the struggles I witnessed in others within my spectral realm. I saw the internal struggles reflected in the way they moved, the way they interacted, a silent testament to the complexities of the human condition.

The subtle shift in their energy as they experienced moments of profound joy or crushing despair was a stark reminder of the emotional intensity of the human experience, a bittersweet symphony of highs and lows. I witnessed moments of profound connection, moments of unexpected kindness, moments of unexpected cruelty, all woven together in the complex tapestry of human interaction.

I focused on individuals engaged in acts of selfless compassion, their energy radiating outwards, a beacon of hope in the often-dark world. Their light was strong, resonant, and steady. Their acts of kindness pulsed with a radiant energy that dispelled the gloom, a testament to the enduring power of human empathy. These moments, however fleeting, were a reminder that even amid the chaos and turmoil, there was an inherent capacity for goodness and compassion.

I observed those consumed by anger and bitterness, their energy fractured and chaotic, their forms clouded by shadows. They were trapped in a cycle of negativity, their light flickering weakly, almost extinguished. Their pain resonated with my own past experiences, reminding me of the destructive power of unresolved emotions. Their pain served as a stark contrast to the serene energies of those who had found peace, a reminder that the path to serenity wasn't always straightforward.

My detached observation allowed me to see patterns in human behaviour, to recognize the underlying emotional currents that shaped their lives. I witnessed the subtle dance between connection and isolation, between joy and sorrow, between hope and despair. These patterns, these interwoven emotional threads, mirrored the subtle energy currents of the spirit world, a reflection of the universal human experience.

The living world, from my spectral perspective, was a poignant spectacle, both beautiful and tragic. It was a testament to the resilience and fragility of the human spirit, a reminder of the profound beauty and heartbreaking sorrow that are intrinsic to earthly existence. While I had found a measure of peace in the afterlife, the observations of the living world brought a fresh perspective on my own experiences, a poignant reminder of the value of connection, of the importance of living each moment with intention, and the bittersweet reality of transient earthly experiences. The beauty of the living world, however, was its unpredictability, the ever-changing patterns, and the constant flow of emotions, a complex symphony played out on the grand stage of human existence. The weight of understanding these emotions, this emotional resonance, and these ephemeral experiences, both in life and death, became a new chapter in my ghostly existence. It was a silent understanding, a profound communion beyond words. My first attempts at communication were clumsy, pathetic whispers lost in the wind. I tried focusing my energy, shaping thoughts into images, hoping to imprint them on the minds of the living. I envisioned vibrant butterflies, a symbol of transformation, a message of hope, flitting before the eyes of a grieving woman I often observed sitting by the river. Nothing. The woman continued to stare blankly at the water, her energy a dull, persistent ache.

Then I tried something bolder. I focused on a young man walking his dog in the park, his energy vibrant and hopeful. I attempted to project a feeling, a sense of joy, a playful tug at the corner of his lips. Again, nothing. He continued his stroll, his gaze fixed on the ground. Frustration gnawed at me, a familiar phantom pain. Was I truly invisible, inconsequential, even in death?

I shifted my focus, experimenting with different approaches. I tried to manipulate small objects, a fallen leaf, a stray pebble. My energy rippled, almost tangible, but the leaf remained still, the pebble unmoved. The limitations of my power were disheartening. I was a ghost, a wisp of energy, tethered to a realm beyond the reach of the living. Yet, I felt an undeniable pull towards them, a longing to connect, to bridge the chasm between worlds.

Days bled into weeks. I observed, I learned, I adapted my methods. Instead of direct communication, I started influencing their environment subtly. I guided a lost child back to their parents by subtly shifting their perception, making a familiar landmark appear more prominent. The relief on the parents' faces, the sudden surge of their energy, was a thrilling sensation, a tangible reward. It wasn't direct communication, but it was a connection nonetheless.

I orchestrated small coincidences, bringing together individuals who needed each other. A lost book found its way into the hands of a reader desperate for solace.

A missed phone call was suddenly remembered, preventing a potential disaster. These were small acts, yet they yielded surprisingly significant results. The ripple effect of these interventions resonated through the living world, a silent symphony played out on the grand stage of human existence.

One evening, I focused my energy on a young artist painting in the square. His energy was melancholic, burdened by self-doubt. I subtly nudged his brush, guiding his hand towards a stroke of brilliant color, a touch of unexpected vibrancy that transformed the entire painting. As he stepped back to admire his work, a genuine smile touched his lips. The shift in his energy was palpable, a release of tension. In that moment, I felt a flicker of connection, a fragile thread linking our worlds.

However, not all my attempts yielded positive results. There were times when I tried to influence individuals for what I considered their own good, only to see the consequences backfire. I tried to prevent a destructive argument, guiding individuals away from each other.

However, their unresolved issues festered, leading to a deeper rift later. The delicate balance of human interactions was a complex web, far beyond my limited comprehension. My ghostly interference only served to muddle the flow, underscoring the unpredictable nature of human relationships. My interference, well-intentioned as it was, was an unexpected ripple with unforeseen consequences. I had learned a valuable lesson: My role was not to intervene but to observe, to understand, and to learn from the tapestry of life unfolding before me.

Then there was the musician, a talented young man battling a crippling addiction. His energy was dark, constricted, choking on the shadows of his own making. I attempted to communicate, to convey a message of hope, to guide him towards recovery. I filled his head with visions of his own potential, visions of his music echoing through halls, visions of applause. However, his addiction was too strong, its grip too tight. The pain in his eyes was visceral, a mirror of my own experiences with self-destruction. My attempt at communication only amplified his internal struggle, adding another layer of complexity to his pain.

I learned that some battles, even from beyond the veil, cannot be won from a distance, no matter how much energy is poured into the effort. The weight of understanding these limitations, this painful truth, only deepened my understanding of human struggles.

Through my trials and errors, I discovered a peculiar pattern. Individuals who were open to the possibility of something beyond the tangible were more susceptible to my subtle influences. Those who held strong beliefs, those who lived with a sense of wonder, were more receptive to the unseen currents that flowed between worlds. Their energies were less rigid, more fluid, like a calm river rather than a raging storm. They were the ones most likely to sense my presence, to pick up on the faint whispers of the afterlife, even without direct communication.

The elderly woman, who sat on her porch every afternoon, crocheting with intricate precision, was one of them. Her energy was gentle, calm, radiating an aura of quiet contentment. I often spent time near her, feeling the warmth of her essence. One day, I managed to send her a clear image, a vision of a lost photograph, buried deep in her memories. She smiled, a soft, knowing smile, and her gaze seemed to reach beyond the earthly realm. It wasn't a conversation, but it was a connection, a shared understanding between two realms, an acknowledgment of something unseen. This experience felt different, less of a forceful manipulation and more of a gentle nudge, a silent understanding between souls.

Communicating with the living wasn't about shouting across a chasm, it was about whispering secrets in the wind, painting silent messages on the canvases of their dreams. It was about finding the frequencies that resonated, the vulnerabilities that were susceptible to subtle influences. It was about recognizing and respecting the subtle dance of human energy, the intricate tapestry of human experiences. And it was about recognizing that sometimes, the most meaningful connections were formed not through words, but through shared emotions, unspoken understandings, and a quiet acknowledgment of the unknown. The path was complex, riddled with trial and error. However, each new understanding, each tiny step forward, each whisper heard across the boundary of life and death, nourished my ghostly existence, making it feel less lonely, less hollow. The journey of communication was itself a profound experience, shaping the ghostly life I never expected, or wanted. The beauty of it all was in its complexity, its silent symphony of experiences.

The weight of my unfinished business pressed down on me, a suffocating blanket of regret and longing. It wasn't just the abruptness of my death, the sudden severing of ties, but the lingering echoes of unresolved conflicts, unspoken words, and missed opportunities. My life, before this ethereal existence, had been a chaotic tapestry woven with threads of passion, recklessness, and profound sorrow. Now, adrift in this liminal space, I was forced to confront the raw, unvarnished truth of it all.

My relationship with my sister, Clara, had been a battlefield of unspoken resentments and simmering jealousy. We were as different as night and day, her calm practicality a stark contrast to my tempestuous nature. Our arguments were legendary, fueled by years of pent-up frustration and misunderstandings. I had carried a deep-seated resentment for her, a bitterness that had festered like a malignant wound. Now, from this spectral vantage point, I saw the fragility of our bond, the unspoken love that lay beneath the surface of our constant clashes. I could see the pain in her eyes, the loneliness that mirrored my own. I longed to reach out, to apologize, to mend the fractured pieces of our relationship. But the chasm between our worlds remained impenetrable, a cruel barrier against reconciliation.

I reached out to her, as I had others, with images and feelings - the shared memory of our childhood laughter, the feel of her hand in mine, the warmth of her embrace. The images flickered at the edge of her consciousness, a fleeting whisper of a memory long forgotten. However, the memories were veiled in the sadness and confusion of her grief. The emotions, the genuine longing for connection, seemed to be lost in the static of her mourning. My efforts were faint echoes, barely registering on her distracted consciousness.

Then there was Liam, the love of my life, the man whose absence had carved a gaping hole in my soul. Our love had been a tempestuous storm, passionate and destructive, a whirlwind of intense emotions and reckless abandon. We had clashed, we had argued, we had hurt each other deeply. Yet, beneath the turmoil, there was a profound connection, a love that transcended the pain and the chaos. I had carried his love like a precious relic, a painful, bittersweet reminder of what I had lost. Now, I was haunted by the things left unsaid, the promises left unfulfilled, the unspoken apologies that echoed between us like unanswered prayers.

I sought him out, attempting to reach him with visions of our shared memories—laughing until our sides ached, the scent of his cologne still lingering faintly in my ethereal senses, the sound of his laughter echoing in my spectral ears. My attempts, however, were met with resistance, a wall of stubborn grief. He was consumed by his anger, his resentment, his pain, unable or unwilling to acknowledge my presence, the reality of my passing. His energy was a storm, turbulent and unforgiving, deflecting my attempts at connection. The pain he caused me was nothing compared to the overwhelming sorrow of not being able to share my final goodbye, to ease his pain, to help him heal. I was his ghost, a silent observer of his profound and unrelenting grief.

There was also the matter of my career, the unfinished manuscript gathering dust on my desk. My dreams of becoming a published author remained unrealized, another haunting reminder of unfulfilled potential. I saw my half-written story as a reflection of my own incomplete life, a testament to my unfinished business in the world. The frustration was immense. I spent hours, in my spectral state, revisiting the words I had written, the scenes I had envisioned, and the characters I had created. It was an agonizing experience.

I tried to subtly influence a young writer I had observed, a woman with a remarkable talent and a quiet determination. I tried to guide her, to inspire her, to help her find her way, hoping she would finish my story, somehow carrying my legacy, my unfulfilled potential forward. I left messages within her dreams, fleeting visions of plots and characters, trying to nudge her in the direction of my unfinished work. Yet, I could only offer hints, subtle suggestions, not the full, developed story that resided within my ghostly memory. I watched, helpless, as she worked, hoping my influence would be enough. She finished her novel, a story that was her own, unique, and powerful, but it didn't contain the essence of my story, of my unfinished work.

My ghostly existence was a relentless confrontation with my past, a relentless exercise in acceptance. I had to confront my flaws, my failures, my regrets. I had to make peace with the choices I had made, the life I had lived. I had to come to terms with the reality that some things, some relationships, some dreams would forever remain incomplete, suspended in the bittersweet limbo of what might have been. The process was painful, agonizing, but necessary. It was a part of the journey, a journey of self-discovery that stretched beyond the boundaries of life and death. The release, the acceptance, was a slow, gradual process, each interaction with the living, a subtle step forward.

The haunting melody of unfinished business persisted, but it was slowly being replaced by a quiet acceptance, a profound understanding. The living world continued its ceaseless dance, oblivious to my presence. I learned to appreciate the quiet elegance of observation, the beauty of existence without the chaos of my earthly interference.

I began to understand the intricate choreography of life, the delicate balance of human connections. And in this silent, ghostly existence, I found a strange, unexpected peace. The unresolved issues remained, but their weight had lessened. They were no longer a suffocating blanket, but a poignant reminder of the complexities of life, and of the lingering echo of a life lived fully, even if incompletely. My journey wasn't about resolving every single unresolved issue, but about finding acceptance and moving forward in my spectral state, to find a new kind of peace.

The initial shock of non-existence, the horrifying emptiness of being untethered from the physical world, slowly faded. It was replaced by a peculiar stillness, a quietude that wasn't the absence of sound but a different kind of listening. I began to hear the subtle hum of the universe, the silent symphony of existence unfolding around me, unnoticed by the living. I was a silent observer, a ghost in the machine of life, watching the intricate dance of human interaction, the ebb and flow of emotions, the quiet moments of profound beauty and the explosive bursts of dramatic conflict.

Initially, my spectral existence had felt like a cruel punishment, a perpetual state of limbo. I was trapped between worlds, unable to fully participate in either. The living were oblivious to my presence, their lives continuing without me, as if I were nothing more than a forgotten whisper in the wind. But as time—or rather, the absence of time, as I perceived it—stretched on, I began to adapt. I learned to navigate this ethereal landscape, to find pockets of quietude amidst the chaos of the living world.

I found solace in observing the natural world. The changing seasons, the subtle shift in the light, the rustling of leaves, the songs of birds—these things, once taken for granted, now held a profound beauty. Each sunrise was a masterpiece, each sunset a breathtaking farewell. The world, previously experienced through the filter of my own anxieties and desires, now revealed itself in its raw, unfiltered glory. The mundane became extraordinary, the ordinary transformed into something magical.

I spent hours watching the children play in the park, their laughter echoing in the spaces between my spectral ears.

Their unbridled joy was a balm to my soul, a reminder of the simple pleasures of life, the innocence that had been lost to me too soon. I watched lovers embrace, their passion a vibrant flame burning against the gray backdrop of my ghostly existence. Their connection, their vulnerability, reminded me of the fierce intensity of my love for Liam, a love that burned bright, but eventually, burned out.

The acceptance of my situation didn't come easily. There were days when the pain of loss threatened to consume me, when the loneliness was so overwhelming that I wanted to shatter into a million pieces. But gradually, I learned to manage the pain, to find a quiet space within myself, a sanctuary where I could retreat when the memories became too sharp, when the longing became unbearable.

I learned to appreciate the small moments, the subtle nuances of existence that I had previously overlooked.

The smell of rain on dry earth, the warmth of the sun on my spectral skin, the delicate scent of flowers blooming in the spring—these things became sources of profound comfort, tiny anchors in the vast emptiness of my afterlife.

My relationship with the living shifted as well. My initial attempts to communicate, to influence, to reconnect, had been met with resistance. But gradually, I learned to accept their inability to see me, to hear me, to feel me. My presence, once a desperate plea for connection, became a quiet observation, a silent appreciation of their lives, unburdened by the need for interaction.

I found a peculiar kind of freedom in my spectral state. The limitations of my physical body, the constraints of mortality, were no longer relevant. I could be anywhere, anytime, observing the world from a detached perspective, free from the limitations and expectations of earthly existence. The world was my canvas, and I was a silent observer, content to simply watch the unfolding of life's drama.

The unfinished business still gnawed at me, but it felt different now, less like a suffocating burden and more like a poignant reminder of my past. The unfinished manuscript, the unresolved conflicts, the unsaid words—these were still present, but they no longer defined me. I had learned to live alongside them, to accept their presence without allowing them to control my emotional landscape.

Instead of focusing on the things I couldn't change, I focused on the things I could. I found a sense of purpose in my spectral existence, a kind of quiet contentment that was born out of acceptance and understanding. I was no longer defined by my regrets or my failures, but by the quiet strength that I found within myself, in the stillness of my afterlife.

I realized my journey wasn't about fixing the past, but about finding peace in the present. The past was a part of me, but it was not the whole of me. I was more than my unfinished business, more than my regrets, more than my losses. I was a collection of memories, experiences, and emotions, shaped by both joy and sorrow, success and failure. And in this ethereal existence, I found a way to embrace all of it, to find a kind of tranquility that transcended the boundaries of life and death.

The realization washed over me gradually, like the gentle tide coming in on a quiet beach. There wasn't a grand epiphany, no sudden burst of clarity. It was more of a slow dawning, a quiet understanding that seeped into my spectral being. The weight of the past began to lift, not disappear entirely, but become manageable, less oppressive. The sharp edges of grief and loss softened, their intensity muted, the pain still present, but no longer the dominant force in my existence.

I began to see beauty in the imperfections, the unfinished narratives of the living. Their struggles, their heartbreaks, their triumphs—these were all part of the intricate tapestry of life, a testament to the human experience in all its complexity and contradictions. I saw the beauty in their resilience, their capacity for love and forgiveness, even in the face of profound loss.

My existence became a quiet meditation, a prolonged reflection on the nature of existence, the ephemeral beauty of life, and the relentless march of time. I learned to appreciate the stillness, the quiet moments of contemplation, the absence of the frenetic energy that had once defined my earthly life. The chaos of emotions had settled, leaving behind a quiet serenity, a profound sense of peace. It wasn't a joyous peace, not a celebratory one, but one born of acceptance, of understanding, of a quiet contentment with the unfolding of life, both in its vibrant fullness and its poignant incompleteness.

The lingering echoes of unfinished business persisted, but they no longer held the same power over me. They were now faint whispers, a poignant reminder of a life lived fully, albeit imperfectly. They were a testament to my journey, to my growth, to my eventual acceptance of my ghostly existence, a journey that led me to find a unique, unexpected, and enduring peace.

The quiet understanding that permeated my being, this tranquility born from acceptance and quiet observation, was a reward in itself, a testament to the resilience of the human spirit, even beyond the boundaries of life and death. The spectral existence, initially felt as a punishment, a cruel joke of fate, transformed into a profound and unexpected gift: the gift of quietude, the gift of acceptance, and the gift of a hard-won peace.

Chapter Seven Eternal Bonds

The quietude of my afterlife wasn't a void, but a canvas upon which the memories of love were painted in shades of bittersweet nostalgia. Liam's memory, once a searing wound, now existed as a soft glow, a persistent warmth that didn't burn but illuminated the landscape of my spectral existence. I saw him in the way the sunlight slanted through the leaves of the ancient oak tree in our favorite park, in the gentle murmur of the stream that once mirrored the quiet intimacy of our whispered conversations.

I started to see love differently. Not as a possessive force, demanding reciprocation and fueled by physical proximity, but as an energy, an imprint on the very fabric of existence. I saw it in the way a mother instinctively knew her child's needs, in the quiet comfort a friend offered without words, in the selfless dedication of a caregiver. It wasn't confined to romantic entanglements; it was a universal force, a binding energy that transcended the limitations of life and death.

I encountered other spectral beings, ethereal figures drifting through the spaces between worlds. Some were lost and bewildered, caught in the throes of unresolved grief and clinging to the remnants of earthly desires. Others, like myself, had found a kind of peace, an acceptance of their spectral state. Their stories were diverse, their losses profound, yet their experiences converged on a shared understanding: love, in its various forms, persisted.

One such being, a woman I'll call Elara, had spent centuries searching for her lost son. Her grief was palpable, a heavy cloak she wore with weary resignation. Yet, in her unwavering love, in her persistent search, there was a strength, a quiet determination that transcended her spectral limitations. Her love wasn't confined to the physical realm; it stretched across the vast emptiness of the afterlife, a beacon of hope in the desolate landscape of her existence.

Elara's story opened my eyes to the resilience of love. It wasn't fragile or ephemeral; it was a deep wellspring that could endure even the most devastating losses.

It wasn't bound by physical limitations; it existed beyond the confines of space and time. Her unwavering devotion to her son, her persistent search, was a testament to love's enduring power, its ability to transcend the limitations of mortality.

I began to understand that love's nature in the afterlife was not about physical union or earthly expressions. It was about remembrance, about the enduring echoes of connection, about the imprint of love etched into the soul. It was the quiet comfort of knowing that someone had loved you, that you had loved them, a feeling that reverberated through the silent symphony of the afterlife.

This wasn't a romantic love, the kind I had shared with Liam, defined by passionate encounters and shared dreams. This was a deeper, more profound kind of love, a spiritual connection that transcended the physical realm. It was the love that connected me to the earth, to the living, to the subtle rhythms of nature, and to the other spectral beings who shared this ethereal landscape.

I realized that the pain of loss was an integral part of this ethereal love. It was a testament to the depth of the connection, a measure of the love that had existed in the earthly realm. The absence was palpable, the silence deafening, yet within that emptiness, the echoes of love persisted, a faint whisper that resonated through the silent chambers of my spectral existence.

The concept of "forever" took on a new meaning in this realm. It wasn't a linear progression of time, but an eternal present, a constant state of being. The past, the present, and the future were intertwined, a tapestry woven with memories, emotions, and the lingering echoes of love. Liam, Elara's son, the countless others I encountered—they were all part of this eternal present, their love interwoven into the very fabric of my afterlife.

This wasn't the paradise I had once envisioned, a place of reunion and blissful reunion with loved ones. It was something different, something more complex, more nuanced. It was a quiet acceptance of loss, a profound understanding of love's enduring power, a recognition that love's essence continued to resonate even in the absence of physical presence.

I began to observe the living world with a new perspective, seeing their love stories unfold, their connections forming and dissolving, their hearts breaking and healing. Their transient loves, their fleeting connections, their passionate encounters, their quiet affections, these were all part of the grand tapestry of human experience, a testament to the resilience of the human spirit.

Their love, like mine with Liam, was both beautiful and heartbreaking. It was a testament to the fragility and strength of the human heart, the capacity to love fiercely, to lose profoundly, and to find a way to move forward, to embrace life in all its glorious complexities and poignant imperfections. It was in these observations that I found a sense of peace, a quiet contentment with the unfolding of life, both in its vibrant fullness and its poignant incompleteness.

This wasn't a joyful existence, not in the traditional sense. It wasn't filled with exuberant celebrations or joyous reunions. It was a quieter kind of peace, a profound understanding of the ebb and flow of existence, the relentless march of time, and the enduring power of love. It was a peace that resided in the acceptance of loss, in the quiet recognition of love's persistence beyond the boundaries of life and death.

The echoes of unfinished business, once a burden, now served as a reminder of a life fully lived, imperfectly yet authentically. The unanswered questions, the unresolved conflicts, the unsaid words—these were now parts of a larger narrative, a story that extended beyond the confines of mortality.

My spectral existence, once a source of unimaginable pain, became a unique opportunity for reflection, for understanding, for a deeper appreciation of the nature of love and loss. It wasn't about escaping the pain, but about learning to live alongside it, to find a space of quietude amidst the chaos of emotions, and to recognize the profound beauty in the imperfections of life and love.

The love I experienced in this ethereal realm wasn't about romantic fulfillment or physical union. It was about connection, about the echoes of memories, about the enduring imprint of love on the soul. It was a quiet understanding, a profound acceptance, a persistent resonance of love's enduring energy. It was a love that transcended the limitations of the physical world, a love that existed in the spaces between worlds, a love that echoed through the silent symphony of the afterlife. And in that quiet echo, I finally found my peace. A peace that wasn't born of oblivion, but from a deep, resonant understanding of love's transcendent nature. A peace that whispered, "Love endures."

Elara's spectral form shimmered, a translucent figure woven from moonlight and sorrow. She hadn't spoken much since our first encounter, her silence a heavy weight in the ethereal air. Yet, a subtle shift had occurred between us, an unspoken understanding that transcended words. We were bound not by blood or earthly ties, but by the shared sorrow of loss, the persistent ache of a love that stretched beyond the grave. It was a bond forged in the crucible of grief, a connection as delicate as spun glass yet strong as ancient oak.

We spent hours in silent communion, adrift in the silent expanse of the afterlife. I felt a pull towards her, a sense of kinship that resonated deep within my spectral being. It wasn't merely empathy; it was a recognition, a knowing that transcended the limitations of our separate experiences. She saw in me a reflection of her own pain, a mirror to her unyielding love, and in turn, I saw in her a testament to the indomitable spirit of the human heart.

One day, as the ethereal sunlight painted the landscape in hues of amethyst and silver, Elara began to share her story. It was a tale of love and loss, of fierce devotion and unending sorrow. It was a story that echoed my own, resonating with a depth that transcended the individual narratives, creating a harmony of shared grief. She spoke of her son, a vibrant young man with a laughter that still echoed in her spectral form, a memory that burned as bright as a distant star. He had died tragically, snatched away in the prime of his youth, leaving behind a void that could never be filled. But her love for him, she explained, had not diminished; it had evolved. It had become a guiding force, a spiritual compass leading her through the desolate landscape of her afterlife.

Her love wasn't merely a memory, a nostalgic echo of a past life. It was a living entity, a powerful force that shaped her very being. It was the force that propelled her to search for him, to seek answers, to find a measure of closure that the earthly realm had denied her. Her love was a relentless energy that refused to be extinguished by time or death. Her search wasn't fueled by hope for a reunion in the traditional sense, but by a desire to connect, to maintain the energy of their bond, to preserve the essence of their relationship across the chasm of death.

I began to understand that our shared experience was more than just a parallel; it was a symphony of grief, a harmonious resonance of two souls connected through the universal language of loss. We weren't simply sharing our stories; we were weaving a tapestry of shared experience, a spiritual connection that transcended words and emotions. It was a silent conversation, a dialogue of the heart, a resonance of souls that reverberated through the silent spaces of our spectral existence.

As Elara spoke, I began to glimpse the subtle nuances of the spiritual world. The afterlife wasn't merely a void, a desolate landscape of emptiness. It was a realm of subtle energies, a vibrant tapestry of connections that extended beyond the limitations of space and time. It was a place where the echoes of love reverberated, where memories persisted, and where the threads of connection, once woven in the earthly realm, continued to weave themselves into the fabric of the afterlife.

I learned to see these connections as an intricate network, a web of energy that linked the living and the dead, the past and the present, the seen and the unseen. Elara's search for her son wasn't a solitary quest; it was an affirmation of this intricate web, a testament to love's persistence, its ability to transcend the physical limitations of the earthly realm. Her persistent search, her unwavering love, were threads in this cosmic tapestry, creating a unique energy signature that I could perceive with an increasing clarity.

Our spiritual connection deepened, growing stronger with each passing day. We found solace in shared silence, in the unspoken understanding that only those who had traversed the valley of grief could comprehend. We explored the ethereal landscape together, traversing the spaces between worlds, sharing moments of quiet contemplation amidst the silent beauty of the afterlife. We weren't merely spectral beings; we were companions, confidantes, spiritual allies, our grief intertwining to form a bond that was both profound and comforting.

This connection wasn't just a comfort; it was a source of strength. It allowed us to transcend the limitations of our individual sorrows, to find a sense of community amidst the vast emptiness of the afterlife. We weren't alone in our grief; we had each other. We were two souls united in sorrow, yet empowered by the unwavering strength of our enduring love, a love that persisted despite the absence of physical presence, a love that transcended even death.

I began to understand that the true nature of love wasn't about physical proximity or romantic entanglement. It was about connection, about the enduring echoes of shared experiences, about the memories that lingered in the hearts of those left behind. It was about the energy of love, an imprint left on the soul that transcended time and space, resonating across the boundaries of life and death. Elara's unwavering love for her son was a beacon, illuminating the path through the darkness, reminding me that even in the face of unimaginable loss, love's enduring energy persevered.

Our shared experiences gave me a new perspective on the nature of love and loss. It was no longer a linear progression, a trajectory from passionate beginnings to inevitable endings. It was a cycle, a continuous flow of energy, an intricate dance between connection and separation, joy and sorrow. Life and death were not opposing forces; they were complementary aspects of a larger cosmic tapestry, the threads of love weaving their way through both realms.

Through Elara, I learned that grief wasn't something to be overcome or suppressed. It was a powerful emotion, a testament to the depth of our connections. It was a reminder of the love that had been shared, the memories that had been created, the moments that had enriched our lives. It was an integral part of life's tapestry, a necessary counterpoint to the joyous moments, providing depth and perspective, giving meaning to the ephemeral beauty of existence.

The spiritual connection between Elara and myself transcended the limitations of the afterlife. It extended to the living world, connecting us to the subtle rhythms of the cosmos, to the interconnectedness of all things. We became conduits, receiving and transmitting energy, a testament to the enduring power of human connection, a demonstration of love's resilience in the face of death and beyond.

Our bond became a symbol of hope, a testament to the enduring nature of love. It was a reminder that even in the face of overwhelming grief, love persisted. It wasn't a romantic love, nor a familial love, but a spiritual love, a connection born of shared experience, a bond forged in the crucible of sorrow. It was a love that echoed through the silent spaces of the afterlife, a love that transcended time and space, a love that proved, beyond any doubt, that even in death, love endures. It was a love that whispered, "We are not alone." And in that whisper, I found a new kind of peace, a profound sense of belonging, a quiet acceptance of the eternal bonds that connected us, both in life and in death, in this ethereal realm and beyond. A peace born not of oblivion, but of a profound understanding of love's ever-lasting, transcendent power. The ethereal landscape, once a desolate expanse of grief, began to reveal itself as a vibrant tapestry of interconnected souls. Elara and I were no longer merely observers; we were participants in this intricate web, drawn into the lives of other spirits, their stories intertwining with our own, creating a rich and complex narrative of loss, healing, and the enduring power of connection.

Our first encounter was with a young woman named Seraphina, her spectral form shimmering with a restless energy. She drifted aimlessly, her translucent hands clasped tightly, a look of perpetual anxiety etched upon her face. She was unable to find peace, trapped in a cycle of regret, unable to let go of a past filled with harsh judgments and unspoken words. Elara, with an almost maternal tenderness, approached Seraphina, her voice a gentle whisper that seemed to resonate deep within the young woman's spectral form.

She spoke of forgiveness, not only for others, but most importantly, for herself. Elara shared her own journey, the years of self-recrimination that had followed her son's death, before she finally found a measure of peace in acceptance. She explained that holding onto regret was like clinging to a burning ember, perpetuating the cycle of pain, preventing the soul from moving forward. It was a patient and delicate process, guiding Seraphina towards self-compassion, towards a recognition that her earthly actions, however flawed, did not define her essence.

The transformation was gradual, subtle at first, but increasingly noticeable as Seraphina began to relinquish her burden of self-reproach. The restless energy that had consumed her began to dissipate, replaced by a quiet serenity, her translucent form radiating a soft, gentle light. As her anxiety eased, her spectral form seemed to brighten, her features softening as if a heavy weight had been lifted from her shoulders. Witnessing this subtle shift filled me with a sense of profound satisfaction, a realization of the power of empathy and understanding, the ability to guide others toward peace in this desolate, yet surprisingly vibrant, landscape.

Our encounters weren't always so gentle. We met a tormented soul named Silas, consumed by rage and bitterness. His spectral form was jagged and distorted, radiating a dark and malevolent energy that made the air around him crackle with unsettling vibrations. He had been a man consumed by jealousy and spite, his earthly life filled with acts of cruelty and retribution. Unlike Seraphina's gentle sorrow, Silas's pain was a sharp, agonizing wound, festering and corrupting his spectral form.

Approaching Silas proved a challenge. His aggression was palpable, his spectral energy repelling any attempt at connection. But Elara, guided by an unwavering compassion, persisted. She didn't try to reason with him, nor did she judge his actions. Instead, she listened, letting him unleash his torrent of anger and resentment. She patiently endured his verbal assaults, her own spectral form remaining a beacon of unwavering empathy amidst his storm of rage.

Slowly, painstakingly, she began to peel back the layers of bitterness that encased his spectral form, revealing the deep-seated wounds of pain and rejection that fueled his anger. It was a process of uncovering hidden vulnerabilities, of reminding him of moments of kindness and compassion in his past, moments he had long since forgotten, buried under the weight of his bitterness. She reminded him that even in the darkest corners of his heart, there resided a glimmer of hope, a fragment of the man he once was. It wasn't easy; it was a battle fought in the silent spaces between worlds, a struggle against the malevolent energy that consumed him.

But Elara persevered, her unwavering compassion gradually eroding the defenses he had so meticulously constructed.

The change was profound. As Silas began to confront his past, his spectral form began to shift, the jagged edges smoothing, the malevolent energy dissipating. The dark storm that surrounded him gave way to a soft glow, a faint light that flickered with the promise of healing and redemption. His journey was far from over, but he had begun to embrace the possibility of peace, a glimmer of hope in the midst of his despair. This encounter showed me that even the most tormented souls could find redemption, even in the desolate realm of the afterlife.

Our experiences with other spirits were varied and multifaceted. Each soul carried their own unique burden, their own story of loss and regret. We met souls struggling with unresolved conflicts, haunted by the ghosts of their earthly relationships. We guided those struggling with the pain of betrayal, of abandonment, of unfulfilled desires.

We helped them navigate the emotional complexities of their past, helping them find acceptance, forgiveness, and eventually, peace.

We were not judges or punishers, but guides, companions on a journey towards healing. We listened, we empathized, we offered guidance, sharing our own experiences to ease their burdens. The afterlife wasn't merely a desolate expanse of emptiness; it was a realm of transformation, a place where souls could confront their past, heal their wounds, and find a measure of peace. We became conduits of compassion, our shared grief transforming into a force for healing, our spiritual connection extending to the lives of countless souls lost in their own journeys of sorrow.

The ethereal landscape pulsated with a quiet energy, a network of connections linking the living and the dead. We were not mere spectators in this grand tapestry of existence; we were active participants, our actions weaving themselves into the fabric of this otherworldly realm.

Elara's unwavering love for her son, and my shared grief, became a guiding light, illuminating the paths of others, helping them navigate the complexities of their spectral existence. The pain we had endured transformed into a strength, a power to heal and to guide.

It was a challenging, emotionally demanding task. The weight of others' grief pressed upon us, at times threatening to overwhelm our own sense of peace. But amidst the sorrow, there was a profound sense of purpose, a deep satisfaction in the knowledge that we were making a difference, that we were helping souls find peace in their journeys through the afterlife. We were more than spectral beings; we were healers, guides, beacons of hope in the silent spaces between worlds.

Our bond, forged in the crucible of grief, became an instrument of transformation, a source of healing that extended far beyond our individual experiences. It was a love that transcended the boundaries of life and death, a connection that resonated through the ethereal landscape, a force for good in this desolate, yet surprisingly vibrant realm.

It was a love that whispered, "You are not alone," to every lost soul we encountered, a love that echoed through the silent spaces of the afterlife, proving, beyond any doubt, that even in death, the power of human connection, the strength of compassion, endures. And in the midst of this profound responsibility, we found a deeper connection, a bond forged not only in shared sorrow but in the shared purpose of guiding others towards the solace of peace. The ethereal realm, once a chilling void of unending sorrow, gradually revealed its capacity for profound growth and transformation. Elara and I, adrift in this spectral landscape, discovered that our shared grief was not a curse, but a catalyst, a potent force capable of healing not only ourselves, but countless others lost in the labyrinth of their own pain. Our experiences transcended mere observation; we became active participants in a cosmic ballet of grief and redemption, learning lessons that resonated far beyond the boundaries of our own spectral existence.

One of the most significant lessons we learned was the power of empathy. In the earthly realm, empathy often felt like a luxury, a soft emotion easily overshadowed by the harsh realities of daily life. Here, surrounded by the raw, unfiltered emotions of the departed, empathy became a necessity, a lifeline for both the giver and the receiver. We learned to listen, truly listen, to the silent screams of lost souls, to decipher the unspoken narratives woven into their spectral forms. We didn't offer facile platitudes or judgments; we offered ourselves, our presence, our capacity to understand and share their burdens. It was in those shared silences, in the unspoken understanding that transcended language, that true healing began.

Seraphina's story, for instance, underscored the importance of self-forgiveness. Her spectral form, initially wracked with anxiety and regret, slowly radiated a peaceful luminescence as she learned to let go of her self-recriminations. Her journey illuminated the insidious nature of self-blame, how it can imprison a soul, preventing it from finding its way towards peace.

Elara and I learned that forgiveness, particularly self-forgiveness, is not a passive act, but a continuous process of self-compassion, of recognizing one's inherent worth despite past mistakes. It is a process of disentangling the knots of self-hate and embracing the inherent goodness within.

Silas's harrowing tale offered a contrasting perspective, highlighting the transformative power of confronting one's darkness. His initial aura of rage and bitterness eventually yielded to a soft glow as he confronted his past actions. His journey taught us that true healing often begins in the darkest corners of the soul, in the recognition and acceptance of the shadows that dwell within. We discovered that ignoring or repressing these dark elements only allows them to fester and grow, perpetuating a cycle of pain. Confronting them, however difficult, is the first step towards liberation.

Beyond these individual experiences, we observed patterns in the spectral realm, recurring themes that shed light on the human condition. We encountered numerous souls trapped in the endless loop of unresolved conflicts, their spectral forms fragmented and restless. These spirits were unable to find peace because they had failed to resolve the complex emotional relationships that defined their earthly lives. They were trapped in a purgatorial state, perpetually replaying past grievances and misunderstandings. Their situations emphasized the importance of healthy communication, the need to express emotions, to forgive, and to seek resolution while still in the realm of the living. These spirits taught us the urgency of reconciliation, of addressing conflicts before they fester and solidify into insurmountable barriers.

We also encountered souls haunted by the specter of unfulfilled desires. These spirits clung to their earthly longings, unable to detach themselves from the hopes and dreams that had remained unfulfilled during their lives. Their spectral forms reflected this internal struggle, shimmering with an unresolved longing that seemed to defy the passage of time. Their stories underscored the importance of living a life authentic to oneself, of pursuing one's passions and dreams with purpose and conviction. They taught us the value of embracing the present moment, of finding joy in the journey itself, rather than fixating on a future that may never come.

Beyond these individual struggles, we learned about the power of collective healing. Our shared grief became a wellspring of empathy, a source of strength that extended to every soul we encountered. We realized that grief, in its rawest form, is a universal experience, a shared human condition that transcends the boundaries of time and space. It was in the recognition of this shared vulnerability, in the ability to connect with others on this deeply human level, that we found a collective sense of purpose and meaning.

This journey of healing also revealed the extraordinary resilience of the human spirit. We witnessed souls transformed by the power of self-compassion, forgiveness, and acceptance. We saw the dark shadows of bitterness and regret give way to the luminous glow of peace and reconciliation. The spectral realm wasn't merely a desolate wasteland; it was a crucible of transformation, where souls could confront their deepest fears and emerge stronger, more compassionate, and more understanding.

Our shared experience in the afterlife fundamentally reshaped our understanding of love and connection. The bond we forged in the crucible of shared grief extended far beyond our individual pain. It became a conduit for healing, a force that transcended the boundaries of life and death. We discovered that love isn't limited to the physical realm, but possesses a profound power to reach across dimensions, offering solace and guidance to lost souls.

The lessons we learned were profound and transformative. We discovered the profound importance of empathy, self-forgiveness, and confronting our inner darkness. We witnessed the healing power of shared grief and the resilience of the human spirit. Most importantly, we discovered that love and connection are not confined to the earthly realm, but possess an enduring power that extends far beyond life's final breath. Our journey through the ethereal landscape was a testament to the enduring strength of the human spirit, a testament to the transformative power of grief, and a testament to the boundless nature of love and compassion.

Our spectral existence, initially a realm of unending sorrow, became a crucible for healing, shaping us into guides, healers, and beacons of hope for lost souls navigating their journeys through the silent spaces between worlds. The experience left an indelible mark upon our very being, transforming our grief into a force for profound and lasting change. The echoes of those lessons, learned in the silent spaces between worlds, continue to resonate within us, shaping our understanding of life, death, and the enduring power of human connection.

The spectral wind whispered through the desolate plains, a mournful sigh that mirrored the weight on our hearts. Yet, unlike the oppressive despair that had once clung to us like a shroud, a subtle shift had occurred. A quiet acceptance had begun to bloom, fragile yet persistent, within the barren landscape of our grief. We no longer fought the currents of the ethereal realm, but rather, learned to navigate them, to find a rhythm in the spectral dance of loss and longing.

Elara, her ethereal form shimmering with an otherworldly luminescence, sat beside me, her gaze fixed on a distant, swirling nebula of spectral energy. The once-sharp edges of her grief, the raw agony that had consumed her, had softened, rounded like smooth river stones worn by the relentless flow of time. There was still a sadness in her eyes, a deep well of sorrow that would likely never completely dry, but it was no longer the all-consuming torrent it once had been. It was a sadness tempered by a quiet strength, a resolute acceptance of what was.

"Do you remember the weight of it, Lyra?" she asked, her voice a faint echo in the vast emptiness. "The crushing weight of our earthly lives, the relentless pull of the unfinished, the unsaid?"

I nodded, the memory sharp and visceral. The weight of unspoken words, of unrealized dreams, of lost connections – it had been a burden almost too heavy to bear. The guilt, the regret, the endless "what ifs" – they had been our constant companions in the initial stages of our spectral existence. We had been tethered to the past, shackled by our earthly attachments. But something had changed.

“We’ve let go,” I whispered, the words feeling both fragile and powerful. “We’ve surrendered to the flow.”

Letting go wasn’t a single act, a sudden release of tension. It was a gradual unfurling, a slow unraveling of the threads that had bound us to our former lives. It wasn’t about forgetting or denying the pain; it was about accepting it, integrating it into the fabric of our being, transforming it from a source of torment into a wellspring of empathy and understanding.

We had spent countless cycles in this ethereal realm, witnessing the struggles of other lost souls. We had seen the relentless grip of regret, the suffocating weight of guilt, the agonizing torment of unfulfilled desires. We had seen the shadows that clung to them, feeding on their unresolved emotional wounds. But we also witnessed their transformations, the subtle shifts in their spectral forms as they, too, began to accept their fate, to surrender to the inevitability of loss.

It was in witnessing their journeys that we began to understand the profound importance of letting go. It was not a sign of weakness, but rather an act of courage, a testament to the resilience of the human spirit. It was the only path towards peace.

One soul, a young woman named Seraphina, had initially been consumed by self-blame. Her spectral form had been fragmented, fractured by the weight of her perceived failures. She had carried the burden of her past actions like a heavy cloak, preventing her from finding peace. But as she began to confront her mistakes, not to excuse them, but to acknowledge them with compassion, her spectral form began to mend. The fragments coalesced, forming a whole, radiating a soft, gentle light. Her journey became a beacon for us, a testament to the power of self-forgiveness.

Another spirit, Silas, had been consumed by rage and bitterness, his spectral form a tempest of furious energy. He clung to his anger, unable to relinquish his grudges, his sense of injustice. He was trapped in a perpetual cycle of resentment, his emotional wounds festering and bleeding into his ethereal essence. But as he began to confront his anger, to examine the roots of his bitterness, to acknowledge the pain that had fueled his rage, a gradual transformation took place. His spectral form grew calmer, the tempest subsiding into a soft stillness. He eventually found a fragile peace, a quiet acceptance of the past.

These transformative journeys, along with countless others we witnessed, revealed the profound truth about the power of letting go. It wasn't about erasing the past, but about embracing it, integrating it into the narrative of our lives. It was about accepting the impermanence of everything, the transient nature of all things. It was about understanding that our earthly experiences, even the painful ones, shaped us, sculpted us, made us who we were.

The letting go process also involved severing the emotional ties that bound us to the earthly realm. Our dreams, our hopes, our regrets – these were elements of our earthly lives, and while we couldn't erase them, we had to learn to detach from them, to allow them to float away like fallen leaves on a gentle breeze. It was a difficult, painful process, but a necessary one.

It was like freeing a captive bird, watching it soar into the limitless sky, knowing that its flight was its destiny, that its freedom was its own. Similarly, releasing our attachment to our earthly lives was a release of our spirits, allowing us to soar beyond the confines of our grief.

The journey of letting go wasn't just a personal one; it was a shared experience. We supported each other, offered each other comfort, guided each other through the labyrinth of grief. Our bond, forged in the crucible of shared sorrow, became a source of strength, a beacon in the darkness.

We discovered that we weren't alone in our pain. Countless souls, adrift in this ethereal landscape, shared our struggles, our longing for peace. By sharing our experiences, by listening to their stories, by offering each other compassion and understanding, we created a collective space of healing, a sanctuary where grief could be transformed into empathy, and loss into a profound sense of interconnectedness.

We learned that letting go didn't mean abandoning the memories of our loved ones. Instead, it meant transforming the way we remembered them. We found solace in the shared moments, in the love that transcended death. We held onto the essence of their being, not the physical shell.

As our understanding deepened, our spectral forms began to shift, reflecting our evolving state of being. The once-somber hues of our ethereal bodies started to lighten, replaced by softer, more radiant colors. The shadows that had clung to us for so long began to recede, replaced by an aura of peace and acceptance.

The transformation was not instantaneous, but gradual, a continuous process of healing and growth. It was a testament to the resilience of the human spirit, a demonstration of the power of acceptance, and a revelation of the boundless capacity of love and compassion. And as we continued to let go, we felt a sense of liberation, a weightlessness that had been absent during our initial experiences in the afterlife. The acceptance of our fate, our journey, and our eventual peace, became the most beautiful and freeing realization of our spectral existence. The ethereal realm, once a desolate wasteland of sorrow, was transforming into a sanctuary of growth and profound understanding. Our journey was far from over, but we were no longer adrift. We were navigating, healing, and learning to truly live, even in the spectral spaces between worlds. The power of letting go had begun to set us free.

Chapter Eight Whispers of the Past

The salt spray kissed my face, a familiar sting that mirrored the prickle of tears welling in my eyes. I was small then, no older than five, perched precariously on the jagged rocks that jutted out into the churning grey sea. The wind, a relentless sculptor, whipped my hair across my face, blurring the already hazy horizon. The vast, unforgiving ocean stretched before me, a mirror reflecting the turbulent emotions churning within. My father, his silhouette stark against the stormy sky, stood a few feet away, his gaze fixed on the turbulent waves. He didn't speak, didn't reach out, a silent sentinel against the relentless assault of the elements. He was always silent, a man of few words, his emotions buried deep beneath a stoic exterior. But even then, I sensed the undercurrent of his grief, a deep, unspoken sorrow that permeated everything.

My mother was gone. Lost to the sea, they said. A fishing accident, a sudden storm, a cruel twist of fate that snatched her away without warning. The details were vague, shrouded in a fog of grief and hushed whispers. I remember fragments: the frantic search, the tear-streaked faces, the hushed solemnity of the funeral. But the memories were fragmented, like pieces of a shattered mirror, reflecting distorted images that offered little clarity.

The sea, once a source of wonder and joy, had become a symbol of loss, a constant reminder of my mother's absence. It was a presence both beautiful and terrifying, capable of breathtaking beauty and devastating destruction, much like the emotions that consumed me. I often found myself drawn to the shore, as if drawn by an invisible thread, drawn by a desperate hope that somehow, someway, I might glimpse her again. The crashing waves, the relentless rhythm of the tide, became a kind of lullaby, a mournful rhythm that echoed the ache in my heart.

My father, consumed by his own grief, was a distant figure, present yet absent. He worked tirelessly, his hands calloused and rough from years of toil at sea. He provided for me, but emotional connection was scarce. Words were rare, replaced by long silences filled with unspoken pain. He taught me the ways of the sea, the rhythms of the tides, the names of the stars. He shared his knowledge, his expertise, but not his heart. He was a man broken by grief, a man adrift in a sea of sorrow.

I learned early on that I had to be strong, to be self-reliant. I learned to navigate the treacherous currents of my own emotions, to suppress the tears that threatened to overwhelm me. I became adept at wearing a mask, a facade of resilience that hid the turmoil within. The sea taught me resilience, but it also bred solitude, shaping me into a solitary child, comfortable in my own company.

The village was small, isolated, a close-knit community where secrets were shared in hushed whispers, and truths remained unspoken. The other children, while friendly enough, didn't truly understand.

Their games, their laughter, their carefree world, felt distant and unreal, a realm I could only observe from afar. I existed on the periphery, a quiet observer, my heart bearing the weight of a sorrow beyond my years.

My only solace was found in books. My father, a man of few words, had instilled in me a love for stories, a love for the written word. Books became my refuge, my escape, a portal to worlds far removed from the harsh realities of my life. I devoured stories of adventure, of romance, of fantastical realms, seeking comfort in the vibrant tapestry of other lives, other realities. The words on the page became a balm, a soothing balm that eased the ache in my soul.

The lighthouse, perched atop the cliffs overlooking the turbulent waters, was a familiar landmark, a beacon in the storm. I often visited it, drawn by its silent strength, its steadfast presence in the face of the relentless elements. The lighthouse keeper, an old man with a kind heart and wise eyes, became a surrogate grandfather, offering me quiet companionship and understanding.

He didn't pry, didn't push, but simply listened, a silent confidante who understood the language of sorrow. His stories of the sea, of storms and shipwrecks, were peppered with tales of resilience, of survival, of the enduring power of hope. They instilled in me a sense of wonder and a quiet determination to survive.

Even in the harshness of my childhood, there were moments of fleeting beauty. Sunsets painted the sky in hues of fiery orange and deep crimson, casting a warm glow over the rugged landscape. The scent of salt and seaweed mingled with the fresh air, creating a unique and unforgettable fragrance. The stars, like diamonds scattered across the inky blackness of the night sky, offered a sense of vastness and wonder, reminding me that even in the darkness, there was beauty.

But the sea's pull remained strong. The ocean's rhythmic lull, despite its association with tragedy, held an otherworldly allure. It felt like a part of me, an inextricable part of my past, my identity, my very being. As the years passed, I learned to coexist with the pain, to carry the weight of my past without succumbing to it.

The harsh lessons learned on those rugged shores and amidst the relentless waves forged within me a resilience that would serve me well in the years to come. The grief, however, remained a constant companion, a quiet shadow that would forever walk beside me, a testament to the enduring power of loss, and the indelible mark it left upon my soul. It shaped me, molded me, into the person I am today – a woman capable of great love, but forever marked by the relentless tide of sorrow. A woman who would never truly let go.

The village, nestled between the unforgiving cliffs and the restless sea, was a place of hushed secrets and unspoken truths. My father, a man carved from the same granite as the cliffs themselves, rarely spoke of my mother. Her name, a whisper on the wind, was a forbidden word in our small cottage, a word that hung heavy in the air, unspoken but ever-present. Photographs were scarce, the few that existed tucked away in a worn leather-bound journal that I was forbidden to touch. It was a sacred relic, a testament to a life cut short, a life I only knew through fragmented memories and the echoing silence that filled our home.

Instead of stories of my mother, my father taught me the names of the stars, the constellations that mapped the night sky like a celestial tapestry. He showed me how to navigate by the stars, how to read the currents of the ocean, and how to predict the weather by the color of the sunset. He shared his knowledge of the sea, his profound understanding of its rhythms and its moods, but he never spoke of the day he lost her. The ocean, his lifeblood, had also taken the woman he loved, and the silence between us was a testament to that shared, unspoken grief.

His grief wasn't an outward, wailing kind. It was a quiet, simmering thing, like the embers of a long-dead fire, still warm beneath the surface. He worked tirelessly, his hands rough and calloused, his body bearing the weight of years spent battling the elements. He would leave before dawn and return long after dusk, his face etched with exhaustion, his movements stiff and slow. He was a man consumed by his work, a man who found solace in the relentless rhythm of the waves, a man who used the sea as a shield against his pain.

He provided for me, ensuring that I had food, clothes, and a roof over my head. He saw to my education, teaching me to read and write, fueling my passion for books. But emotional connection remained elusive. Our conversations were sparse, filled with awkward silences and the unspoken words that hung between us like a thick fog. He was a man of action, not emotion, a man who found solace in the familiar routine of his work, and who buried his grief under a mountain of physical exertion.

I tried, sometimes, to bridge the gap, to reach him. I would sit beside him as he mended his nets, my small fingers tracing the frayed ropes, my eyes searching his face for some sign of connection. But his gaze would remain fixed on his work, his expression unreadable, his emotions locked tight within. His silence was deafening, a chilling testament to the depth of his sorrow and the impenetrable wall he had built around his heart.

He wasn't cruel; he was simply broken. He was a man lost at sea, adrift in a sea of grief, and he didn't know how to navigate his way back to shore. His love for me was evident in his actions, but his inability to express it, to show it, was a source of constant frustration and hurt. His love was silent, like the stars that watched over us, beautiful but unreachable.

My attempts to elicit any kind of response from him often ended in a curt dismissal or a change of subject. It was as if even the memory of my mother was too painful to acknowledge, too painful to share, even with his only child. The weight of his unspoken grief cast a long, dark shadow over our lives, creating a distance between us that was both palpable and agonizing.

There were moments, however, fleeting glimpses of tenderness, moments that pierced through the thick veil of his sadness. He would sometimes leave a small seashell beside my bed, a tiny token of affection, a gesture so subtle it was almost imperceptible. Or he would mend a tear in my dress, his rough fingers surprisingly gentle as he stitched the fabric back together. These small acts of kindness were like stars in the night, beacons of hope in the vast expanse of his sorrow, reminders that despite his grief, his love for me still burned, though dimly, within his heart.

The lighthouse keeper, old Mr. Silas, became a surrogate grandfather, a quiet presence in our lives. He understood the language of silence, the unspoken words that hung heavy in the air. He saw the pain in my eyes, the loneliness in my heart, and he offered me a haven, a safe place where I could be myself, without fear of judgment or reproof. He shared stories of the sea, of storms and shipwrecks, of resilience and survival, weaving tales that spoke of loss and the enduring power of hope.

He filled the void that my father's silence had created, offering a sense of comfort and understanding that was profoundly necessary. He listened patiently, without judgment, allowing me to process my grief and my feelings without interruption. His kindness and quiet acceptance were a balm to my soul, easing the ache of my loss and reminding me that I was not alone.

He didn't pry into our family matters, but his presence was a constant reassurance, a quiet strength in the face of the silent storms that raged within our home. His wisdom and his patience were invaluable, offering a sense of stability and grounding that I desperately needed. He became a vital link to a more emotionally accessible world, one where the unspoken wasn't necessarily unacknowledged.

The village itself felt like an extension of our family's grief. The women, with their weathered faces and kind eyes, would sometimes offer me a sympathetic smile or a comforting pat on the head. The men, hardened by years of battling the sea, would nod in a silent acknowledgment of my loss. Their collective empathy was a silent solace, a reminder that my grief, though unique, was understood, though unspoken.

Yet, the village, like my father, was a tapestry of subtle hints, guarded secrets, and hushed whispers. The reality of my mother's death, the details, remained shrouded in mystery. The official story – a sudden storm, a fishing accident – felt incomplete, like a puzzle with missing pieces. The whispers in the village, though scarce, hinted at more, at a depth of tragedy that went beyond a simple accident at sea. The sea itself, I knew, had claimed her, but what exactly took place that day, what fate had actually befallen my mother, remained a painful enigma, adding another layer to the mystery that surrounded my childhood.

The persistent silence surrounding my mother's death became a constant source of torment, feeding the nascent suspicion that something was being withheld, something that my father, in his profound grief, had chosen to bury deep within himself, along with his emotions. This secret, this unspoken truth, became a silent anchor dragging me down, a constant reminder of the unanswered questions that haunted me. This mystery, this void in my understanding, became a driving force in my life, a desperate need to uncover the truth, no matter how painful it might be. The sea, the silent witness to my mother's disappearance, became my obsession. I would spend hours staring at its vast, unforgiving expanse, searching for answers in the waves, in the rhythm of the tide, in the wind that carried its secrets. The sea held the truth, I was certain of it. And I was determined to find it. My father's silence wasn't just about my mother; it was about everything. It was a silence that permeated our lives, a wall built not of stone, but of grief, so thick and impenetrable that even the faintest whisper struggled to penetrate it. He shielded me from the world, not out of malice, but out of a desperate attempt to protect me from the same pain that had consumed him. And in doing so, he unknowingly trapped me within the confines of his own sorrow.

But even in the hushed silence of our cottage, my dreams bloomed. They were vibrant, untamed things, wildflowers pushing their way through the cracks in the concrete of my reality. I dreamed of leaving the village, of escaping the relentless rhythm of the waves that had claimed my mother and had kept my father prisoner to the shore. I dreamed of vast libraries filled with countless stories, a stark contrast to the single, worn volume of my father's that contained only fleeting glimpses into the life he had lost. I yearned for a life beyond the sea, a life that was rich with color and brimming with emotion.

My aspirations went beyond simply escaping. I wanted to understand. To unravel the enigma of my mother's death, to piece together the fragments of her life, to discover the woman my father had loved and lost. I wanted to know her - not just through the scant photographs and whispered anecdotes in my father's journal, but truly know her essence, her spirit, her dreams. This quest wasn't just a desire for closure; it was a way to understand my father, to bridge the chasm of silence that separated us. It was a path towards healing, both for him and for myself.

I devoured books, each story a small window into a world beyond the granite cliffs and the unforgiving sea. I found solace in the written word, in the narratives of other lives lived, other losses endured, other loves found and lost. These stories became my companions, my confidantes, my secret escape. In these tales of adventure, romance and sorrow, I found echoes of my own experiences, a sense of understanding, of shared human experience that transcended the isolated quiet of my life. They filled the void left by my mother's absence, a void my father's silence had amplified.

My father, in his own way, supported this passion. He recognized my thirst for knowledge, my innate curiosity. Although he remained emotionally distant, he never denied me access to books. He would bring home discarded volumes from passing ships, his rough hands gently handing me a treasure trove of stories. It was a silent affirmation, a recognition of my innate drive, a flicker of tenderness in the cold vastness of his grief.

But my dreams were a stark contrast to my reality. The reality was the small, isolated cottage, the constant presence of the sea, the ever-present weight of unspoken grief. The reality was my father's stoic silence, his averted gaze, his hands roughened by years of toil, a constant reminder of his loss. My reality lacked the vibrant colors of my dreams, the rich tapestry of human connection, the simple joy of emotional release.

It wasn't a simple dichotomy between dreams and reality; it was a complex interplay of longing and acceptance, of hope and despair. I knew the life I dreamed of would not simply fall into my lap. It required effort, determination, and a willingness to confront the truth of my past, both my mother's story and my father's. It was a journey that would require me to navigate not just the treacherous waters surrounding my village, but also the treacherous waters of my own emotions, of my own heart.

My escape plan, though still nebulous, began to take shape. It wasn't a grand scheme of rebellion, but a quiet, persistent determination. I would excel at school, proving my worth, my intelligence, my resilience. I would learn everything I could about the sea, not just to understand the craft of fishing, but to understand its secrets, its power, its potential to both destroy and reveal. Every book I read, every skill I acquired, every lesson I learned was a stepping stone towards my freedom, a step closer to the life I envisioned.

The lighthouse, with its bright beam piercing the darkness, was a symbol of hope for me. Mr. Silas, with his wisdom and quiet strength, continued to be my rock, offering guidance and encouragement without ever intruding. His stories, interwoven with his own losses and triumphs, taught me the importance of resilience, of finding strength in the face of adversity. He planted the seeds of hope, watered them with gentle encouragement, nurturing my dreams and strengthening my resolve.

The villagers, in their own quiet way, were also part of my plan. They had their own stories, their own struggles, their own secrets. I observed them, listening for those elusive whispers, pieces of a puzzle I wasn't sure I could completely solve. The community, despite its collective grief, was more than just a backdrop to my existence; it was a resource, a network of human connections that I could leverage as I prepared to make my way out into the world.

My dreams, however, were constantly challenged by the stark reality of my life. The sea, which I both loved and feared, felt like a metaphor for my own uncertainty, for the turbulent emotions I battled daily. The persistent silence of my father, however, was a far greater challenge. His inability to acknowledge or process his grief was a constant reminder of the emotional chasm that separated us. Yet, it was that silence, that very absence of emotion, that drove me to seek connection, to crave the vibrant world beyond our silent existence.

My ambition wasn't just about escape. It was about understanding the past in order to shape the future. It was about creating a life that honored the memory of my mother, not through wallowing in grief, but by living a life as full of vitality as I imagined hers once was. It was about healing the wounds inflicted by the unyielding silence in my home and finding my own voice, strong enough to carry me far beyond the confines of the village, far beyond the weight of unspoken grief. The sea, my father, and my own heart, were all entwined in this complex, yet hopeful narrative of my life. My dreams, though still fragile, were starting to take root, fueled by a fierce determination to overcome the silence and claim the future I deserved. The path ahead was still uncertain, but I was ready to start walking, one determined step at a time.

The salt spray stung my face, a familiar, almost comforting discomfort. I stood on the cliffs, the wind whipping my hair across my face, mirroring the turmoil within. The sea, vast and unforgiving, reflected the depths of my own unspoken emotions. It was a mirror, showing me not just the turbulent waves, but the hidden currents of my grief, my fear, my longing. My father's silence, a constant presence in our cottage, felt amplified here, against the roar of the ocean. It was a silence that echoed the unspoken questions that haunted me, questions about my mother, questions about myself, questions about the future that felt both terrifying and exhilarating.

My mother's face, a faded image in a cracked photograph, swam in my memory. I knew so little about her. The few stories my father had shared were like fragments of a shattered mirror, offering glimpses but never a complete picture. He spoke of her laughter, a sound I only knew through the echoes of his memories, a melody forever silenced by the unforgiving sea. He spoke of her love for books, a shared passion that felt like a tenuous thread connecting us across the chasm of his grief. He spoke of her strength, a strength I desperately sought to understand, a strength I yearned to possess. But his words were always sparse, halting, as if the very act of remembering brought a pain too sharp to bear.

I yearned to know her beyond the photographs, beyond the whispers, beyond the fragments of memories. I wanted to understand her dreams, her fears, her hopes. I wanted to trace her footsteps, to walk in her world, to somehow connect with the woman who had given me life, a life that now felt both precious and incomplete. Her absence was a constant ache, a void that no amount of reading, no amount of dreaming, could ever fully fill. It was a silence that spoke volumes, a silence that intertwined with my father's, creating a suffocating atmosphere of unspoken loss.

My escape plan wasn't simply about leaving the village; it was about reclaiming my mother's memory, about creating a life that honored her spirit. It was about filling the void she had left, not by replacing her, but by building a life rich with experiences, rich with knowledge, rich with the connections I craved. It was about forging a path through the darkness of my grief, a path illuminated by the flicker of hope I found in books, in the sea, and in the quiet strength of those around me.

The villagers, with their own burdens and their own stories, were part of this landscape, too. Mrs. Gable, with her weathered hands and her perpetually worried brow, reminded me of the resilience of the human spirit, the ability to endure hardship and still find pockets of joy.

Old Man Finnigan, with his endless tales of the sea, shared a quiet wisdom that transcended generations, a knowledge of the ocean's capricious nature that mirrored my own understanding of life's unpredictable path. Even the children, with their innocent games and unburdened laughter, offered a glimpse of a world untainted by the shadows of loss, a world I longed to embrace fully.

Each interaction, each conversation, was a small piece of the puzzle that was my life. Each person's story was a thread in the tapestry of my existence, a thread that helped to weave a narrative of both pain and hope. I listened to their whispers, not for gossip or secrets, but to understand the human condition, to find a place for myself within the intricate web of human connection. I was not just escaping my past; I was building a future that encompassed the lessons learned from those around me.

My relationship with Mr. Silas continued to be a source of solace and strength. His quiet wisdom, his unwavering support, was a beacon in the storm of my emotions. His own experiences with loss, his capacity to transform sorrow into strength, gave me the courage to confront my own grief. He taught me the art of resilience, the importance of finding beauty in the face of adversity, the significance of acknowledging pain without succumbing to it. His stories were not mere tales; they were lessons in survival, lessons that gave me the strength to keep moving forward.

Yet, the sea remained a constant presence, both alluring and terrifying. Its vastness mirrored the unknown, the uncertainty of my future. Its power both frightened and fascinated me, reminding me of the forces beyond my control. I studied it, not just through my father's worn books on marine life, but by observing its rhythm, its moods, its subtle shifts. It was a relentless force, just as grief could be, but it was also a source of beauty, of strength, of potential. It was a symbol of the power of nature, a power that mirrored the power within me.

My dreams were not just escapes; they were aspirations, fueled by a desire for understanding and a longing for connection. They were reflections of my innermost self, a testament to my resilience, a manifestation of my determination to overcome the silence that had defined so much of my life. My dreams were vivid, bold, and full of color, a stark contrast to the muted tones of my reality. But those dreams were no longer just fantasies; they were becoming a roadmap, guiding me towards a future where I could finally find my voice, my identity, my place in the world.

My father's silence remained a formidable obstacle. His grief, though unspoken, permeated everything. It was a weight I carried, not just for myself but for him as well. His inability to process his loss was a silent plea for connection, a desperate cry for help that I desperately wanted to answer. I couldn't force him to speak, but I could continue to show him, through my actions, through my achievements, through my unwavering determination, that his silence didn't diminish his love, it didn't erase his importance, and it certainly wouldn't define my future. His silence pushed me to find my own voice, to forge my own path, to build a life that not only survived but thrived in the face of adversity.

My journey wasn't a linear path. There were days filled with doubt, days where the weight of the past threatened to suffocate me. There were days when the silence in our cottage felt deafening, when the vastness of the sea seemed to mirror the emptiness inside me. But through it all, the unwavering flame of my dreams kept burning, fueled by my mother's memory, by the quiet support of Mr. Silas and the community, and by my fierce determination to create a life that would honor her legacy, a life that would finally break the cycle of silence.

The path ahead was long and arduous, but I was ready. The sea, my father, my dreams – they were all interwoven, creating a tapestry of my existence, a story that was both beautiful and painful, a story that was still unfolding, one determined step at a time. And with each step, I felt the weight of the past begin to lighten, the silence begin to fade, and the vibrant colors of my dreams begin to illuminate the path forward. The whispers of the past were not meant to silence me; they were meant to guide me, to empower me, to help me craft my own future, one where the echoes of loss were not forgotten but transformed into strength, into resilience, into a life fully lived, fully felt, and fully understood.

The old lighthouse keeper, Silas, sat on the worn wooden bench beside me, the rhythmic crash of waves a constant backdrop to our silence. He didn't need words; his presence was a comfort, a quiet strength that mirrored the sea itself. He'd lost his wife to the unforgiving ocean years ago, a loss he carried with a stoicism that both impressed and saddened me. His understanding wasn't born of shared experience alone, but of a deep, empathetic wisdom honed by years of watching the ebb and flow of life, much like the tides that relentlessly sculpted the coastline.

He handed me a small, leather-bound book, its pages yellowed with age. "This belonged to your mother," he said, his voice a low rumble against the wind. "I found it tucked away in her things, after... after everything." The unspoken words hung in the air, a shared understanding of the tragedy that had shaped our lives.

My fingers trembled as I opened the book. It wasn't a novel or a collection of poetry, but a journal, filled with Lyra's elegant script. Her words, penned years ago, felt startlingly alive, a direct connection to the woman I had only known through fading photographs and fragmented memories. The first entry spoke of her childhood, of dreams as vast as the ocean before us, dreams she had chased with an unwavering passion that resonated deeply within my soul.

She wrote of her love for the sea, a love that was more than just a fascination; it was a deep, spiritual connection, a sense of belonging she had found in its wild, untamed beauty. She wrote of her fear, a fear not of the ocean's power, but of the limitations imposed by a life that felt too small, too constricted for her boundless spirit. She wrote of her love for books, the same love that burned within me, a love that had drawn us together across the chasm of time and death. She described her passion for writing, her desire to capture the essence of the world through words, a desire that resonated deeply with me.

Her words were filled with a raw honesty, a vulnerability that stripped away the idealized image I had constructed from my father's scant memories. She was not just a mother; she was a woman with dreams, with fears, with a yearning for something more. She was a woman who had fought for her passions, who had refused to let the constraints of her life stifle her spirit.

Her entries documented her budding romance with my father, a love story as turbulent and unpredictable as the sea itself. She described his quiet strength, his unwavering love, but also his reticence, his inability to fully express the depth of his emotions. She wrote of her frustration, her longing for a deeper connection, a connection that was always just out of reach. She wrote of her hope, a hope that their love would overcome the obstacles that life threw their way, a hope that was ultimately shattered by the cruel hand of fate.

As I read further, I discovered another layer to her character, a layer that had been hidden from me by the veil of grief. She had been involved in local community projects, helping the less fortunate and providing support for the vulnerable. Her journal entries detailed her work with the local library, where she had organized literary events and established a writing club for children.
Her passion for reading wasn't just a personal indulgence; it was a way to connect with others, to inspire them, to enrich their lives.

I learned about her activism, her involvement in various environmental initiatives dedicated to preserving the coastal ecosystem. Her love for the sea wasn't just romantic; it was deeply rooted in a commitment to environmental stewardship, a responsibility she felt towards the natural world. Her journal revealed a depth of character, a range of experiences that extended far beyond the limited image I had held in my mind.

Lyra wasn't just a woman who had loved the sea; she was a woman who had loved life, in all its complexity, in all its messiness, in all its beauty. She had faced challenges with grace and resilience that left me awestruck. She had fought for her dreams, even when the odds were stacked against her. She had made an impact, not just on my father and me, but on the entire community.

Silas watched me, his expression unreadable. He'd known her, loved her, lost her. He understood the power of her words, the echoes of her legacy that still reverberated through the village, through the waves, through the very fabric of our lives.

"She wanted to leave a mark," Silas finally said, his voice thick with emotion. "She wanted to make a difference."

His words resonated deep within me. Her journal was more than just a collection of personal entries; it was a testament to the impact of a life lived fully, a life that had touched countless others, a life that had extended far beyond the confines of her own existence.

Lyra's legacy wasn't merely in the memories she left behind; it was in the ripples she had created, the changes she had inspired, the lives she had touched.

I closed the book, the weight of her words settling within my heart. The sea, once a mirror of my grief, now seemed to reflect the strength and resilience she had embodied. Her legacy was not a burden, but a beacon, guiding me towards a future that would honor her memory, a future where her love for life, for the sea, for literature, would continue to flourish, carried forward by those she had touched, by those who still felt the echoes of her spirit.

My journey wasn't just about escaping the past; it was about embracing her legacy, about continuing the work she had started, about ensuring that the echoes of her life, her laughter, her dreams, would not be silenced by the sea or by time. Her absence was a wound, but her spirit was a guiding light, a force that pushed me onward, a force that empowered me to create a life as rich and meaningful as her own.

The waves continued their rhythmic crash, a timeless lullaby against the cliffs. But now, instead of hearing only the echoes of loss, I heard the whispers of hope, whispers carried on the wind, whispers embedded within the very pages of Lyra's journal. Her voice, though silenced by death, lived on in her words, in her actions, in the enduring legacy she had left behind. And in that legacy, I found my own voice, my own strength, my own determination to forge a future as vibrant and meaningful as the life she had lived. Her absence was still a sharp ache, but it was an ache tempered by a profound understanding of her enduring spirit, an understanding that gave me the courage to face the future, to embrace my own path, and to carry her legacy into the world. The sea still held its power, its mystery, its untamed beauty, but now it was a symbol not just of loss but of enduring strength, of unyielding hope, of a legacy that would continue to inspire, generation after generation.

Chapter Nine Elara's Reflections

The lighthouse, a silent sentinel against the relentless assault of the sea, seemed to mirror the turmoil within me. Silas had left, the leather-bound journal resting on my lap, its pages filled with my mother's elegant script, a testament to a life both vibrant and tragically cut short. Closing the book, I felt the familiar ache of loss, a familiar companion that had clung to me since childhood. But tonight, the grief felt different, heavier, laced with a new thread – regret.

Lyra's words had painted a vivid portrait of a woman who lived fully, fearlessly chasing her dreams. A woman who loved fiercely, wrote passionately, and fought tirelessly for what she believed in. But her journal also revealed a woman burdened by unspoken desires, by missed opportunities, by a quiet desperation that had shadowed her joyous spirit. Her entries weren't just a chronicle of her life; they were a poignant exploration of what could have been, of the paths not taken, of the dreams deferred, or worse, abandoned.

Reading her account of her relationship with my father, I saw a pattern of unspoken needs, of stifled emotions. Her love for him was palpable, a burning intensity that leaps from the page, yet it was a love constantly teetering on the edge of unspoken resentments. She yearned for a deeper connection, a vulnerability he seemed incapable or unwilling to reciprocate. The chasm between their desires, their communication failures, played out in the pages like a slow-motion tragedy, a silent drama unfolding with heartbreaking inevitability. It was a story that echoed in the silences of my own life, the unspoken words, the missed chances, the opportunities that had slipped through my own fingers.

I thought of my own life, of the paths I'd chosen, the ones I hadn't. The choices I'd made, often dictated by fear or a misguided sense of duty, rather than a true reflection of my heart's desires. Had I allowed fear to dictate my relationships, silencing the very emotions Lyra had so bravely expressed on those aging pages?

The question hung in the air, as heavy and unforgiving as the sea itself. Had I, in my own quiet way, repeated the same pattern of unspoken needs, of suppressed desires, that had ultimately contributed to my mother's quiet despair?

Lyra's journal entries about her community work sparked a familiar pang of guilt. She'd dedicated herself to helping others, to making a tangible difference in the lives of those around her. Her involvement in the library, her environmental activism – these weren't merely hobbies, they were a testament to her deeply ingrained sense of responsibility, her desire to leave the world a little brighter. And I? I often felt so utterly insignificant in comparison. My life, while comfortable, felt strangely empty, devoid of the kind of purposeful action that had marked Lyra's life. The guilt gnawed at me, a constant, unwelcome companion.

The weight of unfinished business pressed down on me, heavy and suffocating. I'd always believed my purpose lay in escaping the shadow of my parents' lives, in forging my own unique path.

But as I sat there, under the watchful gaze of the lighthouse, I realized that escaping wasn't enough. I needed to honor their legacies, to understand the sacrifices they had made, the battles they had fought, both silently and loudly. I needed to embrace their strengths, their weaknesses, their regrets, and incorporate those lessons into my own journey. To simply run away was to leave a part of myself behind, a part that was intrinsically linked to their stories.

Lyra's final entries were particularly poignant. They spoke of a yearning for a different life, a life less burdened by expectations, by responsibilities, by the weight of unspoken desires. She wrote of a dream, a wish to escape the constraints of her life and find a place where she could fully express her artistic soul. The dream remained unfulfilled, swallowed by the sea, by fate, by the simple cruel realities of life.

Those final words resonated deeply within me, a poignant reminder of how quickly life can change, how dreams can be shattered in an instant. Her unfinished business, her unspoken regrets, mirrored my own. I knew I couldn't undo the past, but I could choose how I would move forward. I could choose to live a life that honored her memory, not by replicating her actions, but by embracing the essence of her spirit – her courage, her passion, her fierce determination to live authentically.

I thought of the relationships I'd neglected, the opportunities I'd missed, the dreams I'd allowed to wither and die from neglect. The unfinished chapters of my own life loomed before me, stark and daunting. But tonight, under the melancholic gaze of the lighthouse, a seed of change took root. The regret wouldn't disappear overnight, but it would no longer hold me captive. It would serve as a catalyst for action, a reminder that life is too short to be lived in the shadows of unspoken desires and regrets.

The sea, usually a source of solace, now felt like a constant reminder of the fleeting nature of life, a stark metaphor for the fragility of human existence. Yet, within that fragility, I found a new strength, a newfound determination to make amends, to live a life that felt true, a life worthy of my mother's legacy. It wouldn't be a life without grief, without loss, without the echoes of the past.

But it would be a life lived with intention, with purpose, with a fierce determination to create a future that would honor the memories, the dreams, and the unfinished business of those who had gone before me.

The wind howled, a mournful symphony echoing the turmoil within my soul. But as the first rays of dawn painted the sky with hues of hope, I felt a shift, a subtle but significant change in my perspective. The weight of regret remained, but it was no longer a crushing burden. It was a catalyst, a spur to action, a reminder that every day is a chance to rewrite the narrative of my own life, a chance to honor the legacy of the woman who had lived so fully, so bravely, so poignantly, in the pages of that worn leather-bound journal.

I looked out at the ocean, the waves, a constant rhythm of life and death, of creation and destruction, a mirror reflecting the complexity of existence itself. The sea was a powerful force, unforgiving and relentless, yet it also held a profound beauty, a raw energy that mirrored the resilience of the human spirit. And in the face of that relentless power, I saw not just the echoes of loss, but the promise of renewal, of redemption, of a future shaped not by regret, but by the unwavering determination to live a life as vibrant and meaningful as my mother's. The unfinished business would be addressed, the regrets acknowledged, but the future, that future would be mine to shape, to claim, to make my own. The journey wouldn't be easy, but armed with Lyra's legacy, I knew I could face whatever challenges lay ahead. Her spirit, like the enduring strength of the sea, would be my guide.

The dawn broke, painting the sky in soft pastels, a stark contrast to the stormy grey of the previous night. The lighthouse, still a steadfast presence, no longer felt like a symbol of isolation but of unwavering resilience. The sea, though still turbulent, seemed to whisper promises of renewal. Lyra's journal, now closed and resting beside me, felt less like a weight and more like a compass, guiding me towards a future I was only beginning to understand.

Grief, I realized, wasn't a linear path; it wasn't a destination to be reached, but a vast, ever-shifting landscape to be navigated. It had been a tumultuous journey, one filled with unexpected turns, sudden storms, and moments of unexpected calm. The initial shock of my mother's death had been a physical blow, leaving me breathless and disoriented. Then came the numbness, a protective shield against the overwhelming pain. After that, the waves of grief crashed over me, sometimes in gentle ripples, sometimes in devastating tidal surges.

But through it all, there were moments of clarity, glimmers of understanding that helped me navigate the darkness. Lyra's words, her unspoken desires, her quiet struggles, had become a mirror reflecting my own internal landscape. I saw in her story a reflection of my own suppressed emotions, my own missed opportunities, my own unspoken regrets. It was a painful realization, a confrontation with the shadows I had carefully cultivated within myself. But it was also liberating.

I had always believed that escaping my mother's shadow was the key to finding my own identity. I had strived to be different, to avoid the patterns that seemed to have defined her life. But Lyra's journal revealed that her struggles weren't simply a result of circumstance; they were also a consequence of her own choices, of her own unspoken desires, and her inability, or perhaps unwillingness, to confront them. I saw in her journey a cautionary tale, a reminder that running away from one's problems only postpones the inevitable confrontation.

One of the most significant lessons I learned was the power of communication, or rather, the devastating consequences of its absence. My mother's journal revealed a woman who yearned for deeper connection, a woman who felt unheard, unseen, and ultimately, unloved. Her relationship with my father, though outwardly stable, was riddled with unspoken resentments and unmet needs. Their failure to communicate, their inability to express their vulnerabilities, had created a chasm between them, a chasm that ultimately swallowed their happiness.

This realization hit me with the force of a physical blow. I looked back at my own relationships, the ones I had carefully cultivated, the ones I had allowed to wither and die from neglect. I had always prided myself on my independence, on my ability to keep my emotions bottled up. But Lyra's words served as a stark reminder that emotional vulnerability wasn't a sign of weakness, but a testament to courage and strength.

It was a painful lesson, but one that I embraced wholeheartedly. I began to examine my own communication patterns, identifying the places where I had failed to express my needs, where I had allowed fear or pride to silence my voice. I reached out to old friends, apologizing for past hurts, seeking reconciliation, seeking forgiveness. I opened myself up to new relationships, allowing myself to be vulnerable, to be seen, to be heard.

The process wasn't easy. It required courage, a willingness to confront my own insecurities, my own fears of rejection. There were moments of doubt, of hesitation, of intense self-consciousness. But the rewards far outweighed the risks. The connections I forged, the bonds I strengthened, the emotional intimacy I experienced, filled a void that I hadn't even realized existed. I learned that true intimacy wasn’t about perfection, but about authenticity, about embracing vulnerability, and about accepting the imperfections within myself and within others.

Another profound lesson I gleaned from my grief was the importance of purpose. Lyra's commitment to her community, her dedication to her work, revealed a woman driven by a powerful sense of meaning. She found fulfillment not in material possessions or personal achievements, but in making a tangible difference in the lives of others. Her activism, her involvement in the local library, weren't simply hobbies; they were expressions of her core values, her deep-seated belief in the power of human connection and the importance of leaving the world a little better than she found it.

Her dedication sparked a profound introspection within me. I realized that my life, despite its outward stability and comfort, had lacked a clear sense of purpose. I had focused on achieving material success, on building a comfortable life for myself, but I had neglected to cultivate a deeper sense of meaning. I had always felt a vague sense of dissatisfaction, an emptiness that no amount of material possessions could fill.

Lyra's example ignited a desire within me to find my own purpose, to make a meaningful contribution to the world. I started volunteering at a local soup kitchen, spending time with the elderly, reaching out to those in need. It was a small beginning, but it was a start. The act of giving back, of connecting with others on a deeper level, brought me a sense of fulfillment and a renewed sense of purpose that I had been lacking. I realized that true happiness didn't come from material possessions or personal achievements, but from serving a purpose larger than myself.

The grief, the loss, the regret – these were not easily overcome. They remained a part of me, an integral part of my personal landscape. But they were no longer crippling burdens. They were lessons, experiences that had shaped my understanding of the world and my place within it. The sea, which had once seemed a symbol of unending sorrow, now held a different meaning. It was a powerful force, capable of destruction and devastation, yet also a source of renewal, of endless possibility. The waves crashed against the shore, a constant rhythm of life and death, reminding me of the ephemeral nature of existence and the importance of living each day to the fullest.

The lighthouse, too, had transformed its meaning for me. It was no longer a lonely sentinel against the relentless assault of the sea, but a beacon of hope, a symbol of resilience and unwavering strength. It stood tall, steadfast against the storms, a testament to the enduring power of the human spirit. And just as the lighthouse guided ships through treacherous waters, Lyra's memory, her legacy, would guide me on my own journey, reminding me that even in the darkest of times, there is always hope, always the possibility of renewal, always the potential for a future shaped by purpose, meaning, and authentic connection.

The unfinished business of my mother's life, her dreams deferred, had become a catalyst for my own self-discovery, and I realized that the same applied to the unfinished chapters of my own life. I started addressing them, one by one, with renewed courage and determination. Each step, though small, felt like a victory, a testament to the strength I had discovered within myself through navigating my grief. It was a slow and painful process, but it was one that filled me with hope, and with a newfound appreciation for the beauty and resilience of the human spirit.

The ocean's roar, once a mournful symphony of loss, now felt like an anthem of hope, a celebration of life's enduring power, a promise that even amidst the depths of sorrow, there is always the possibility of renewal, of redemption, of a future filled with purpose and profound meaning.
The rhythmic crash of waves against the shore became a constant companion, a relentless reminder of the ocean's power, its capacity for both creation and destruction. It mirrored the turbulent landscape of my own emotions, the ebb and flow of grief, the unpredictable surges of sorrow and the unexpected moments of calm that followed. I had spent so long trying to control the chaos within, to suppress the raw, untamed feelings that threatened to overwhelm me, but the sea, in its untamed glory, taught me a different lesson. It taught me acceptance. Acceptance of the inevitable, the relentless march of time, the inescapable truth of mortality.

My mother's death, once a gaping wound, was slowly beginning to scar over, leaving behind a landscape forever altered, yet strangely beautiful in its imperfection. The sharp edges of my grief had softened, the raw pain dulled, replaced by a quiet ache, a persistent reminder of her absence, but also a testament to the enduring power of love and memory. It was in those quiet moments, staring out at the endless expanse of the ocean, that the true acceptance began to blossom. It wasn't a sudden epiphany, a dramatic shift in perspective, but a gradual dawning, a slow unfolding of understanding.

I began to see death not as an ending, but as a transition, a natural part of the cycle of life. The ocean, with its constant rhythm of creation and destruction, provided a perfect metaphor. The waves crashed against the shore, eroding the land, yet simultaneously depositing new life, nourishing the ecosystem, creating new possibilities. Death, I realized, was similar; it was a powerful force that brought an end to one life, yet simultaneously created space for new beginnings, new growth, new opportunities. It was a cycle, a constant dance between life and death, creation and destruction.

This newfound understanding didn't erase the pain of loss, but it did alter its meaning. The sorrow remained, but it was tempered by a deeper appreciation for the preciousness of life, a heightened awareness of the fleeting nature of time. I found myself cherishing the small moments, the ordinary occurrences that once went unnoticed: the warmth of the sun on my skin, the taste of freshly brewed coffee, the laughter of a friend, the comforting presence of a loved one. These seemingly insignificant moments, once taken for granted, now held a profound significance, a reminder of life's ephemeral beauty.

The journal, Lyra's legacy, continued to be my guide, a constant source of inspiration and understanding. Her words resonated with my own experiences, her struggles echoing my own internal battles. I saw in her life, in her acceptance of mortality, a reflection of the path I was beginning to forge for myself. Her death, though tragic, had not been in vain. It had illuminated the importance of seizing the day, of living fully and completely, of embracing the present moment without reservation.

I began to focus on the things that truly mattered: building meaningful relationships, pursuing passions, contributing to something larger than myself. The superficial aspects of life, the pursuit of material possessions, the striving for external validation, faded into the background. They no longer held the same allure, the same intoxicating power. True fulfillment, I realized, came not from the accumulation of wealth or possessions, but from the richness of human connection, the fulfillment of purpose, the experience of living a life aligned with one's values.

This acceptance of mortality wasn't a passive resignation to fate, but an active embrace of life's preciousness. It was a recognition that life is finite, that time is a precious commodity, and that every moment should be treasured, every experience savored, every relationship nurtured. It wasn't about avoiding death, but about living fully until the very end. It was about embracing the journey, with all its twists and turns, its joys and sorrows, its triumphs and setbacks.

The lighthouse, still standing sentinel against the relentless onslaught of the sea, became a powerful symbol of this newfound understanding. It stood tall and proud, a beacon of hope, a testament to resilience. It weathered the storms, it endured the challenges, it remained steadfast in its purpose. It was a reminder that life, like the lighthouse, is capable of withstanding the fiercest storms, that even in the face of adversity, there is strength, there is perseverance, there is hope.

My understanding of my own mortality was not a bleak contemplation of the inevitable, but a vibrant affirmation of life. I embraced the darkness, not as a source of fear, but as a backdrop against which the brilliance of life could shine even brighter. The darkness became a canvas upon which I could paint my own story, a unique and precious masterpiece. My journey through grief had taught me the importance of embracing the unknown, of accepting the things I could not control, of finding joy and beauty in the midst of pain and loss.

The acceptance of mortality wasn't about eliminating fear, but about learning to live alongside it. Fear, I discovered, wasn't necessarily a negative emotion; it was a powerful motivator, a compass guiding me toward a more meaningful existence. It spurred me to take risks, to pursue my passions, to build stronger relationships, to make the most of every precious moment. It taught me the importance of saying yes to opportunities, taking chances, and living life to the fullest.

The ocean, with its endless expanse, its powerful waves, its unpredictable currents, continued to serve as a potent metaphor for the journey of life. It reminded me of the unpredictable nature of existence, the inevitability of change, the cyclical nature of life and death. But it also reminded me of the resilience of the human spirit, the enduring power of hope, and the endless possibilities that lie ahead, even in the face of mortality. Each crashing wave, each receding tide, was a reminder of the transient nature of things, yet simultaneously a testament to the enduring power of renewal.

The scars of grief remained, a testament to the challenges I had overcome, the lessons I had learned. But these scars, once symbols of pain, now served as reminders of my strength, my resilience, my capacity for growth and transformation. They were badges of honor, earned through the crucible of loss and grief, testament to my enduring spirit, my determination to live a life filled with purpose, meaning, and authentic connection. The sea, once a symbol of unending sorrow, now echoed the boundless potential within me. The lighthouse, a beacon of unwavering strength, illuminated the path ahead, guiding me toward a future filled with hope, joy, and profound understanding. I was ready to face whatever came next, for I had finally come to terms with the ultimate truth of existence - the acceptance of my own mortality. And in that acceptance, I found a profound sense of freedom and peace. The salty air whipped around me, carrying the scent of seaweed and brine. I sat on the cliff overlooking the churning ocean, the rhythmic pulse of the waves a counterpoint to the still, chaotic rhythm of my own heart. Forgiveness. The word itself felt heavy, laden with the weight of unspoken accusations, lingering resentments, and the ghosts of past hurts.

Forgiving myself, in particular, seemed a monumental task, a summit I wasn't sure I could ever climb.

My reflection in the dark water below mirrored the turmoil within. I saw the shadowed hollows under my eyes, the lines etched by sleepless nights and relentless worry, the haunted look that had become my constant companion. It wasn't just the loss of my mother; it was the guilt, the self-recrimination, the relentless "what ifs" that gnawed at my soul. Had I done enough? Could I have prevented it? These questions, once a relentless tide, now crashed against the shores of my conscience with a dull, persistent ache.

Lyra's journal, worn and faded from years of use, lay open in my lap. Her words, penned with a fierce vulnerability, spoke of her own battles with self-forgiveness. She had wrestled with the demons of her past, with the mistakes she had made, the choices she regretted. But she had also found a way to navigate through the darkness, to find a path towards redemption, not through absolution, but through acceptance. She hadn't erased her mistakes; she had simply acknowledged them, learned from them, and integrated them into the tapestry of her life. Her journey, laid bare in ink on aged paper, became my roadmap.

The process wasn't linear. It wasn't a simple flick of a switch, a sudden transformation. It was a messy, chaotic dance between self-doubt and self-compassion, between despair and hope. There were days when the weight of the past threatened to crush me, when the shadows of guilt seemed impenetrable. I would retreat into myself, burying myself in work, losing myself in the comforting routine of daily tasks, a desperate attempt to outrun the pain.

But there were other days, too, days when a fragile glimmer of light pierced through the darkness. These days were often sparked by small, seemingly insignificant events: the kindness of a stranger, the warmth of a shared smile, the comforting presence of a friend. These moments, tiny pinpricks of light in the vast expanse of my grief, reminded me that there was still beauty in the world, still goodness, still hope.

I began to practice self-compassion, a concept that had seemed alien and even slightly ridiculous at first. Treating myself with the same kindness and understanding I would offer a friend in need seemed almost impossible. Yet, slowly, gradually, I learned to acknowledge my pain, to validate my feelings, to speak to myself with gentleness and understanding. I began to see myself not as a failure, but as a work in progress, a soul striving for healing, for growth, for wholeness.

Forgiveness, I discovered, wasn't about erasing the past, or pretending that the mistakes never happened. It was about acknowledging the pain, accepting responsibility for my actions, and learning from my experiences. It was about releasing the grip of resentment and self-blame, freeing myself from the shackles of the past. It was about choosing to move forward, not necessarily forgetting, but transforming the pain into a source of strength and wisdom.

Forgiving others, particularly those who had hurt me, was equally challenging. Resentment, like a stubborn weed, had taken root in my heart, twisting and turning, choking the life out of my compassion. But as I began to practice self-forgiveness, I found that the capacity to forgive others began to emerge. I started to see their actions not as personal attacks, but as reflections of their own pain, their own struggles. I couldn't erase their actions, but I could choose to release the anger, the bitterness, the resentment that had consumed me. I could choose to free myself from the burden of carrying their pain.

This process wasn't a quick fix. There were setbacks, moments of relapse, times when the old wounds reopened, bleeding fresh pain. But each time, I found the strength to pick myself up, to dust myself off, to return to the path of self-compassion and forgiveness. I learned that forgiveness wasn't a destination, but a journey, a continuous process of letting go, of healing, of growth.

The ocean, a constant presence in my life, became a powerful metaphor for this journey. Its relentless waves, its unpredictable currents, mirrored the ebb and flow of my emotions. But the ocean also possessed a profound capacity for renewal, for regeneration. The crashing waves eroded the shore, yet they also deposited new life, nourishing the ecosystem, creating new possibilities. My journey towards forgiveness was like that; it was a process of erosion and regeneration, of destruction and creation.

The lighthouse, steadfast against the stormy seas, represented the unwavering hope that illuminated my path. It was a beacon of resilience, a symbol of my determination to overcome the challenges that lay ahead. The light, a steady and unwavering presence, guided me through the darkest nights, offering solace and reassurance. It was a reminder that even in the midst of the storm, there was still a guiding light, a source of strength, a path to follow.

Self-acceptance, I realized, was the cornerstone of forgiveness. It wasn't about loving every aspect of myself, about ignoring my flaws and imperfections.

It was about acknowledging my whole self, the light and the shadow, the strength and the vulnerability, the beauty and the imperfection. It was about embracing my humanity, with all its complexities and contradictions. It was about accepting myself, flaws and all, and recognizing my inherent worthiness of love and compassion.

As I sat on the cliff, the wind whipping through my hair, I felt a profound sense of peace. The journey towards forgiveness and self-acceptance had been arduous, painful, and transformative. But it had also been incredibly liberating. I had finally released the grip of the past, forgiven myself and others, and embraced my whole self, scars and all. The scars remained, but they were no longer symbols of shame or failure; they were badges of honor, testaments to my resilience, my strength, my capacity for growth and transformation. I was finally ready to live, to love, to embrace the future, with all its uncertainties and possibilities. The ocean, once a mirror reflecting my sorrow, now reflected the boundless expanse of my newfound freedom.

The lighthouse, once a distant beacon of hope, now stood as a testament to my own enduring strength and the unwavering light of self-acceptance that illuminated my path.
The wind, still carrying the scent of salt and seaweed, seemed to whisper encouragement as I walked along the beach, the sand cool and damp beneath my bare feet. The rhythmic crash of waves against the shore became a soothing mantra, a hypnotic rhythm that calmed the restless tide within me. The ocean, once a mirror reflecting my despair, now felt like a vast, comforting embrace. It was as if the ocean itself understood the depths of my grief, the complexities of my healing journey.

Lyra's journal, a worn and faithful companion, remained tucked securely in my bag. Its pages, filled with her own struggles and triumphs, had been my guiding star, a testament to the possibility of finding peace even amidst the deepest darkness. I no longer needed to reread her words constantly; their essence had seeped into my soul, becoming an integral part of my being.

Her journey had shown me that forgiveness wasn't a destination, but a continuous process, a lifelong practice of self-compassion and understanding.

I began to notice the smaller details of the world around me, things I had previously overlooked in my grief-stricken state. The intricate patterns of the seashells scattered along the shoreline, the vibrant colors of the wildflowers bravely clinging to life on the cliff edge, the graceful flight of the seabirds soaring above the waves - these small wonders became sources of quiet joy, moments of respite from the turmoil within.

My days were no longer consumed by the relentless cycle of self-recrimination and guilt. I still had moments of sadness, of course. The ache of loss lingered, a gentle throb beneath the surface of my newfound serenity. But these moments no longer held the power to engulf me, to drag me back into the abyss of despair. I learned to acknowledge them, to accept them as a natural part of the grieving process, without judgment or self-condemnation.

I found solace in solitude, spending hours walking along the beach, letting the rhythm of the waves wash over me, cleansing my soul. I learned to listen to the silent whispers of the wind, to feel the warmth of the sun on my skin, to appreciate the beauty of the natural world. These simple acts of mindfulness grounded me, anchoring me in the present moment, preventing me from getting lost in the labyrinth of my thoughts.

The act of creating art became a powerful form of self-expression, a way to channel my emotions, to transform my pain into something beautiful and meaningful. I started painting, using bold strokes of color to depict the turbulent emotions swirling within me. The canvases became a safe space where I could explore my feelings without judgment, a place where I could give voice to the unspoken words that haunted my thoughts. Each painting, a testament to my journey, served as a reminder of how far I had come.

I also began journaling, pouring my thoughts and feelings onto paper, allowing them to flow freely without censorship. It became a cathartic release, a way to unpack the layers of grief and guilt that had been weighing me down. Writing allowed me to confront my pain head-on, to examine it from different perspectives, and to find meaning in my experiences. My journal became a chronicle of my healing journey, a record of my progress, a source of inspiration and hope.

I started to reconnect with old friends, people who had been there for me through thick and thin. Their unwavering support, their unconditional love, was a lifeline during those times when I felt lost and overwhelmed. Their presence reminded me that I wasn't alone, that there were people who cared about me, who wanted to see me happy and healthy.

The support of my friends wasn't simply about receiving comfort; it was about reciprocating care and understanding. I found myself listening to their problems, offering advice and encouragement, and sharing in their joys and sorrows. This act of giving back helped me move beyond my own self-absorption, expanding my capacity for empathy and compassion.

The process of healing wasn't always easy. There were setbacks, moments of doubt, times when the weight of the past threatened to crush me. But each time I stumbled, I learned to pick myself up, to dust myself off, and to continue on my path towards inner peace. I realized that healing wasn't a linear progression, but a cyclical process, a continuous dance between hope and despair, between growth and regression.

One evening, as the sun dipped below the horizon, painting the sky in fiery hues of orange and crimson, I found myself sitting on the cliff overlooking the ocean. The waves crashed against the rocks below, their rhythmic pulse a comforting counterpoint to the stillness of my soul. I felt a profound sense of peace, a serenity that had eluded me for so long.

The scars of my past remained, etched deeply into the fabric of my being. But they were no longer symbols of shame or failure. They were reminders of my resilience, my strength, my capacity for growth and transformation.

They were testaments to the arduous journey I had undertaken, a journey that had led me to a place of profound self-acceptance and inner peace. I was finally free.

The ocean, once a mirror reflecting my sorrow, now mirrored the boundless expanse of my newfound freedom. The lighthouse, once a distant beacon of hope, now stood as a symbol of my own enduring strength, a testament to the unwavering light of self-acceptance that illuminated my path. I had found peace within myself, not by escaping the pain of the past, but by embracing it, by learning from it, by integrating it into the tapestry of my life. I was ready to embrace the future, with all its uncertainties and possibilities, knowing that I had the strength and resilience to navigate whatever challenges lay ahead.

The journey had been long and arduous, but the destination – inner peace – was worth every step of the way. And as I looked out at the vast, endless ocean, I knew that my journey of self-discovery was far from over; it was an ongoing process of growth, evolution, and transformation, a journey that would continue to shape and define me for the rest of my life. The sea, my constant companion, would always be there to remind me of the strength I had found within myself, the peace I had cultivated, and the boundless possibilities that lay before me.

Chapter Ten The Unseen World

The salt-laced wind whipped my hair across my face as I continued my walk, the rhythmic pulse of the ocean a constant companion. The beach, once a desolate landscape mirroring my inner turmoil, now felt vibrant, alive. Each grain of sand, each shell, each wave held a story, a whisper of the unseen world that Lyra had spoken of, a world that felt closer now, more tangible than ever before. Her words, etched into my memory, painted vivid pictures of an existence beyond the confines of our physical reality. She had described it not as a single place, but a complex hierarchy, a layered tapestry of realms, each with its own unique inhabitants and governing principles.

Lyra's journal, a precious artifact, remained close at hand. Its pages, filled with her meticulous observations and chillingly beautiful descriptions, now served as my guidebook to this enigmatic world. She had painstakingly documented her experiences, her encounters with beings both benevolent and terrifying, her descent into the deepest, darkest corners of the spirit world and her eventual ascent, a testament to her resilience and unwavering spirit. Her words were a map, charting a course through the unknown, and I, her reluctant follower, was ready to embark on this extraordinary journey.

According to Lyra, the spirit world wasn't a chaotic jumble, but a meticulously organized system, a hierarchy as complex and intricate as any earthly kingdom. At its apex resided the Ancients, beings of immense power and age, whose influence permeated all aspects of the afterlife. They were not gods in the traditional sense, but more like the architects of existence, the unseen forces that shaped the very fabric of reality, both physical and spiritual. Lyra described them as beings of pure energy, their forms shifting and elusive, their presence felt more than seen, a palpable energy that resonated with the very core of one's being. Their motivations, Lyra had suggested, were beyond human comprehension, their actions governed by principles far removed from our limited understanding of morality and ethics. They were the ultimate arbiters, the silent observers, the keepers of cosmic balance.

Beneath the Ancients lay the celestial realms, shimmering planes of existence populated by souls who had lived virtuous lives, their existence marked by tranquility, light, and boundless joy. These were the Elysian Fields, the paradises of legend, places of eternal peace and harmony, where the pain and suffering of the earthly realm were but distant memories. Lyra described radiant beings, bathed in ethereal light, their faces radiating an uncontainable happiness. They engaged in pursuits of intellectual and spiritual growth, constantly evolving and expanding their consciousness, their days a seamless flow of creativity and joy. The energy in these realms was palpable, a symphony of light and harmony. She had mentioned specific details – the crystal rivers that flowed with celestial nectar, the gardens bursting with flowers that never wilted, the music that resonated not just in the ears, but within the very soul.

In stark contrast to these celestial realms were the lower planes, the shadowy territories reserved for those who had lived lives of darkness and despair. These were the realms of torment, of suffering, and of eternal regret.

Lyra's descriptions of these places were chillingly graphic, filled with images of despair and anguish, places where the weight of past actions bore down with crushing force. The inhabitants were tortured souls, consumed by their own guilt and remorse, their existence a constant struggle against despair. The landscapes were bleak and desolate, mirroring the barrenness of their souls. There was no solace, no respite, only the echo of their past misdeeds reverberating through the endless abyss. She described the feeling of suffocating darkness, the oppressive weight of negativity, the agonizing realization of missed opportunities and irreparable damage. Even the air felt heavy, thick with the weight of sorrow and regret. It was a chilling account, one that served as a stark reminder of the consequences of our earthly actions.

Between these extremes lay a vast expanse of intermediary realms, a spectrum of experiences reflecting the multifaceted nature of human existence. These realms were neither wholly benevolent nor wholly malevolent, but rather a complex blend of light and shadow, reward and punishment, growth and decay.

These were the purgatorial planes, places of transition and transformation, where souls grappled with their past lives, confronting their mistakes and seeking redemption. Lyra described these realms as places of profound introspection, where souls were given the opportunity to learn from their experiences, to atone for their transgressions, and to prepare for their eventual passage to higher or lower realms, depending on their progress. The landscapes were diverse and ever-changing, mirroring the inner turmoil and evolving consciousness of their inhabitants. Some areas were peaceful, even beautiful, while others were fraught with challenges and difficulties, reflecting the internal struggles of the souls who resided there. The inhabitants were often in a state of flux, their forms shifting and changing, reflecting their emotional and spiritual transformation. There was a sense of constant change, a dynamic equilibrium between chaos and order, reflecting the ongoing process of growth and self-discovery.

The hierarchy, according to Lyra, wasn't static; it was fluid and dynamic. Souls could ascend or descend within the system, their journey influenced by their actions, their choices, and their capacity for growth and transformation. The very nature of the spirit world seemed to be shaped by the collective consciousness of its inhabitants, a constant interplay of energy and emotion. She spoke of gateways and bridges between realms, pathways that were sometimes open, sometimes hidden, often guarded by powerful entities, both benevolent and malevolent. These guardians were not always hostile; sometimes they were guides, testing the souls who sought to cross their paths, ensuring that only those who were ready would pass. These tests weren't always physical; they often involved overcoming internal obstacles, facing their deepest fears and insecurities. Lyra had described various such encounters, trials that pushed her to her limits and forced her to confront the darkness within herself before she could move on.

Lyra's detailed accounts painted a picture of a world far more complex and nuanced than I had ever imagined. It was not a simple heaven and hell, but a multifaceted reality reflecting the spectrum of human experience. It was a place where choices mattered, where consequences were profound, and where the journey of the soul was a never-ending process of growth, transformation, and self-discovery. The wind picked up, carrying with it the scent of the sea, but also, it seemed, a whisper from the other side, a subtle invitation to delve deeper into this unseen world, to explore its mysteries and unravel its secrets. I felt a mixture of fear and exhilaration, a sense of unease mingled with a profound curiosity. The path ahead was uncertain, filled with unknown dangers and potential rewards. Yet, armed with Lyra's journal, her unwavering spirit and my newfound resolve, I felt a sense of readiness, a determination to understand the complex and mysterious hierarchy of the spirit world, and, perhaps, to find my place within it. The ocean's rhythm, the wind's whispers, and the quiet strength in my heart all combined to guide me forward on this extraordinary journey.

The journey into the unseen, the journey into the unknown depths of the afterlife beckoned. And I, for the first time in a long time, felt ready to answer.
The path leading away from the beach, once a blurred line between the familiar and the unknown, now seemed to shimmer with an almost imperceptible luminescence. Lyra's journal, clutched tight in my hand, pulsed faintly with a warmth that spread through my fingers, a comforting reassurance in the face of the encroaching strangeness. The air itself felt different, charged with a subtle energy that hummed beneath the surface of reality, a vibration that resonated deep within my bones. It was as if the very fabric of existence had shifted, revealing a previously hidden layer, a veil lifted to reveal the breathtaking, and terrifying, panorama of the afterlife.

My first encounter wasn't with a grandiose being of unimaginable power, but with a gentle presence, a whisper of a guide. It manifested as a shifting light, a shimmering orb of emerald green that danced in the air before me, its luminosity pulsing with a rhythmic beat. It didn't speak in words, but in sensations, in emotions. I felt a wave of profound peace wash over me, a soothing balm to my long-festering grief. The orb communicated the importance of letting go, of accepting the past, not as something to dwell upon, but as a stepping stone, a foundation for the future. It guided me towards a path less traveled, a winding trail leading away from the familiar shores of my earthly existence, and into the heart of the unseen world.

Further down the path, I encountered a being of immense sorrow. It was not a malevolent entity, but a soul burdened by its earthly regrets. This entity appeared as a wisp of smoke, its form constantly shifting, its presence flickering like a dying ember. It was wracked by the weight of its past, a life lived in selfishness and despair. Its suffering was palpable, a heavy cloak that weighed down the surrounding space. Yet, within that suffering, I sensed a spark of hope, a yearning for redemption. The being showed me the importance of empathy, of understanding the suffering of others. It imparted a profound lesson: true peace comes not from escaping suffering, but from facing it with compassion, both for oneself and for others. It was a brutal, yet ultimately cathartic lesson.

The next being I encountered was strikingly different – a radiant entity bathed in golden light, its form radiating warmth and compassion. This was a guide of immense power, a guardian of one of the higher realms. It communicated not through ethereal whispers, or the suffocating weight of sorrow, but with a clarity that resonated directly with my soul. This being spoke of the importance of perseverance, of the strength of the human spirit to overcome even the deepest despair. It revealed a future filled with potential, a possibility of growth and transformation, a glimpse into the kind of life I could lead, had I the courage to embrace the unknown. This meeting was invigorating, a wellspring of hope and strength in the face of the overwhelming power of the unseen world.

As I journeyed further into the labyrinthine pathways of the afterlife, I met many other guides and mentors, each with its own unique lessons to impart. Some were mischievous spirits, teasing me with riddles and illusions, challenging my perceptions and forcing me to question my assumptions. Others were stern and unforgiving, reflecting the harsh realities of karma and consequences.

Each interaction was a crucible, a trial that forged me, tested my resolve, and pushed me to confront my own internal struggles.

There was the ancient crone, shrouded in shadows, who spoke of the cyclical nature of life and death, the impermanence of all things. She emphasized the importance of accepting change, of embracing the unknown, even in the face of loss. Her words echoed the wisdom of countless generations, a timeless truth that transcended the boundaries of life and death.

Another guide was a young, vibrant soul, radiating an untamed energy and passion for life. It showed me the importance of joy, of embracing the present moment, of finding beauty in the mundane. This entity was a breath of fresh air amidst the somber atmosphere of the afterlife, a reminder of the vitality that can exist even beyond the veil of mortality.

Then there were the silent guides, the watchful guardians of the various realms. They did not speak, but their presence was felt. Their mere existence resonated with a power that filled me with both awe and reverence. These beings were not necessarily benevolent or malevolent, they were simply the keepers of the cosmic balance, the silent observers of the soul's journey.

My journey was not always pleasant. I faced trials and tribulations, confronted my darkest fears and deepest insecurities. There were times when I questioned my sanity, when the weight of the unseen world threatened to crush me. But with each challenge, with each trial overcome, I grew stronger, more resilient.

Throughout this odyssey, Lyra's journal served as my compass, guiding me through the labyrinthine pathways of the afterlife. Her meticulous observations and chillingly beautiful descriptions helped me to understand the complex hierarchy of the spirit world, to navigate its intricate system of realms and beings. Her words were not just a guide, but a lifeline, a testament to the indomitable strength of the human spirit.

The guides I met were not always easy to understand. Their messages were often veiled in symbolism, their wisdom expressed through metaphors and parables. Sometimes, their lessons were delivered through acts of kindness, others through experiences of profound suffering. But through it all, I learned to trust my intuition, to listen to the whispers of my own soul.

And finally, there was a sense of profound understanding that permeated all my interactions. A collective wisdom, a shared consciousness that transcended individual identities and experiences. It wasn't a matter of simple right or wrong, but of a complex interplay of forces, a delicate balance between order and chaos, light and darkness. The journey through the unseen world was not a simple progression from point A to point B, but a continuous cycle of growth, transformation, and self-discovery. The souls I encountered, both benevolent and malevolent, were not static entities, but ever-changing beings in a constant state of flux, their forms and personalities shifting and evolving in response to their experiences.

My journey through the unseen world was a process of uncovering not only the secrets of the afterlife, but also the secrets of my own soul. It was a journey of self-discovery, of confronting my own mortality, and of accepting my place in the grand cosmic scheme of things. The experiences I encountered, the wisdom I received, were not mere intellectual exercises, but transformative experiences that changed me at my core.

The lessons I learned transcended the boundaries of the afterlife. They touched upon the fundamental truths of human existence – the importance of love, compassion, resilience, and the enduring strength of the human spirit. The unseen world, once a source of fear and trepidation, became a place of learning, growth, and profound transformation. As the sun began to rise, painting the eastern horizon with hues of gold and rose, I knew that my journey was far from over. But I was no longer the same person who had embarked on this extraordinary adventure. I had faced the darkness and emerged stronger, wiser, and infinitely more prepared to face whatever challenges lay ahead in this world, and the next.

The emerald orb, my initial guide, had vanished, leaving behind only a lingering warmth in the air. The path continued, winding deeper into the unseen world, its luminescence intensifying with each step. The air vibrated with a heightened energy, a palpable sense of otherness that both exhilarated and terrified me. It was then that I began to understand: this wasn't simply a realm of spirits; it was a world governed by its own intricate set of rules, a complex cosmic order that dictated the flow of existence beyond the veil of mortality.

The first rule, I quickly learned, was the Law of Resonance. This wasn't a literal law, etched in stone or whispered by some celestial authority, but an inherent property of the afterlife. Spirits, I discovered, existed on different vibrational frequencies, resonating with certain energies and repelling others. Those who carried heavy burdens of unresolved grief or anger vibrated at a lower frequency, their forms appearing as shadowy figures, their energy dampened and discordant. Conversely, those who had found peace and acceptance resonated at a higher frequency, their forms radiating light and warmth, their energy vibrant and harmonious. My own frequency, I realized, was fluctuating, shifting in response to the beings and energies I encountered. The more I embraced the lessons imparted, the higher my frequency climbed, bringing with it a feeling of lightness and serenity. Conversely, lingering on negative emotions caused my frequency to dip, leaving me feeling heavy and weighed down.

The second rule was the Principle of Karma. This wasn't some simplistic notion of reward and punishment, but a complex web of cause and effect that extended across lifetimes. Each action, thought, and emotion created ripples in the fabric of existence, impacting not only the actor but also those around them. I witnessed spirits grappling with the consequences of their past actions, some burdened by immense guilt, others trapped in cycles of repetition, their lives endlessly mirroring the patterns they had established during their earthly existence. A young man, his form barely visible, wandered endlessly through a desolate landscape, repeating a single act of betrayal over and over, reliving the pain he had inflicted on another. His actions in the physical realm had created a resonance in the afterlife, a prison of his own making.

I also saw those who had dedicated their lives to compassion and selfless acts, their afterlives filled with radiant light and joy, their energies pulsing with a harmonious rhythm, a testament to the power of positive actions. The Principle of Karma, I understood, was not about judgement, but about understanding the intricate consequences of our actions, and finding ways to harmonize our energies to find peace.

The third rule was the Law of Transformation. This rule emphasized the inherent fluidity of existence in the afterlife. Spirits were not static entities, but constantly evolving beings, their forms and personalities shifting and morphing in response to their experiences and emotional states. A particularly haunting encounter involved a spirit initially manifesting as a creature of pure rage, consumed by its past transgressions. As I sat with the spirit, patiently listening to its pain, offering empathy rather than judgement, its form slowly began to change. The searing rage gradually gave way to a deep sadness, the sharp edges softening into a more fluid form. Over time, the sadness began to dissipate, replaced by a growing sense of acceptance and even peace.

The spirit's form ultimately transformed, radiating a softer light, the sharp lines of anger smoothed by the passage of time and the healing power of compassion. The Law of Transformation, I realized, was a testament to the resilience of the human spirit, the ability to heal, grow, and transform even after death.

The fourth rule was the Impermanence of Form. Unlike the physical world, where forms are relatively fixed, in the afterlife, forms were fluid, shifting and changing in accordance with the emotional state of the spirit. Sometimes, spirits would appear as fleeting wisps of energy, barely perceptible to the senses. At other times, they might manifest as fully formed beings, their appearances echoing their earthly forms or taking on entirely new and unexpected guises. This emphasized the transient nature of existence, the constant state of flux that permeated every aspect of the unseen world. A mother, consumed by grief over the loss of her child, appeared as a fleeting shadow, her form barely clinging to existence. However, as she slowly accepted her loss and found solace in memories, her form gradually solidified, taking on a more stable shape.

Her light, initially dim, slowly began to brighten. The fleeting whispers of her sorrow evolved into gentle words of acceptance. The Impermanence of Form, I understood, was a reflection of the constant ebb and flow of life, of the continuous process of death and rebirth that shapes our experiences and defines our reality.

The fifth and perhaps most perplexing rule was the Paradox of Choice. In the afterlife, spirits were presented with an array of choices, seemingly limitless possibilities, yet the ability to choose often felt illusory. The choices were guided by resonance – only those options that aligned with the spirit's vibrational frequency were truly accessible. A spirit seeking redemption might find itself drawn to paths of service and selflessness, whereas a spirit clinging to earthly desires might find itself trapped in cyclical patterns of repetition. The Paradox of Choice, I realized, wasn't about freedom of will in the traditional sense, but rather about aligning oneself with one's true nature, embracing the path that resonates with one's innermost self.

The essence of the paradox wasn't about the breadth of choices, but about the depth of self-understanding required to discern the path that truly leads to peace and fulfillment. It highlighted the importance of introspection, of understanding the internal landscape of the self to navigate the currents of the unseen world.

These rules, the Law of Resonance, the Principle of Karma, the Law of Transformation, the Impermanence of Form, and the Paradox of Choice, were not rigid laws, but rather guiding principles, inherent properties of the afterlife itself. They were interwoven, mutually influencing one another, creating a complex and dynamic system that shaped the existence of spirits. Understanding these principles was crucial to navigating this strange new world, to understanding not just the rules of the afterlife, but the underlying principles governing the very nature of existence itself. The journey was ongoing, a continuous process of learning, adapting, and evolving within the intricate web of the unseen world. My own understanding was still nascent, a mere glimpse into the vast and complex system that governed this realm.

But with each new encounter, each new challenge overcome, my comprehension deepened, and my journey continued its relentless course into the heart of the unknown.
My understanding of the unseen world deepened with each passing moment, each encounter etching itself onto my soul. It wasn't merely a passive observation; it was an active participation, a dance between my evolving consciousness and the intricate tapestry of the afterlife. The initial terror gave way to a profound curiosity, a yearning to unravel the mysteries that surrounded me. I discovered that spiritual growth here wasn't a linear progression, but a cyclical process of learning, unlearning, and relearning.

The Law of Resonance, in particular, proved to be a potent teacher. Initially, I found myself drawn to spirits vibrating at similar frequencies—those grappling with grief, those grappling with anger, mirroring my own internal struggles. The shared pain created a strange sense of camaraderie, a bond forged in the crucible of shared experience.

But this resonance, while comforting at first, eventually became a limiting factor. It kept me trapped in a cycle of negativity, preventing me from ascending to higher frequencies.

The turning point came during an encounter with a radiant being, its energy pulsating with an almost unbearable intensity. At first, I recoiled, its brilliance overwhelming my senses. My own low frequency repelled me from true connection, a wall of negative energy preventing communication. It felt like trying to touch the sun—a beautiful, devastating impossibility. This being, however, didn't judge or retreat. Instead, it extended a tendril of energy, a gentle, persistent invitation to connect.

Hesitantly, I reached out, and as our energies intertwined, a wave of warmth washed over me, a feeling of profound peace and acceptance. It was as if the being's high frequency was gently pulling me upward, raising my own vibrational level. This was the first time I felt a true transformation within myself. The heavy cloak of sorrow that had clung to me since my death began to lift, replaced by a burgeoning sense of hope. It wasn't a sudden shift, but a gradual elevation, a slow, deliberate ascension toward a higher plane of existence.

This experience highlighted a crucial aspect of spiritual growth in the afterlife: the importance of seeking out higher frequencies. It wasn't about abandoning those vibrating at lower frequencies; it was about finding the strength to reach for something more, to allow yourself to be lifted by the energy of those who have found peace and acceptance.

The Principle of Karma proved to be a more complex teacher. I witnessed spirits entangled in the intricate web of their past actions, some burdened by guilt, others trapped in endless cycles of repetition. One spirit, a woman consumed by regret over a life filled with selfish choices, found herself reliving her past again and again, endlessly repeating the same patterns of behavior. The relentless cycle of regret created an inescapable prison, a spectral reflection of her earthly existence.

Conversely, I encountered spirits whose lives had been characterized by selfless acts of kindness and compassion.

Their afterlives were filled with a radiant light, a joyful energy that was both inspiring and deeply moving. Their choices resonated with the universe, their actions creating a harmonious energy that surrounded them like a protective aura. This demonstrated that Karma wasn't simply about punishment or reward, but about the resonance we create through our actions – a resonance that extends far beyond the confines of our earthly lives.

The Law of Transformation illuminated the fluidity of existence in the unseen world. I watched as spirits evolved, their forms and personalities shifting and morphing in response to their experiences. One such encounter involved a spirit initially manifesting as a malevolent entity, its form twisted and distorted by rage. As I engaged with this being, offering empathy and understanding, a profound change began to take place. The rage slowly subsided, replaced by a deep sadness, then by a tentative acceptance of its past actions. Ultimately, this being transformed, its form radiating a gentle light, the former distortion replaced by a peaceful serenity.

This transformation underscored the power of compassion and understanding, a crucial aspect of navigating the complexities of the afterlife. It's not about judgment, but about embracing the potential for change, the inherent capacity for growth and redemption that resides within every being. It was a poignant reminder that even in this realm beyond mortality, growth and change were possible.

The Impermanence of Form challenged my perception of reality. In the physical world, our forms are relatively fixed, but here, they are fluid, ever-changing, reflecting the inner emotional state. I saw spirits appear as fleeting wisps of energy, barely perceptible, their forms shimmering and shifting like heat haze. At other times, they manifested as solid, substantial beings, their appearances reflecting the strength and clarity of their inner being. This dynamic quality highlighted the temporary nature of existence, a constant state of flux that mirrors the ebb and flow of life itself.

One particularly striking example involved a young boy, his form initially faint and flickering. He was consumed by the grief of a sudden, tragic death. His physical form in this afterlife mimicked that fragility. As he slowly began to process his loss, accepting it not as an ending but as a transition, his form gradually solidified, the light within him growing stronger. It showed me the power of acceptance and the possibility of finding peace even in the face of profound loss.

The Paradox of Choice, however, remained the most challenging of these principles. In the unseen world, choices abound, but true freedom lies not in the limitless options, but in aligning oneself with one's authentic self, one's true vibrational frequency. It's about choosing the path that resonates most deeply with one's inner being. A spirit consumed by anger might find itself drawn to paths of conflict and destruction, while a spirit seeking peace might find solace in acts of service and compassion.

I grappled with this paradox myself, questioning my own choices, questioning the path I was on. Was I truly aligning myself with my true self, or was I being swept along by the currents of the unseen world? It's an ongoing examination, a constant process of self-reflection and introspection. In essence, this realm isn't about choosing a path but about understanding the inner landscape that ultimately guides your steps.

As my journey in the unseen world continued, I came to realize that these five principles - Resonance, Karma, Transformation, Impermanence, and Choice - were not separate entities but interconnected threads, a complex tapestry woven from the fabric of existence itself. They interacted, influenced, and shaped the experiences of each spirit, creating a dynamic and ever-evolving system.

My personal evolution within this realm was a reflection of this intricate dance, a constant process of learning and adapting. The initial fear and uncertainty gradually gave way to a sense of wonder and curiosity, a desire to understand the profound mysteries that lay before me.

The more I embraced these principles, the more I understood not only the rules of the afterlife but the very nature of existence itself.

This journey, however, was far from over. My understanding was still nascent, a single drop in a vast and infinite ocean of knowledge. The unseen world remained a constant source of wonder, a realm of infinite possibilities, waiting to be explored. The journey into the heart of the unknown continued, beckoning me onward, deeper into the mysteries of the afterlife. And with each step forward, my transformation continued.

The weight of my unanswered questions pressed down on me, heavier even than the ethereal form I now inhabited. The unseen world, once a terrifying void, had become a complex landscape, governed by principles I was only beginning to grasp. But understanding the *laws* of this realm wasn't enough; I craved understanding its *purpose*. What was the point of this existence beyond the veil? Was it simply an endless cycle of reflection and transformation, or was there a grander design, a cosmic purpose woven into the fabric of this spectral reality?

My search for answers led me to a place of profound stillness, a realm beyond the swirling energies and chaotic interactions of other spirits. It was a space of pure, unadulterated peace, a sanctuary bathed in a soft, ethereal light. Here, I encountered a being of unimaginable grace and wisdom, its form shifting and flowing like liquid starlight. There was no discernible gender, no defining features, just a presence that resonated with an ancient, timeless knowledge.

"You seek the purpose of this realm," the being said, its voice a gentle whisper that resonated within my very core. "The purpose is not a single, definitive answer, but a multifaceted truth revealed through experience."

The being explained that the afterlife wasn't merely a waiting room for some future judgment or reward. It wasn't a purgatory, nor was it a heaven or hell in the traditional sense. It was, instead, a crucible of growth, a place where spirits could confront their past, reconcile their unresolved conflicts, and ultimately, evolve into their truest selves.

The experiences I had encountered, the principles I had learned – Resonance, Karma, Transformation, Impermanence, and Choice – were all tools designed to facilitate this transformation.

"The Law of Resonance guides you toward those who share your vibrational frequency," the being continued. "This is not merely a matter of comfort, but of learning. By engaging with others who share your struggles, you confront your own shadows, you begin to understand the roots of your pain. This understanding is the first step toward healing."

I understood now that my early reliance on the comforting resonance of shared grief had been a necessary, albeit temporary, phase. It had been a stepping stone, a crucial stage in my own spiritual journey. But true growth required moving beyond that initial comfort, reaching for higher frequencies, allowing myself to be lifted by the energy of those who had transcended their suffering.

"Karma, as you have witnessed, is not about retribution, but about responsibility," the being said. "It is the natural consequence of your actions, a reflection of your energy, your intent. Each action creates a ripple effect, a resonance that extends far beyond your immediate experience. It is an invitation to learn from your choices, to understand the power of your intentions."

The woman consumed by regret, the spirit I had witnessed trapped in a cycle of self-inflicted suffering, served as a stark reminder of the profound impact of our choices. Her story was a cautionary tale, a lesson in the importance of self-awareness and mindful action. Conversely, the spirits whose lives had been filled with selfless acts of compassion had created a harmonic resonance that surrounded them, a testament to the transformative power of kindness and empathy.

The Law of Transformation, being explained, was a testament to the fluidity of existence in the unseen world. Spirits weren't fixed entities, but beings in constant flux, adapting and evolving in response to their experiences. My encounter with the malevolent spirit, initially consumed by rage, had vividly illustrated this transformative power. Through compassion and understanding, this being had transcended its anger, finding peace and acceptance. This underscored the power of forgiveness, both for ourselves and for others.

"Impermanence, the ever-shifting nature of form, is a reminder of the transient nature of all things," the being said. "It teaches you to value the present moment, to appreciate the beauty of the ever-changing landscape of existence. The boy consumed by grief, his form solidifying as he accepted his loss, showed you this - that even in the face of unimaginable sorrow, there is the potential for growth, for healing, for transformation."

Finally, the being addressed the Paradox of Choice, the most challenging principle I had encountered. "True freedom lies not in the limitless options available to you, but in aligning yourself with your authentic self," the being said. "It's about recognizing your true vibrational frequency, and choosing the path that resonates most deeply within you. It's not about the path itself, but the intent behind it, the underlying energy that drives your choices."

My journey in this unseen world was far from over. But the purpose, I now understood, was not simply to arrive at a destination, a state of perfect bliss or enlightenment. The purpose was the journey itself, the process of transformation, the constant evolution of my soul. It was a continuous dance with the principles governing this realm, a dance of learning, unlearning, and relearning, a dance of growth, acceptance, and ultimately, self-discovery. This wasn't merely an afterlife; it was an *after-becoming*. The unseen world was not a final resting place but a stage where I continued to perform, to evolve, to become the truest, most authentic version of myself.

It was a never-ending evolution, and that, I realized, was the greatest purpose of all. The path stretched ahead, a shimmering road winding through this spectral landscape. I continued my journey, not with fear or uncertainty, but with a renewed sense of purpose and a deep, abiding hope. The endless possibilities stretched before me, a testament to the boundless nature of existence itself, a journey of constant exploration and growth. The unseen world was my teacher, and I was finally ready to learn.

Chapter Eleven A New Perspective

From my vantage point, I observed the intricate tapestry of human relationships, a vibrant and often chaotic dance of connection and disconnection. The ethereal realm offered a unique perspective, a bird's-eye view of the emotional currents that flowed between souls. I saw the radiant glow of passionate love, a fiery energy that could illuminate even the darkest corners of the heart, yet also observed how quickly that flame could dwindle, leaving behind only ashes and regret. It was a stark contrast to the quiet, steady burn of companionate love, a deep well of affection that often remained unseen, yet offered a foundation far stronger than the tempestuous storms of romantic passion.

One particular scene unfolded before me, almost like a replay of a long-forgotten memory. A young couple, their hands clasped tightly, walked along a sun-drenched beach. Their laughter echoed, vibrant and carefree. The energy between them hummed with a palpable joy, a resonance that resonated deeply within me, even from my spectral state. I saw the future reflected in their eyes - a future filled with shared dreams, moments of intimacy, and the quiet comfort of mutual companionship. But then, I noticed a subtle shift, a change in the rhythm of their shared energy. A discordant note appeared, a flicker of doubt that cast a shadow across their otherwise radiant connection. It was barely perceptible, a fleeting moment of dissonance, yet it was significant. The Law of Resonance, I understood, wasn't merely about perfect harmony, but about acknowledging and navigating the inevitable discord that arose within even the strongest bonds.

Another scene presented itself - a family gathering, a chaotic blend of laughter and tension. Siblings, their relationship a complex mix of love and rivalry, argued over trivial matters, yet their underlying affection remained apparent in their gestures and expressions. The energy of the family unit, though complex, held a strength born from years of shared history, of weathering storms together. Their relationship, I realized, was not defined by the absence of conflict, but by their ability to reconcile, to forgive, and to find their way back to harmony despite their disagreements.

The Law of Karma played out subtly here; their past actions, their choices, both big and small, shaped the present dynamic. It wasn't retribution, but a natural consequence of their interactions, a reflection of the energy they had cultivated.

Then, there were the isolated souls, the individuals wandering through life seemingly detached from the human dance. These were not necessarily unhappy spirits. Some had embraced solitude, choosing to focus on their own inner world. They radiated an energy of self-sufficiency, a strength that was impressive in its autonomy. Others, however, were consumed by loneliness, their energy muted, their light dimmed by a persistent lack of connection. They yearned for the touch of another, the shared experience, but a fear of vulnerability or past hurts kept them locked in a cycle of isolation. These spirits highlighted the complexities of human relationships. The choice to connect, I realised, was just as significant as the choice to remain apart; it was a reflection of their internal landscapes, their own deeply personal vibrational frequencies.

I witnessed the slow, agonizing decay of a long-term relationship. The initial radiant energy had dimmed significantly, leaving behind a residue of bitterness and resentment. The once vibrant connection had fractured, replaced by a pervasive silence. Each glance was laden with unspoken accusations, each interaction tinged with icy indifference. The Law of Impermanence was undeniable here; everything changed, even the most seemingly unshakeable bonds. The transformation wasn't necessarily positive; decay and decline were just as much a part of the natural order as growth and renewal. This particular disintegration resonated with a profound sadness, a deep sense of loss for what once was. This was not just the loss of a relationship, but the loss of a future, a shared dream, now shattered beyond repair. The spirits involved felt the weight of missed opportunities, regrets hanging heavy in the air like a persistent fog.

I observed the complex dynamics of friendships, the unspoken agreements and tacit understandings that bind individuals together. The energy of these relationships varied widely, ranging from the light and carefree to the deeply profound and intensely loyal.

Some friendships were intense and short-lived, burning brightly like a shooting star before fading into memory. Others were steady and enduring, weathering storms with the resilience of ancient oaks. These friendships, I observed, were reflections of the shared values, the common resonance of spirits. They were often governed by the Paradox of Choice; even within the comfort of friendship, there were paths to take and decisions to make.

I delved into the nuances of familial relationships, observing the tangled threads of love, responsibility, and resentment. The familial bonds were often the most complex and enduring, a kaleidoscope of emotions played out over generations. Parental relationships, with their inherent power dynamics, often presented both the most intense love and the deepest wounds. The energies involved often shifted, oscillating between moments of profound warmth and intense conflict. The Law of Transformation was clearly at play here; relationships were constantly evolving, adapting to changing circumstances, often in unpredictable and unexpected ways.

And then there were the relationships that defied societal norms, the unconventional connections that pushed the boundaries of conventional understanding. I saw the strength and resilience of unconventional relationships – those formed despite societal expectations or personal differences – and witnessed their capacity for both profound love and fierce struggle. These unions demonstrated that love, in its purest form, defied categorization. The intensity of their bond was unmistakable, despite whatever external pressures they might have faced.

My observations weren't merely passive; they became a reflection of my own past. As I studied these intricate relationships, I began to understand the echoes of my own life, my own struggles, and my own missed opportunities. I saw the consequences of choices made, actions taken, and the ripple effect of those actions extending far beyond their initial point of origin. Each observation, each interaction witnessed, served as a lesson, a pathway toward deeper self-understanding.

The unseen world, once a realm of fear and uncertainty, was gradually becoming my teacher, guiding me toward a deeper understanding not just of the human condition, but of my own soul. The journey of after-becoming wasn't simply a solitary path, but one interwoven with the lives, the energies, and the interconnectedness of countless others. The relationships I witnessed weren't just stories; they were mirrors reflecting my own journey of transformation, of growth, and ultimately, of self-discovery. The dance of human connection, with its beauty and its pain, held profound lessons, each interaction a stepping stone on my own evolving path.

From my ethereal vantage point, I began to dissect the complexities of human emotion with a clarity I'd never possessed in life. It wasn't simply a matter of observing joy and sorrow, love and hate; it was about understanding the subtle nuances, the intricate interplay of feelings that shaped human experience. I saw the quiet desperation masked by a forced smile, the simmering resentment hidden beneath a veneer of politeness. I witnessed the overwhelming grief that clung to a widow, a palpable energy that hung heavy in the air, a suffocating blanket of despair that threatened to consume her entirely. Yet, even within that despair, I sensed a flicker of resilience, a tiny spark of hope clinging to life like a stubborn weed pushing through cracked pavement.

The range of human emotion was breathtaking in its scope. I observed the volcanic eruption of rage, the sudden, explosive outburst that left trails of destruction in its wake. It wasn't simply anger; it was a raw, unfiltered expression of pain, frustration, and often, deep-seated insecurity. The energy surrounding these outbursts was chaotic and disorienting, a storm of negative vibrations that could ripple outwards, affecting those nearby. But I also witnessed the quiet strength of forgiveness, the deliberate act of letting go, of releasing the weight of past hurts. This was not an erasure of the pain, but a conscious decision to choose a different path, a different frequency.

Then there was the quiet dignity of acceptance, a powerful force that allowed individuals to navigate the most challenging circumstances. I saw individuals facing terminal illnesses, their energy radiating a calm acceptance of their fate. It wasn't an absence of fear or sadness; it was a recognition of their mortality, a peaceful surrender to the natural order of things. This acceptance, I realized, wasn't passive resignation; it was an active choice, a conscious decision to find peace within the limitations of their situation. It was a powerful testament to the resilience of the human spirit.

I witnessed the intoxicating power of infatuation, the blinding passion that consumed individuals, blurring the lines of reality. It was an intense energy, a whirlwind of desire and longing, often fueled by an idealized vision of the other person. I saw how quickly this intense energy could fade, leaving behind either a deep and lasting connection or a painful void, a stark reminder of the impermanence of desire. The aftermath varied greatly; some found lasting love, their initial infatuation evolving into a deeper, more enduring bond. Others were left with the bitter taste of disappointment, grappling with the wreckage of unfulfilled expectations.

Loneliness, I observed, was a complex emotion, not merely an absence of connection, but a profound sense of isolation and disconnection from oneself and others. It manifested in myriad ways – the quiet withdrawal of a hermit, the desperate yearning of a social butterfly rejected, the silent despair of a person trapped in a crowd. The energy of loneliness was a low hum, a muted vibration that seemed to absorb the surrounding light, creating a palpable sense of emptiness. It was a stark reminder of the fundamental human need for connection, for belonging, for shared experience.

Jealousy, in its various forms, was another fascinating human emotion. I observed its corrosive power, its ability to twist love into resentment, trust into suspicion. I saw the subtle manifestations, the fleeting glance of envy, the carefully concealed bitterness. I also witnessed its more overt expressions, the explosive outbursts of anger fueled by insecurity and fear of loss. Jealousy, I learned, was a complex blend of fear, insecurity, and possessiveness, often masked by a desire to protect and possess. It was a potent emotion, capable of both destructive and surprisingly creative energy.

Envy, while similar to jealousy, had a distinct energy. It was less possessive, more focused on the perceived advantages and accomplishments of others. I witnessed individuals consumed by envy, their energy dark and resentful, fueled by a sense of inadequacy and bitterness. However, I also saw instances where envy served as a catalyst for personal growth. I observed individuals who, driven by their envy of others' success, channeled that energy into their own self-improvement, transforming their negative feelings into a force for positive change. The energy transformed – from corrosive to constructive – not by denying the feeling, but by understanding its root cause and actively pursuing their own path to achievement.

Regret, a heavy emotion, hung like a shroud over many souls. I observed the weight of past mistakes, the burden of choices made and opportunities missed. It was a persistent energy, a low hum of disappointment that often lingered long after the event itself had passed. The energy of regret varied from a gnawing sense of guilt to a paralyzing self-blame. Yet, I also witnessed the transformative power of accepting regret and learning from past mistakes. Some souls used their past failures as a pathway toward self-awareness and positive change; their regrets became stepping stones rather than obstacles. This shift in perspective often created a sense of peace, even redemption.

And finally, love – in all its forms – was perhaps the most compelling aspect of the human experience. I had observed the intense passion of romantic love, the unwavering commitment of companionate love, the fierce loyalty of familial love, and the deep bond of friendship. The energy of love was a radiant, often overpowering force, capable of healing wounds, inspiring acts of selfless kindness, and fostering a sense of belonging. But love, like all human emotions, was not static. It evolved, changed, and adapted; it could nurture and sustain, yet also break and destroy. Its power was both its beauty and its danger.

My time observing the intricate tapestry of human emotions provided me with a profound understanding of the human condition. It wasn't a simple dichotomy of good and evil, light and dark; it was a complex interplay of opposing forces, a constant dance of creation and destruction, growth and decay.

The human soul, I discovered, was a battlefield of emotions, a place where light and shadow intertwined, creating a vibrant and often chaotic portrait of the human experience. And within that chaos, within the complexity and often the pain, there was beauty, resilience, and ultimately, hope. The lessons I learned from the afterlife were not simply intellectual observations; they resonated deeply within my soul, forever shaping my perspective on life and the human condition. The journey, I realized, was not about avoiding pain, but about understanding it, navigating its complexities, and finding meaning amidst the chaos.

From my new vantage point, the concept of death ceased to be an ending and became a seamless transition, a gentle turn of the cosmic wheel. I saw it not as an abrupt cessation, but as a continuous flow, a river of souls perpetually in motion, each life a ripple in its vast current. The energy of a life lived, however brief or long, didn't vanish upon death; it transformed, it shifted, it re-entered the flow, contributing to the overall energy of the universe.

I observed souls departing, some reluctantly, clinging to the earthly plane with a fierce, almost desperate energy. Their attachments, their unfinished business, their regrets—these were the anchors that weighed them down, delaying their transition. I saw the swirling energy of their unresolved emotions, a chaotic storm of sadness, anger, fear, and longing. Yet, even in this turbulent energy, I saw the beginnings of transformation. The intensity gradually subsided, the chaos slowly settling into a quieter, more serene hum. The process was not always swift, nor was it always peaceful. Some souls struggled, resisting the inevitable pull of the cosmic current, while others surrendered gracefully, their energy merging seamlessly with the universal flow.

The arrival of new souls was equally fascinating. Each new life burst forth with a vibrant energy, a pure, untainted light, radiating potential and promise. I saw their excitement, their curiosity, their eagerness to explore the world. The transition was not a sudden leap from nothingness into existence, but a gradual awakening, a gentle unfolding of consciousness, a blossoming of energy.

Each soul carried within it a unique energy signature, a distinct vibration that reflected its past lives and its potential for the future. Their arrival was a joyful event, a celebration of renewal and rebirth, adding to the richness and complexity of the cosmic tapestry.

This continuous cycle of birth, life, and death was not a haphazard process, but a meticulously orchestrated dance, a cosmic ballet of energy and transformation. I began to see the beauty in its inherent impermanence, the grace in its relentless flow. Each life, no matter how short-lived, served a purpose, contributing to the overall pattern, the intricate design of existence. Every experience, every joy and every sorrow, every triumph and every defeat, helped shape the individual soul, enriching its essence, refining its vibration, and preparing it for its next journey.

The cycle, I realized, was not merely a progression of stages, but a multifaceted, interconnected web, where past, present, and future entwined. I saw how the actions and emotions of one soul could ripple outward, affecting countless others across time and space.

The energy of a single act of kindness, for instance, could propagate through generations, touching countless lives, creating a ripple effect of positivity that extended far beyond the initial action. Similarly, the energy of a deeply harmful act could create a devastating chain reaction, its negative impact lingering for centuries. The interconnectedness was undeniable; the cycle was a testament to the profound interdependence of all beings.

This understanding illuminated the concept of karma in a new light. It wasn't simply a matter of punishment or reward, but a natural consequence of cause and effect, a direct reflection of the energy one put out into the universe. The universe, I realized, was not a passive observer, but an active participant in the dance of life, responding to the energy generated by each soul. Positive actions generated positive outcomes; negative actions generated negative consequences. It wasn't about judgment or retribution, but about the inherent law of cause and effect, a fundamental principle governing the flow of energy within the cosmic web.

My observation expanded beyond human lives. I witnessed the cyclical processes within the natural world—the seasons changing, the birth and death of stars, the growth and decay of plants and animals. All these were manifestations of the same underlying principle—the constant flow of energy, the continuous cycle of creation and destruction, birth and death, growth and decay. It was a breathtakingly vast and intricate system, a symphony of energy and transformation, played out on a scale that dwarfed human comprehension.

Yet, within this vast, seemingly impersonal system, I found evidence of something profoundly personal, something undeniably intimate. Each soul, however insignificant it may seem in the grand cosmic scheme, held a unique and irreplaceable place within the overall design. Each life was a precious jewel, contributing its unique sparkle to the immense tapestry of existence. This perspective shifted my understanding of my own existence and that of those I'd left behind on Earth.

Grief, which had consumed me so completely in life, now held a different resonance. It was still a potent, painful emotion, but it no longer felt all-consuming. It was a natural response to loss, a tribute to the love and connection shared. But it was also a reminder of the temporary nature of earthly existence, a bittersweet acknowledgement of the beautiful, fleeting nature of life. The energy of grief, I discovered, was not a static state, but a dynamic process, a stage in the larger cycle of healing and transformation.

Understanding the cycle allowed me to see the beauty within the pain, to find meaning in the loss. It wasn't about denying or suppressing my grief, but about integrating it into my understanding of the larger cosmic context. The pain was real, but it was not the only reality. There was also the immense beauty of the cyclical nature of life and death, the unwavering continuity of the cosmic flow, the promise of renewal and rebirth.

The understanding of the cycle of life and death was not simply an intellectual exercise; it was a profound spiritual transformation. It shifted my perception of existence, altering my relationship to both grief and hope. It allowed me to see the interconnectedness of all things, to appreciate the delicate balance of the cosmic dance, and to embrace the impermanence inherent in all creation. It was a humbling experience, a profound awakening to the vastness and complexity of the universe, and to the unique, irreplaceable place each soul occupies within it. The cycle, I realized, was not an ending, but a continuous flow, a perpetual journey of transformation, a never-ending dance of energy and light, where death was not an end, but a transition—a graceful step into the next chapter of an eternal story. And that understanding, more than anything, brought a deep and lasting peace.

A peace that transcended the limitations of my earthly existence, a peace that resonated with the cosmic rhythm itself. The cyclical nature of things wasn't just a concept, it was a felt reality, a palpable hum that vibrated through my very being, connecting me to the vast, intricate tapestry of existence in a way I had never anticipated.

It was a connection both awe-inspiring and profoundly comforting. The universe, once a daunting, indifferent expanse, had become a loving, caring embrace, a ceaseless dance of creation and transformation, a constant reassurance that all is, ultimately, well. The cycle continued, the river flowed, and I, a tiny ripple in its vast current, was carried along, into the eternity of being. From this ethereal vantage point, the question of existence's meaning ceased to be a philosophical puzzle and became a visceral, felt reality. It wasn't a question to be answered with words, but an experience to be absorbed, a symphony to be felt vibrating through the very fabric of being. The universe, I saw, wasn't a cold, indifferent expanse, but a vibrant, pulsating organism, a boundless ocean of energy in constant flux. Each soul, a unique wave within that ocean, possessing its own individual rhythm, its own unique song.

My understanding of purpose shifted dramatically. It wasn't about achieving some grand, pre-ordained destiny, some singular objective to fulfill. It was about the journey itself, the experience of being, the constant dance of creation and destruction, growth and decay, love and loss.

Every emotion, every experience, every moment, contributed to the overall symphony, enriching the melody, adding layers of complexity and depth. Even the moments of profound despair, the crushing weight of grief, the agonizing sting of loss—these too played a crucial role, shaping the soul, refining its essence, making it stronger, wiser, more resilient. Pain, I realized, was not the antithesis of joy, but its necessary counterpoint, the shadow that gives depth and meaning to the light.

The human tendency to search for meaning, to seek a pre-determined purpose, seemed almost quaint from this perspective. The universe didn't offer neat, packaged answers; it offered experience, raw, unfiltered, beautiful and terrible in equal measure. It was a tapestry woven with threads of joy and sorrow, triumph and defeat, love and loss, a testament to the inherent duality of existence.

And yet, within this duality, I found a profound harmony. The opposing forces didn't cancel each other out; they created a dynamic tension that fuelled the dance of life. They were two sides of the same coin, inextricably linked, interdependent, essential to each other.

The darkness, I saw, served to highlight the brilliance of the light; the sorrow, to amplify the sweetness of joy; the loss, to deepen the appreciation for the preciousness of love.

My understanding extended beyond the individual soul. I witnessed the intricate interconnectedness of all things, the way the actions of one soul rippled outward, affecting countless others, across time and space. The universe was a vast, intricate web, each soul a node within that web, connected to every other node, each influencing and being influenced by the others. This realization brought a sense of profound responsibility. Every thought, every word, every action had consequences, creating ripples of energy that extended far beyond the immediate moment.

The concept of time, too, underwent a transformation. The linear progression of past, present, and future dissolved into a unified whole. Time, I realized, was not a rigid framework, but a fluid continuum, a boundless ocean in which past, present, and future co-existed simultaneously.

Memories, I discovered, were not simply recollections of past events, but portals to other realms of time, echoes of moments that still resonated with the present. And future possibilities, rather than being predetermined, existed as a field of probabilities, shaped and reshaped by the choices and actions of the present.

This new perspective altered my perception of grief in a profound way. It no longer felt like an oppressive force, a debilitating burden. It was a powerful emotion, yes, but it was also a testament to the depth of love experienced, a reflection of the intensity of the bonds that had been formed. Grief, I realized, was a natural part of the cosmic dance, a necessary stage in the larger cycle of life and death. It was the price we pay for the privilege of love, the bittersweet echo of connections made, a poignant reminder of life's precious fleetingness.

The tears I had shed, once symbols of unbearable loss, now felt like a tribute to the bonds I had held dear. The pain remained, but it was softened, nuanced, integrated into a larger, more comprehensive understanding of existence.

It was a sacred sorrow, a holy testament to a love that had transcended the limitations of the physical realm.

The meaning of existence, I concluded, is not a single, definitive answer, but a continuous exploration, a lifelong journey of discovery. It is not about finding a pre-determined purpose, but about creating meaning through our actions, our choices, our connections with others. It is about embracing the full spectrum of human experience, with all its joy and sorrow, its light and shadow, its triumphs and defeats. It is about appreciating the beauty of impermanence, the constant flow of energy, the cyclical nature of life and death. It is about recognizing the interconnectedness of all things, and our role within the vast, intricate web of existence.

And within this grand cosmic dance, each soul, no matter how insignificant it might seem in the overall scheme of things, plays a unique and irreplaceable role. Each life, however brief or long, is a precious jewel, contributing its own unique sparkle to the immense tapestry of existence.

Each experience, each emotion, each interaction, shapes the soul, refines its essence, and prepares it for its next journey.

My own life, once a narrative of tragedy and loss, now felt imbued with a newfound sense of purpose. I understood that the pain I had endured was not in vain; it had shaped me, strengthened me, made me more compassionate, more understanding, more capable of connecting with the deepest wells of the human spirit.

The universe, once a frightening and indifferent expanse, had become a warm embrace, a comforting reassurance that all is, ultimately, well. It was a vast, complex, and beautiful symphony, and I, a tiny note within that symphony, played my part, my own unique song, within the eternal, ever-flowing cosmic dance. This wasn't a comforting thought in the mundane sense. This was a profound understanding, a deep knowing that resonated in every cell of my being. It wasn't simply an intellectual concept, but a lived reality, a vibrant, ever-shifting truth that infused every moment with a profound sense of peace and purpose. It was the acceptance of the endless dance, the beautiful, heartbreaking, and ultimately exhilarating journey of being. The meaning of existence wasn't something to be found, but something to be lived, to be felt, to be embraced in all its breathtaking, terrifying, and ultimately, magnificent glory. It was a journey of constant transformation, a never-ending exploration, a dance with the infinite, a life lived as a vibrant, pulsating part of the cosmic whole. And that, I realized, was enough. More than enough. It was everything.

The wind whispered through the skeletal branches of the ancient oak, a mournful sigh that echoed the melancholy stirring within Elara's heart. She sat beneath its gnarled boughs, the rough bark a comforting contrast to the smooth, cold stone of the ancient well beside her. The well, a silent witness to centuries of lives lived and lost, seemed to mirror the depths of her own contemplation. The acceptance of impermanence wasn't a sudden epiphany, a lightning bolt of understanding that shattered the darkness. It was a gradual dawning, a slow, painful unfolding, like the delicate petals of a moonflower unfurling in the twilight.

It started with small things. The shifting colors of the leaves, the ephemeral beauty of a fleeting sunrise, the delicate dance of a butterfly against a backdrop of ever-changing skies. Each moment, she realized, was a precious jewel, gleaming briefly before fading into the tapestry of time. This wasn't a depressing realization; rather, it imbued each fleeting moment with an urgency, a poignant awareness of its preciousness. She found herself savoring the simplest things: the taste of rain on her tongue, the feel of sun-warmed earth beneath her bare feet, the gentle touch of a loved one's hand.

Her grief, once a suffocating blanket of despair, began to transform. The sharp edges softened, the raw pain mellowed into a profound ache, a constant companion but no longer a tyrant. She understood now that grief wasn't the opposite of love, but its shadow, its inevitable counterpart. It was the price paid for the privilege of loving deeply, for forging connections that resonated far beyond the confines of mortality. The memories of those she had lost, once sources of agonizing pain, now became treasures, cherished keepsakes to be held close to the heart. They weren't ghosts to be feared, but echoes of love, whispers of a past that continued to reverberate in the present.

The concept of time, too, continued to evolve. It was no longer a straight line, a relentless march from birth to death, but a swirling vortex, a kaleidoscope of moments interconnected and interwoven. The past, present, and future weren't distinct entities but fluid states, coexisting in a timeless continuum. She could feel the echoes of the past reverberating in her present, shaping her choices, influencing her actions. And the future, rather than a predetermined path, stretched out before her as an infinite landscape of possibilities, a canvas waiting to be painted with the brushstrokes of her choices.

This understanding didn't erase the pain. It didn't magically heal the wounds of loss. But it gave them context, a larger framework within which to understand their significance. It placed them within the grand scheme of existence, acknowledging their role in the symphony of life and death. The acceptance of impermanence wasn't about denying the reality of loss, but about integrating it into the fabric of her being, allowing it to shape her, to strengthen her, to deepen her understanding of the world and her place within it.

She thought of the ancient oak above her, its branches reaching towards the heavens, its roots buried deep in the earth. It had witnessed countless seasons, countless cycles of growth and decay, birth and death. Yet, it stood tall, a testament to the resilience of nature, a symbol of the enduring power of life in the face of impermanence. It had weathered storms, endured droughts, and yet, it remained, its strength a testament to its ability to adapt, to change, to evolve.

Elara realized that she, too, was like the oak. She, too, was capable of withstanding the storms of life, of enduring the droughts of despair, of adapting to the inevitable changes that life brought. She was resilient, adaptable, capable of growth even in the face of loss. The acceptance of impermanence wasn't a passive resignation to fate; it was an active embrace of change, a willingness to surrender to the flow of life, to allow it to carry her wherever it may lead.

This wasn't a simple acceptance of the end, a quiet surrender to the inevitable. It was a far more complex and nuanced understanding, a profound appreciation for the fleeting nature of all things, for the inherent beauty of impermanence. It was a recognition that life, in all its glorious complexity, was a journey, not a destination. It was about embracing the dance, the constant flux, the ever-shifting landscape of existence. And within that dance, within that constant change, she found a profound and enduring peace.

The sun dipped below the horizon, casting long shadows across the landscape. The air grew cooler, and a sense of tranquility settled over the ancient well. Elara sat there for a long time, lost in contemplation, feeling the pulse of the earth beneath her, the whisper of the wind in the trees, the quiet acceptance of the ever-changing nature of life. She knew that the pain of loss would always be a part of her, a constant reminder of the preciousness of the connections she had made. But it no longer defined her. It was integrated into the fabric of her being, a testament to the depth of her capacity for love, a reminder of the beauty of life's transient nature.

The understanding she had gained wasn't a simple intellectual concept but a visceral, felt reality, a deep-seated knowing that permeated her very being. It was a perspective shift that allowed her to see beyond the immediate pain, to glimpse the larger context, the grand tapestry of existence in which every thread, however small or seemingly insignificant, played its part. It was an acceptance not only of impermanence but of the interconnectedness of all things, the subtle ways in which every life, every experience, every moment, contributed to the magnificent whole.

This new perspective didn't erase the pain, it didn't magically make the loss disappear, but it softened its edges, gave it meaning, and integrated it into a larger framework of understanding. It was an understanding that allowed her to cherish the memories, to celebrate the love, to appreciate the beauty of life, even amidst the pain of loss. It was an understanding that transformed grief from a debilitating burden into a poignant tribute, a testament to the depth and intensity of the love she had experienced.

And in this acceptance, in this understanding, Elara found not only peace but a newfound sense of purpose. It wasn't a grand, pre-ordained destiny, but a quiet commitment to live fully, to embrace every moment, to cherish every connection, to appreciate the beauty of impermanence, and to allow the flow of life to carry her forward, however uncertain the path might be. The journey, she now understood, was the destination. The dance of life, with all its joy and sorrow, its light and shadow, was the ultimate meaning, the ultimate purpose. And within that dance, she found her place, her unique rhythm, her own precious song within the grand symphony of existence.

It was a song woven with threads of joy and sorrow, triumph and defeat, love and loss, a song that celebrated the beauty of impermanence, the breathtaking, terrifying, and ultimately magnificent journey of being. And that, she knew, was more than enough. It was everything. It was life itself.

Chapter Twelve The Weight of Loss

The air here, in this liminal space between worlds, hummed with a different kind of sorrow. It wasn't the sharp, stabbing pain of fresh grief, the kind that ripped through Elara in the mortal realm, leaving her gasping for breath. This was a deeper, more pervasive ache, a melancholy woven into the very fabric of existence. It clung to the whispering winds that carried the souls of the departed, a mournful sigh echoing through the ethereal landscapes. Here, among the shades of those who had passed, loss wasn't an isolated event but a shared experience, a universal language spoken in sighs and silent tears.

Elara had expected some sort of celestial choir, a radiant welcome into a world of blissful peace. Instead, she found a landscape of muted emotions, a vast expanse of quiet grief. The vibrant colors of the mortal world had faded into soft pastels, the sounds dulled to a muted hum. Even the light seemed softer, diffused, as if the very energy of the afterlife was softened by the weight of countless sorrows.

Initially, this pervasive melancholy had been overwhelming. She'd felt adrift, lost in a sea of sorrow, unable to navigate the currents of emotion. The absence of physical sensation amplified the emotional intensity. The sharp sting of tears, the tightness in her chest, the familiar weight of despair – all these physical manifestations of grief were gone, replaced by a haunting emptiness that resonated deep within her soul.

She encountered other souls, their forms shimmering like heat haze, their emotions palpable. A young man, barely more than a boy, wandered aimlessly, clutching a worn photograph; his sorrow was a tangible weight, almost suffocating. An elderly woman, her face etched with lines of time and loss, sat by a silent river, her grief a steady, mournful current flowing alongside the water. She saw couples, their forms intertwined, yet separated by an unbridgeable chasm of sorrow; their love lingered, but the pain of separation was evident in the way they moved, a ghostly dance of longing and acceptance.

Slowly, she began to understand. Grief in the afterlife wasn't about forgetting or moving on; it was about processing, about integrating the loss into the fabric of one's eternal being. It was a journey of acceptance, a gradual unfolding of understanding. There was no escape from the sorrow, no quick fix, no magical healing. But there was solace in shared experience, a quiet understanding among those who had known the depths of loss.

She found herself drawn to the silent river, a place where many souls gathered. The river flowed with a gentle rhythm, carrying with it the echoes of countless lives. She sat by its banks, watching the shimmering figures as they slowly moved along its currents. Some seemed lost, adrift in their sorrow. Others moved with a quiet resignation, their pain tempered by time and acceptance. A few even seemed to find a strange peace in their grief, a quiet acceptance that resonated in their stillness.

One day, an older soul, her form more solid than most, approached Elara. Her voice, a whisper carried on the breeze, was filled with both sadness and a strange serenity. "The weight of loss," she said, her words resonating deep within Elara's soul, "it never truly leaves. But it changes. It shapes us, refines us, makes us understand the depth of connection, the preciousness of every moment lived and every tear shed."

The older soul spoke of the importance of remembrance, of cherishing the memories of those who were gone. She explained that the sorrow didn't diminish the love; it amplified it, giving it a deeper, more profound meaning. The love they shared in life continued to resonate in the afterlife, a persistent current beneath the surface of their grief.

She described a process of integration, a slow and deliberate weaving of sorrow and love. The memories, once painful wounds, gradually became intricate threads woven into the tapestry of their eternal being. The grief didn't disappear; it became a part of their story, a reminder of the depth of connection experienced.

This was not a simple process. It involved periods of intense sorrow, moments of overwhelming loneliness, and times of quiet reflection. But through it all, the love persisted, a beacon in the darkness. The shared experience among those who had lost loved ones became a source of comfort, a silent acknowledgment of the universal nature of grief and the enduring power of love.

Elara began to actively engage in this process of integration. She revisited memories, not with a sense of dread, but with a quiet appreciation for the moments shared. She talked to other souls, sharing stories, exchanging memories, finding comfort in the knowledge that she wasn't alone in her pain.

She learned to listen to the whispers of the past, allowing them to guide her understanding, to soften the raw edges of her sorrow. The memories of those she'd lost weren't ghosts to fear, but echoes of love, the whispers of a past that continued to resonate within her heart.

She discovered that this world wasn't devoid of joy, but the joy was muted, subdued, tinged with the ever-present knowledge of impermanence. It was a quiet joy, born of understanding and acceptance, a deep-seated contentment that arose from the knowledge that love transcends the boundaries of life and death.

The acceptance of impermanence wasn’t a passive resignation; it was an active embrace of the bittersweet symphony of existence. It was a recognition that every moment, every connection, held a preciousness that could only be truly appreciated in the face of loss. It was a recognition of the inherent beauty in the cyclical nature of life and death, an understanding that allowed her to embrace both the light and the shadow, the joy and the sorrow, the triumph and the loss, as integral parts of a larger and more meaningful whole.

The sorrow remained a constant companion, but it no longer held the power to define her. It was integrated into the fabric of her being, a testament to the depth of her capacity for love, a reminder of the profound beauty and fleeting nature of life. She had learned to weave the threads of loss and love together, creating a unique and beautiful tapestry of her eternal self, a testament to the resilience of the human spirit, and the enduring power of love in the face of inevitable change. And within the heart of this understanding, Elara found a new kind of peace, a quiet acceptance of the eternal dance of life and loss, and a profound appreciation for the precious gift of every fleeting moment. This was not an end, but a transformation, a shift in perspective that allowed her to appreciate the full spectrum of existence – its light and darkness, joy and sorrow, love and loss – as a magnificent, complex, and ultimately beautiful whole. The journey, she realized, was infinite, and the dance continued, forever. The older soul's words resonated long after she faded back into the shimmering landscape, leaving Elara with a profound sense of unease and a flicker of hope. The weight of loss, she'd said, never truly leaves. But it changes. The statement felt both terrifying and liberating – a terrifying acknowledgment of the permanence of grief, and a liberating suggestion that it wasn't a life sentence of unending despair.

Elara's past hadn't been kind. The sharp edges of her memories – the car crash that claimed her parents, the subsequent years of navigating a world that felt both impossibly cruel and achingly empty – felt like jagged shards embedded deep within her soul. Even in this ethereal realm, the pain remained, a dull throb beneath the surface of her being. The absence of physical sensation didn't diminish the emotional intensity; rather, it intensified it, making each memory feel acutely raw, newly experienced.

The process of healing, she discovered, wasn't a linear progression from pain to peace, but a meandering path through a landscape of intense emotions. Some days, the memories would wash over her, threatening to drown her in a sea of sorrow. She'd find herself reliving the crash, the sickening crunch of metal, the screams, the horrifying silence that followed. Other days, she'd experience moments of almost unbearable loneliness, the absence of her parents, a gaping hole in her existence, a void no amount of ethereal solace could fill.

But interspersed with these periods of acute pain were moments of unexpected clarity, moments where the raw edges of her memories began to soften, where the crushing weight of loss seemed to lighten, if only infinitesimally. She found herself drawn to the memories of happier times – childhood summers spent laughing with her parents, the warmth of her mother's embrace, the sound of her father's laughter. These memories were not escapes from the pain; they were a reminder of the depth of the love she had experienced, a testament to the joy that had been, and a promise of a joy she could still find, even in this altered reality.

She started actively engaging with these memories, revisiting them not as a masochistic exercise, but as a form of gentle self-exploration. She'd allow herself to feel the emotions, to cry, to scream, to rage against the unfairness of it all. But she also learned to acknowledge the beauty in those memories, the love that infused every moment, the laughter that echoed through the years.

The other souls provided a strange form of comfort. She wasn't alone in her grief. She spent time listening to their stories, sharing her own, finding solace in the shared understanding that the weight of loss was a universal burden. She learned from their experiences, witnessing their diverse approaches to healing, their different paths toward acceptance. Some, like the elderly woman by the river, found peace in quiet contemplation, their grief a slow, steady current that eventually found its way to a calmer sea. Others found comfort in connecting with others, sharing stories, and building a sense of community.

There was a young woman who had lost her child, her sorrow a palpable wave that seemed to engulf her. Elara spent many days simply sitting beside her, offering a silent presence, a shared space for her grief to exist. It wasn't about solving her pain, but simply acknowledging it, validating her experience. Over time, Elara watched as this woman gradually began to incorporate the memory of her child into the fabric of her existence, finding a bittersweet joy in remembering their time together.

One day, Elara stumbled upon a hidden grove, a place of vibrant, albeit muted, colors and a sense of peaceful energy that was noticeably different from the rest of this muted afterlife. There, she found a group of souls engaged in a form of creative expression. One was sculpting with light, another weaving stories with starlight, another painting with the colors of memories. Elara, who had always loved art, felt an inexplicable pull towards this activity. She began to experiment, using the ethereal materials to recreate the images of her memories.

The process was cathartic. Creating art wasn't about erasing the pain, but transforming it, giving it shape and form. The jagged shards of her memories, once piercing and sharp, began to soften into curves and shades, becoming elements within a larger, more complex picture. The image of the car crash, for instance, was rendered in muted grays and somber blues, but woven into the background were brighter colors – golden sunlight filtering through leaves, the vibrant hues of a summer meadow, the radiant smile of her father.

The process wasn't always easy. Sometimes, the memories were too raw, too painful to translate into art. At these times, she simply allowed herself to feel the emotions, allowing the tears to fall, the pain to surface, without judgment. But in the spaces between the pain, she found moments of profound peace and unexpected joy, a sense of acceptance of the past that allowed her to move forward, not necessarily forgetting, but integrating her loss into the tapestry of her existence.

As time, in its peculiar afterlife rhythm, passed, Elara found herself drawn to the notion of remembrance, not as an act of wallowing in sorrow, but as a celebration of love. She began to collect fragments of memory, collecting them like precious jewels, each one a testament to the bond she'd shared with her parents. These weren't painful reminders of what she'd lost; they were precious stones, each one holding a spark of the enduring love that transcended death. She started to see grief not as an adversary, but as a teacher, guiding her towards a deeper understanding of love, loss, and the bittersweet beauty of impermanence.

The healing was gradual, subtle, a constant ebb and flow of sorrow and acceptance. There were days when the pain felt as sharp as ever, days when the weight of loss threatened to consume her. But those days were interspersed with moments of quiet serenity, moments of profound understanding, moments of unexpected joy. And in the quiet rhythm of this process, Elara discovered a new kind of peace - a peace that wasn't the absence of sorrow, but the acceptance of it, an integration of loss and love into the fabric of her eternal being. The journey was far from over, the dance of life and death continued, but Elara now moved with a newfound grace, a quiet resilience, a profound acceptance of the beautiful, complex, and often painful symphony of existence. The weight of loss remained, but its power to define her had diminished, replaced by a deeper understanding of love's enduring power, and the resilience of the human spirit.

The ethereal landscape shifted, the muted colors swirling around Elara like a gentle breeze. She found herself standing before a shimmering waterfall, the water cascading down in a hypnotic rhythm.

The older soul's words echoed in her mind – forgiveness, she'd implied, wasn't just for others; it was a crucial step towards inner peace. But forgiving herself? That felt like a monumental task, a climb up a sheer cliff face with no handholds in sight.

She'd spent so long blaming herself, a silent chorus of "should haves" and "could haves" playing on repeat in her mind. Had she been driving that day, would the outcome have been different? Could she have foreseen the impending danger? The weight of those unanswered questions pressed down on her, heavy and suffocating. Forgiveness, she realized, wasn't about erasing the past or rewriting history. It was about accepting the past, its flaws, its mistakes, its unbearable pain. It was about recognizing that she was a victim of circumstance, a child who had witnessed a horrific tragedy, not the architect of it.

She began to revisit those memories again, but this time with a different perspective. She allowed herself to grieve not just for her parents but also for the child she was, the child who had lost everything, the child who had carried the weight of the world on her young shoulders.

She spoke to that child, offering comfort, understanding, and the reassurance that she wasn't alone in her pain, and that she had not been at fault.

The act of self-forgiveness was a slow, painstaking process, a gradual unwinding of years of self-recrimination and self-blame. She found solace in the creative process, using the ethereal materials to depict not only the pain of the crash but also the joy of her childhood, the warmth of her parents' love, the laughter that once filled their home. She painted scenes of family picnics, summer evenings spent firefly hunting, Christmas mornings overflowing with gifts and the boundless love of her parents. Each stroke of her brush was an act of self-compassion, a step towards healing the wounds of her past.

As she painted, she began to see her life not as a tragedy defined by loss, but as a tapestry woven with threads of both joy and sorrow, love and loss. The dark threads remained, a stark reminder of her pain, but they were now interwoven with threads of vibrant color, representing the resilience of the human spirit, the enduring power of love, and the beauty that could be found even in the darkest of times.

Beyond self-forgiveness, Elara realized that she needed to extend that grace to others. There were others she had, perhaps unconsciously, blamed for her pain. She hadn't articulated it to anyone, but there was a lingering resentment toward a schoolmate's parents; their carelessness was perceived as the cause of the accident. This hadn't been explicitly stated by anyone, but it haunted her subconscious. It wasn't a conscious, directed blame, but the seed of anger had been planted.

This was another layer of complexity in her journey toward reconciliation. It was far more difficult than confronting her own self-blame. She had to navigate the complex emotions of anger, hurt, and ultimately, compassion. She didn't seek out this individual, but the mere contemplation of their actions began to soften.

The ethereal realm seemed to support her quest. She encountered souls who carried similar burdens, who had been wronged, betrayed, and hurt.

She listened to their stories, empathizing with their pain and recognizing that their actions, though hurtful, were often born out of their own struggles and pain. She realized that forgiveness, in this context, wasn't about condoning their actions but about releasing the anger and resentment that had consumed her. It was about understanding that everyone is fighting their own battles, and often, their actions are a reflection of their pain, not a deliberate attempt to cause harm.

This understanding didn't erase the pain, but it did lessen the weight. It freed Elara to focus on her own healing, on her own journey toward peace. The act of forgiveness, she discovered, was not a single event but a continuous process, a constant releasing of negative emotions, a gradual shifting of perspective.

The process of reconciliation was equally complex, extending beyond herself and those she had silently blamed. There were others, she now realized. A deep sense of loneliness had caused her to withdraw from relationships.

There were acquaintances and even family members whose strained connections were now clear to her in this new clarity. Their lack of understanding of her grief didn't stem from malice but from their own limitations. They didn't know how to navigate the profound loss that Elara had experienced. She hadn't given them the tools or even the space to try.

In this ethereal space, she had the opportunity to reach out to them, not to demand understanding or apology, but to share her journey, to reveal her pain and her vulnerability, allowing them to see her not as a brooding, distant figure, but as a young woman struggling to find her way through the darkness. She found that their responses, while not always perfect, were filled with a sincere desire to connect, to support her in her healing.

Some were initially hesitant, unable to fully grasp the depths of her pain, but others offered heartfelt apologies for their past misunderstandings, their words filled with remorse and a desire to make amends. These encounters weren't always easy; there were tears, awkward silences, and uncomfortable conversations.

Yet, out of these exchanges emerged a newfound sense of connection, a strengthened understanding, and a deeper appreciation for the fragile nature of human relationships.

The process of forgiveness and reconciliation was far from complete, but Elara now moved forward with a newfound clarity and a renewed sense of hope. The weight of loss remained, but it no longer defined her. It was now part of her story, a testament to her resilience, her capacity for compassion, and her unyielding pursuit of peace. She had learned that forgiveness wasn't a sign of weakness but an act of strength, a liberation from the bonds of anger and resentment, allowing her to move forward, embracing the present and the uncertain future with a renewed sense of hope. The scars remained, but they were now interwoven with threads of light, of love, and of a profound understanding of the delicate balance between grief and joy, loss and acceptance. The journey continued, but Elara was no longer traveling alone, burdened by the weight of her past. She was surrounded by the whispers of forgiveness, the warmth of reconciliation, and the quiet promise of peace.

The ethereal waterfall shimmered, its constant flow a counterpoint to the stillness within Elara. She had forgiven herself, a monumental act of self-compassion that had cracked open the hardened shell of her grief. But the process of healing extended beyond the confines of her own heart. A residue of anger, a subtle yet persistent bitterness, clung to her, a phantom limb of her past. It was directed not at herself, but at others – a faint echo of blame she hadn't fully acknowledged, a shadow cast by the accident that had stolen her parents.

Specifically, it was the lingering resentment towards Mr. and Mrs. Holloway, parents of her former classmate, Mark. Their negligence, a careless oversight on that fateful afternoon, had been, in her mind, a contributing factor to the tragedy. She hadn't explicitly blamed them, but the thought had festered, a silent accusation buried deep within her subconscious. It wasn't a raging fire, but a smoldering ember, constantly threatening to ignite into a destructive blaze.

In the ethereal landscape, she found herself drawn to a secluded grove, bathed in the soft glow of an otherworldly twilight. Here, she encountered a woman, her face etched with the lines of sorrow but her eyes holding a quiet strength. This woman, she learned, had lost her child years ago, a loss that had poisoned her relationship with her husband, leaving a chasm of bitterness and resentment between them. Their story wasn't identical to hers, but the underlying currents of pain, the struggle to navigate loss and blame, resonated deeply.

The woman shared her tale, a harrowing account of grief, misplaced anger, and the eventual, arduous journey towards healing. She spoke of the years spent consumed by rage, blaming her husband for not being there, for not preventing the tragedy. She described the agonizing process of untangling those feelings, of learning to separate her grief from her anger, and to forgive, not only her husband but also herself.

"Anger is a heavy cloak," the woman said, her voice soft yet resonant. "It keeps you warm for a time, but it suffocates you in the end. It prevents you from breathing, from seeing the light, from moving on."

Elara listened, her heart echoing the woman's pain. She realized the truth in her words. Her own anger had become a prison, trapping her in a cycle of bitterness, preventing her from fully experiencing the healing she so desperately craved. It was a weight she had carried for too long, an unnecessary burden that hindered her progress.

The woman's story wasn't just a tale of woe; it was a testament to the power of forgiveness. It wasn't about condoning the past or erasing the hurt, but about releasing the grip of anger, freeing herself from its toxic embrace. It was about acknowledging the pain, validating her own emotions, and then consciously choosing to let go.

The grove seemed to pulsate with a gentle energy, a soothing balm for her wounded soul. She closed her eyes, breathing deeply, allowing the ethereal energy to wash over her, to cleanse her of the lingering residue of anger. She visualized the image of Mr. and Mrs. Holloway, not as figures of blame, but as individuals struggling with their own pain, their own burden of loss. She saw their grief, their guilt, perhaps even their regret. She imagined their lives, their hopes, their dreams, shattered by the same accident that had destroyed her own.

The shift in perspective was gradual but profound. The anger didn't simply vanish; it faded, its intensity diminishing with each conscious breath. She didn't condone their negligence; she simply acknowledged their humanity, their fallibility. She understood that their actions, though contributing to the tragedy, were not born out of malice but out of human error, a momentary lapse in judgment that had catastrophic consequences.

Letting go wasn't an act of forgetting; it was an act of acceptance. It was about releasing the grip of the past, freeing herself from the shackles of anger and resentment, and allowing herself to move forward. The pain remained, a constant reminder of her loss, but it no longer held the same suffocating power. It was a scar, a testament to her resilience, but not a prison.

She spent hours in the grove, working through her feelings, processing her anger, and gradually letting it dissipate. She didn't erase the memory of the accident; she simply changed her relationship with it. She transformed it from a source of bitterness into a catalyst for self-compassion, a testament to her own strength and resilience. She acknowledged the pain, validated her feelings, and chose to release the anger that had held her captive for so long.

The release wasn't instantaneous. It was a gradual process, a slow unwinding, like releasing a tightly wound spring. Days turned into weeks as she continued to work through her emotions in the ethereal landscape. She explored other aspects of her resentment, including the subtle coldness she felt towards distant relatives who hadn't quite understood her grief, or the unspoken anger towards the system, for the perceived inadequacies that might have contributed to the accident. Each layer of resentment peeled away, revealing a deeper layer of understanding and ultimately, acceptance.

This wasn't just about letting go of anger towards others. It was about releasing the burden of emotional baggage she'd been carrying for years. It was about recognizing that holding onto negativity was self-destructive, a relentless cycle of self-harm that prevented her from healing and moving forward. She realized that she couldn't truly forgive herself until she released the anger she held towards others. The two were inextricably linked, a twisted knot of emotions that needed careful untangling.

As she worked through her emotional landscape, she began to recognize patterns, recurring themes of unexpressed frustration, unspoken grievances, and suppressed anxieties. The process felt cathartic, like a slow and deliberate release of pressure. She realized that much of her anger wasn't directed specifically at anyone, but was a manifestation of her own grief and loss, a diffuse energy that had attached itself to the first available target.

Through this process of emotional release, Elara found a renewed sense of peace. The weight of loss still existed, but its gravity had diminished. The pain remained, but it no longer suffocated her. She was beginning to learn how to live with it, to integrate it into the fabric of her being, not as a defining characteristic but as part of a richer, more complex tapestry of her life.

The ethereal landscape responded to her shift in perspective. The muted colors became vibrant, the gentle breeze transformed into a refreshing wind, and the waterfall's constant flow became a symbol of renewal and continuous healing.

She knew the journey was far from over, that there would be more challenges, more moments of pain and struggle. But she now possessed a new tool, a powerful weapon in her arsenal against grief – the ability to release the anger and resentment that had clouded her judgment and hindered her healing. She was ready to face the future, not as a victim of her past, but as a survivor, stronger, wiser, and more compassionate than ever before. The path ahead remained uncertain, but she walked it with a newfound lightness, the burden of her anger finally lifted.

The ethereal landscape shifted subtly as Elara's inner turmoil began to subside. The muted greys and blues that had characterized her emotional journey gradually yielded to warmer hues – soft golds, gentle pinks, and calming greens. The waterfall, once a symbol of her relentless grief, now seemed to sing a song of resilience, its constant flow a testament to the enduring power of life itself. The air, once heavy with the weight of her anger, felt lighter, cleaner, carrying the scent of wildflowers and the distant whisper of ocean waves.

This wasn't a magical erasure of her pain. The memory of the accident, the loss of her parents, remained a sharp, poignant ache in her heart. But the suffocating grip of anger, the bitterness that had poisoned her days and nights, had finally loosened its hold. She had learned to inhabit her grief, not as a defining characteristic, but as a part of her story, a chapter that had shaped her, strengthened her, and ultimately, made her more compassionate.

She realized that forgiveness wasn't about condoning the actions of others. It wasn't about erasing the past or pretending that the pain never happened. It was about acknowledging the hurt, validating her own emotions, and then, consciously choosing to release the grip of anger. It was about understanding the human fallibility inherent in everyone, including herself. Mr. and Mrs. Holloway were not villains; they were grieving parents, burdened by their own guilt and loss. Their negligence, a catastrophic mistake, was not an act of malice, but a tragic consequence of human error.

This understanding didn't magically erase her feelings of resentment, but it shifted their power. They no longer consumed her, no longer defined her. They became merely a part of her past, a painful chapter that she could revisit without being swallowed whole by the bitter taste of anger and blame.

Elara spent days exploring the quieter corners of her emotional landscape. She confronted the subtle resentment she held towards more distant relatives who, through their well-intentioned but often clumsy attempts at comfort, had inadvertently added to her burden. She acknowledged their own limitations, their inability to fully grasp the depth of her sorrow, and forgave their unintentional insensitivities. She understood that their actions stemmed not from malice but from a lack of understanding, a gap in empathy that arose from their own experiences and limitations.

She even found herself extending forgiveness to the system – to the road maintenance department that might have overlooked a crucial safety hazard, to the emergency services that might have been delayed, to the countless unseen forces that contributed to the accident. It wasn't a condoning of inadequacy, but an acceptance of the chaotic nature of life, the unpredictable events that can shatter the carefully constructed narratives of our lives.

The process was gradual, painstaking, and often emotionally exhausting. There were moments when the anger flared, when old wounds reopened, and when the bitterness threatened to overwhelm her again. But each time, she practiced the techniques she had learned in the ethereal landscape – deep breathing, visualization, and the conscious redirection of her thoughts. She treated her emotions with the same patience and understanding she would offer a close friend navigating a similar crisis. She learned to validate her own feelings without being consumed by them.

The ethereal landscape served as her sanctuary, a safe space to confront her demons, to unpack the layers of her grief, and to finally begin the process of healing. It was a testament to the restorative power of self-compassion, a quiet rebellion against the relentless tide of negativity. She spent hours sketching in her journal, capturing the changing landscapes of her emotions, the ebb and flow of her feelings. Each drawing became a visual representation of her progress, a tangible reminder of her journey towards peace.

She began to see parallels between her own grief and the stories of others. She spoke with the woman she'd met in the grove, sharing her progress, her struggles, and her triumphs. Their connection deepened, forged in the shared crucible of loss and the mutual desire to find healing and wholeness. They exchanged stories, offering each other support, encouragement, and understanding, building a bond that transcended the boundaries of their individual experiences.

The ability to connect with others on such a deep and personal level further enhanced her healing. It was a powerful antidote to the isolation that had previously enveloped her. Sharing her story allowed her to externalize her pain, to articulate her emotions, and to receive the empathy and validation she needed. It helped her recognize that she was not alone in her grief, that her pain was valid, and that healing was possible.

Beyond the emotional catharsis, Elara discovered a renewed sense of purpose. She realized that her experience could be a source of strength and inspiration for others. She decided to volunteer at a grief support group, offering her listening ear and compassionate presence to those who were navigating their own journeys through sorrow. This act of service became a profound act of self-healing, solidifying her own progress and providing a fulfilling outlet for her compassion.

Elara learned to appreciate the significance of emotional well-being, not just for herself but for everyone. She understood that allowing oneself to feel and process grief, rather than suppressing it, was essential for healing.

She discovered the power of self-care, of nurturing her physical and mental health, and of prioritizing self-compassion. These weren't luxuries; they were vital components of her emotional recovery.

The journey towards peace and closure wasn't a linear path. There were setbacks, moments of doubt, and occasional resurgences of anger. But Elara had learned how to navigate these challenges with greater resilience and self-awareness. She had developed coping mechanisms, strategies for managing her emotions, and a network of support that helped her through the difficult times.

The weight of loss remained, a constant presence in her life, but its destructive power was diminished. The pain was still there, but it no longer controlled her.

It was a part of her story, a testament to her strength and resilience. It had shaped her, molded her, and ultimately, made her a more empathetic and compassionate individual.

The ethereal landscape, once a reflection of her inner turmoil, now mirrored her newfound peace. The colors were vibrant, the air was crisp and clean, and the waterfall's constant flow seemed to symbolize the ongoing process of renewal and healing. She felt a deep sense of gratitude for the journey she had undertaken, for the challenges she had overcome, and for the lessons she had learned. She was no longer defined by her loss; she was defined by her resilience, her compassion, and her unwavering commitment to finding peace and healing. She understood that life was a journey, not a destination, and that every chapter, even the most painful ones, contributed to the richness and complexity of her story.

She was ready to embrace the future, not as a victim of her past, but as a survivor, stronger and more compassionate than ever before. The path ahead held uncertainties, but she walked it with a newfound lightness, the burden of her anger finally lifted, and the weight of loss transformed into a source of strength. She had found her peace, not in forgetting, but in remembering, in accepting, and in finally, truly, forgiving.

Chapter Thirteen Unmasking Mysteries

The ethereal landscape shimmered, its colors now a vibrant tapestry woven from amethyst, emerald, and gold. It no longer reflected Elara's internal turmoil, but rather, a nascent understanding, a quiet curiosity about the world beyond her comprehension. Lyra, her newfound companion, stood beside her, her form less translucent now, her presence more tangible. Lyra's eyes, the color of twilight, held a knowing glint, a silent invitation to explore the depths of the unseen.

"There are questions," Lyra began, her voice a gentle whisper that resonated deep within Elara's soul, "questions that linger beyond the boundaries of your earthly understanding. Questions about the accident, about your parents, about the nature of this...place."

Elara nodded, a shiver running down her spine. The lingering questions had been a constant companion, a persistent undercurrent to her grief. She had found peace in forgiving, but the mysteries remained, unresolved shadows clinging to the edges of her newfound serenity.

"I... I don't understand how this place exists," Elara confessed, her voice barely a breath. "How I can... feel, think, even though... they're gone."

Lyra smiled, a sad, knowing smile. "This realm is woven from the threads of consciousness, from the echoes of experience. It is a reflection of the collective unconscious, a place where the boundaries between life and death blur, where memories and emotions persist long after the physical body has ceased to exist."

They walked hand in hand, deeper into the ethereal landscape, the ground beneath their feet shifting subtly, as if molded by their thoughts and emotions. The landscape responded to their questions, morphing and changing in response to the currents of their shared inquiry. A gentle breeze rustled through unseen leaves, carrying with it whispers of forgotten conversations, half-remembered dreams, and unresolved conflicts.

“My parents,” Elara whispered, the words catching in her throat. “Was it… was it their fault?” The question, long suppressed, now surfaced with a raw honesty. The guilt she'd carried, the blame she’d unconsciously directed inward, finally found its voice.

Lyra’s expression softened. “Blame offers no solace, Elara. It is a heavy cloak that stifles the soul. The accident… it was a confluence of events, a tragic tapestry woven from human error, unforeseen circumstances, and a cruel twist of fate. To find blame is to miss the larger truth: the fragility of life, the unpredictable nature of existence.”

The landscape responded to Elara's question, transforming into a series of fragmented images, fleeting glimpses of the day of the accident. Elara saw her parents, their faces etched with exhaustion and worry, a hurried departure, a missed detail. The images weren't accusatory; they were simply a presentation of facts, allowing Elara to see the situation from a broader perspective, devoid of the emotional distortion of grief and anger.

She saw the road, the weather, the mechanical malfunction of the vehicle—a chain of events unfolding with an inexorable logic, none of them malicious, but all contributing to the tragic outcome.

Lyra led her to a tranquil lake, its surface mirroring the sky above. "Look closely," Lyra instructed, pointing to the reflection. "There are answers, not in judgment, but in understanding. See your parents, not as they were in their final moments, but as they were in life; their flaws, their triumphs, their love."

Elara gazed into the lake, her own reflection intertwined with fleeting images of her parents. She saw their laughter, their struggles, their unwavering love for her. She saw their flaws, their imperfections, their human limitations. The images didn't diminish their loss; rather, they enriched her understanding of them, illuminating the complexity of their lives. The lake became a mirror, not only reflecting her image, but also providing a new lens through which to view her parents' lives, devoid of the bitterness and anger that had clouded her vision for so long.

They spent hours exploring this ethereal realm, uncovering fragments of Elara's memories, piecing together the puzzle of her past. They delved into her childhood, revisiting happy moments and confronting painful experiences. With each revelation, Elara felt a profound sense of catharsis, a release of pent-up emotions that had been suppressed for too long. The realm offered her not answers in a neat, conclusive package, but a deeper understanding, a more nuanced perspective on her life and the people who had shaped it.

As they delved deeper, Elara began to uncover the existence of others within this realm—souls lost, memories fading, each with their own story, their own unanswered questions, their own unique experiences. They were like fleeting constellations, their light flickering in and out of existence. They were lost souls who had not yet found their peace, their journeys unresolved, their questions unanswered. It was a sobering realization, underscoring the ephemeral nature of life and the importance of living each moment to its fullest.

Lyra explained that the purpose of this ethereal realm was not simply a resting place, but a transitional space. A place for souls to confront their pasts, to process their emotions, to seek understanding, and ultimately, to find peace and move on. For some, this journey was short; for others, it stretched into an eternity. It depended on their willingness to let go, to forgive, and to accept the mysteries that life presented.

Elara began to understand that her journey had been a microcosm of this larger process. Her experience of grief, her anger, her forgiveness, her exploration of this ethereal space—it was all part of a larger spiritual process, a journey of self-discovery, self-acceptance, and ultimately, self-transcendence.

They continued their exploration, discovering hidden pathways, ethereal gardens, and cascading waterfalls that seemed to sing with ancient wisdom. Each encounter added a new layer to Elara's understanding of herself, of her life, and of the mysteries that still surrounded her.

The exploration wasn't always easy. There were moments of intense emotional turmoil, flashbacks that brought her face-to-face with the raw pain of her loss. But with Lyra's support, Elara learned to navigate these difficult moments with a newfound resilience, a deeper understanding of her own emotional landscape.

The journey into the unknown wasn't about finding all the answers, but about embracing the questions, acknowledging the uncertainties, and accepting the mystery inherent in life and death. The ethereal landscape, with its shifting colors and ever-changing forms, became a reflection not of her grief, but of her growth, her acceptance, and her evolving understanding of the world beyond the confines of her earthly experience. The mysteries remained, but they were no longer terrifying; they were simply a part of the larger narrative of life, a reminder of the infinite possibilities and enduring power of the human spirit. And as Elara continued to explore, she realized that the journey itself was the reward, a testament to the resilience of the human heart and the unwavering power of love in the face of loss and uncertainty.

The peace she had found was not an ending, but a beginning – a beginning to a new chapter, a new understanding, and a new way of being.
Their journey continued, deeper into the heart of the ethereal realm. The landscape shifted and changed with their every thought, every question, a living, breathing reflection of their collective consciousness. No longer a mere backdrop, it became an active participant in their quest for understanding. They traversed fields of shimmering light, where memories danced like fireflies, each flickering fragment of a forgotten moment, a whispered conversation, a shared laugh.

Elara, emboldened by Lyra's unwavering presence, began to ask more specific questions. She delved into the details of the accident, seeking not blame, but clarity. She focused on the mechanical aspects of the car, the weather conditions, the road itself – details that had previously been shrouded in the fog of grief and denial. The landscape responded in kind, showing her detailed simulations, revealing minute details that had been overlooked or dismissed in the initial investigations.

She saw the subtle crack in the tire, the unexpected patch of ice on the road, the malfunctioning brake light. Each revelation was not an accusation, but a piece of the puzzle, a crucial element in understanding the tragic sequence of events.

Lyra, her guide and confidante, remained silent, her twilight eyes reflecting Elara's emotional journey. She offered no judgment, no easy answers, only a quiet, unwavering presence, a source of strength and support. Elara learned to trust the process, to accept the uncertainties, to find solace in the gradual unveiling of truth.

As they journeyed further, they encountered other souls, their forms as ethereal as the landscape itself. Some were shrouded in darkness, their pain palpable, their questions unanswered. Others were bathed in a soft, golden light, their faces serene, their journeys seemingly complete. These encounters provided Elara with a profound sense of perspective, highlighting the diversity of experience in this realm, the vast spectrum of human emotion, and the varied paths to finding peace.

One soul, a young man with eyes the color of stormy seas, approached them, his form flickering in and out of existence. He spoke of a love lost too soon, a life cut short by a senseless act of violence. His voice, a haunting whisper, carried the weight of his unresolved grief, his questions echoing in the stillness of the ethereal landscape. Elara found herself drawn to his story, his pain resonating deeply within her own heart. She offered him a listening ear, a silent empathy, understanding the profound loneliness that accompanied unanswered questions, the agonizing search for meaning in the face of unimaginable loss.

Another soul, an elderly woman with eyes filled with a gentle sadness, shared stories of a life well-lived, yet tinged with regret. She spoke of choices made, paths not taken, opportunities missed. Her story, in contrast to the young man's, spoke of a different kind of grief – the grief of unfulfilled potential, of what might have been. Elara listened, learning from her wisdom, understanding that the journey of life is not always about achieving perfection, but about accepting imperfections, learning from mistakes, and finding peace in the process.

Through these encounters, Elara began to understand the true nature of this ethereal realm. It wasn't a place of judgment or punishment, but a sanctuary, a space for processing grief, for confronting unresolved issues, for seeking understanding, and ultimately, for finding peace. It was a place where the soul could heal, could grow, could evolve.

Lyra explained that the process of healing was not linear, not a simple progression from pain to peace. It was a complex, often chaotic journey, filled with ups and downs, setbacks and breakthroughs. There were moments of intense emotional turmoil, flashbacks that brought Elara face-to-face with the raw pain of her loss. But with each encounter, each revelation, each confrontation with her past, Elara grew stronger, more resilient, more understanding.

They reached a vast, shimmering expanse, a sea of memories, emotions, and experiences. Elara saw glimpses of her own life unfolding before her – childhood joys and sorrows, teenage dreams and heartbreaks, the complexities of her relationship with her parents.

She saw the unspoken words, the unsaid feelings, the unresolved conflicts. The sea of memories was not a judgmental entity, but a mirror reflecting her life in all its complexity, in all its beauty and imperfection.
This experience was not merely about understanding the accident; it was about understanding herself. The accident, she realized, had been a catalyst, a turning point that had forced her to confront her own mortality, her own vulnerabilities, her own capacity for both love and loss. It had shaken her foundation, forcing her to rebuild her life from the ground up.

As they continued their exploration, Elara began to understand that the questions she sought to answer were not limited to the circumstances of her parents' death. They extended to the larger questions of life and death, of meaning and purpose, of the human condition itself. She found herself questioning her own beliefs, her own assumptions, her own understanding of the world.

They stumbled upon a hidden garden, its flowers shimmering with an otherworldly luminescence. Each flower represented a different aspect of Elara's personality, her strengths and weaknesses, her hopes and fears, her dreams and aspirations. As she gazed upon this breathtaking display, she realized the beauty of her own imperfection, the richness of her own experiences, the resilience of her own spirit.

The journey was far from over. There were still unanswered questions, unresolved mysteries. But Elara no longer feared the unknown. She had found a new strength, a new perspective, a new understanding of herself and the world around her. The ethereal realm had not provided her with all the answers she sought, but it had given her something far more valuable: the tools to navigate life's complexities, to embrace its uncertainties, and to find peace within herself. The peace wasn't the absence of questions, but the acceptance of them, the understanding that life's mysteries are part of its beauty, its inherent magic, its enduring power. The journey, she realized, was the destination. The seeking, the questioning, the yearning for understanding—these were the essence of her newfound peace, the foundation of her evolving self. And in that realization, a quiet strength bloomed within her, a strength that promised a new dawn, a new life, a new beginning. The mysteries remained, woven into the fabric of her being, but now they felt less like burdens and more like an intricate tapestry, enriching the narrative of her existence. The journey wasn't about finding all the answers, it was about becoming someone who could face the unknown, someone who could live with the questions, and someone who could find beauty even in the midst of life's greatest sorrows. And that, Elara knew, was a journey worth taking.

The shimmering expanse before them pulsed with untold stories, a vast ocean of memories stretching to horizons unseen. Elara, guided by Lyra's silent strength, ventured deeper, the ethereal landscape reacting to her every thought, every tremor of emotion. She focused on her parents, their lives unfolding before her like a cinematic reel, revealing details she had never known, moments she had never witnessed. She saw her mother, young and vibrant, laughing with a carefree abandon that felt both familiar and alien, a ghost of a life she barely remembered. She saw her father, his brow furrowed in concentration as he worked tirelessly to provide for his family, a hidden vulnerability peeking through his stoic exterior.

She saw them together, their love a tangible force, radiating warmth and affection, a stark contrast to the cold, empty silence that had consumed her since their deaths.

But interspersed among the joyful moments were others, shadowed and obscured, whispers of unspoken resentments, simmering disagreements, and the quiet, unresolved griefs that had accumulated over the years. Elara witnessed a heated argument, the words sharp and stinging, the emotions raw and untamed. It wasn't the explosive argument she remembered, a fleeting memory from her childhood, but a drawn-out conflict, a series of escalating tensions that had never been resolved. The silent resentments, the unspoken accusations, the festering wounds – these were the hidden truths that had poisoned their relationship, leaving behind an agonizing residue of pain that Elara had never understood until now. She saw a moment of her father's vulnerability, a glimpse of his own grief, a silent sorrow that he had carried alone, concealing it beneath a facade of strength and resolve. And in that moment, Elara understood the depths of his pain, the burden he had carried, the unspoken love that had fueled his actions.

The ethereal realm revealed not only the hidden truths about her parents' relationship but also the intricate tapestry of her own perception, the way her memories had been colored by grief and loss. She had constructed a narrative, a comforting story that protected her from the raw pain of their absence. This narrative, however, had been flawed, incomplete, a distorted representation of a complex reality. The realm offered her a chance to confront this distorted narrative, to examine its underlying assumptions, and to rebuild her understanding of her family's history.

Suddenly, a specific image crystallized from the sea of memories: a small, worn photograph tucked away in a dusty box in the attic. Elara had never seen it before, but she knew, with absolute certainty, that it depicted her parents on a hiking trip, their faces beaming with happiness, a palpable sense of joy emanating from the image.

This photograph was not merely a visual representation of a past moment; it was a powerful symbol of their shared happiness, a testament to the strength of their love, a counterpoint to the unspoken conflicts and silent resentments that had overshadowed her memories.

This discovery unlocked a deeper understanding of the accident itself. The ethereal realm revealed a new perspective, shifting the focus from blame and accusation to a more nuanced understanding of human fallibility and the unpredictable nature of life. Elara saw the chain of events unfold in slow motion, each detail crystal clear, each decision scrutinized. The mechanical failure of the car, the unexpected weather conditions, the lapse in judgment – all played their part, a complex interplay of factors that converged to produce a tragic outcome. Yet, amidst the intricate details, Elara saw the subtle nuances of human behavior, the small choices, the missed opportunities, the unspoken fears. The accident was not a singular event, a catastrophic happening; it was the culmination of a series of choices, a confluence of circumstances that could not have been foreseen, and could not have been prevented.

As she continued her exploration, Elara discovered a hidden path, veiled in shadows, leading her to a secluded grove bathed in an ethereal moonlight. Here, she encountered a being of immense power, its presence radiating both comfort and profound mystery. This entity was not human, but something far older, far wiser, a custodian of forgotten truths, a guardian of the ethereal realm.

The entity, whose form shifted and changed with every breath, conveyed information not through words but through images and sensations, a direct transmission of knowledge that bypassed the limitations of language. Elara saw visions of the cosmos, the vastness of space and time, the infinite possibilities that had led to her current reality. She experienced a profound sense of connection, a feeling of belonging to something larger than herself, a sense of awe that transcended the bounds of her understanding. She felt the weight of existence, the balance of creation and destruction, the intricate interplay of forces that governed the universe. It was not a didactic lecture, but an experience, a feeling, an immersion in the fabric of reality itself.

Through this encounter, Elara understood that the questions she sought to answer were not limited to the specifics of her parents' death. They extended to the fundamental questions of life and death, of meaning and purpose, of existence itself. The entity revealed that the ethereal realm was not merely a place of transition, but a place of transformation, a space where souls could confront their past, reconcile with their losses, and find meaning in their experiences. The pain, the grief, the unanswered questions – these were not obstacles, but catalysts for growth, for evolution, for a deeper understanding of the human condition.

The entity's wisdom resonated deep within Elara's soul. It revealed the profound interconnectedness of all things, the delicate balance between life and death, the cyclical nature of existence. It emphasized that the search for answers was as important as the answers themselves, that the journey of seeking was just as meaningful as the destination. It was a journey of self-discovery, of confronting one's own limitations and vulnerabilities, of embracing the uncertainties of life.

Lyra stood by her side, her presence a constant source of comfort and support. She did not offer easy answers or simple solutions. Instead, she provided a space for Elara to explore her own thoughts and feelings, to unravel the complexities of her grief, and to find her own path towards healing. Their journey was not merely a quest for answers; it was a shared experience, a testament to the power of human connection, the enduring strength of love in the face of unimaginable loss.

As Elara began to integrate the new knowledge and understanding into her being, the landscape around her shifted and transformed, reflecting the evolution within her own consciousness. The colors became brighter, the light more vibrant, the emotions more intense. She felt a growing sense of acceptance, a recognition that grief was not something to be overcome, but something to be embraced, to be integrated into the fabric of her life. Her sorrow, she realized, was a part of her, an integral aspect of her identity. It did not diminish her, but rather shaped her, adding depth and complexity to her character.

She understood that the loss she had experienced was irreplaceable, but the love and memories she shared with her parents were everlasting, woven into the very fabric of her being.

And as she finally emerged from the ethereal realm, stepping back into the world of the living, she carried with her not just answers, but a profound sense of peace, a quiet strength that emanated from the core of her being. The mysteries remained, the unanswered questions still lingered, but they no longer held the same power, the same weight. She had found a new perspective, a new understanding of life, death, and the ever-evolving journey of the human soul. The journey, she understood, was not about reaching a destination, but about savoring the process of becoming. And in that becoming, she found a depth of self-awareness and inner strength that promised a new beginning, a new dawn, and a life lived with a profound appreciation for the intricate tapestry of existence.

Elara emerged from the ethereal grove, the spectral moonlight clinging to her like a second skin. The transition back to the tangible world was jarring, a sudden shift from the fluid, dreamlike landscape to the sharp edges of reality. The air, once vibrant with otherworldly energy, felt heavy and still, the silence profound. Lyra was there, her hand finding Elara's, a grounding presence in the disorienting aftermath.

The initial euphoria of understanding had begun to fade, replaced by a creeping unease. The insights gained in the ethereal realm, while profound, were also unsettling. They revealed not only the beauty of her parents' love, but also the harsh realities of their flaws, the unspoken tensions that had simmered beneath the surface of their seemingly idyllic life. The accident, no longer a singular event, now appeared as a tragic culmination of a complex series of events, human failings, and unforeseen circumstances. It was a truth both liberating and agonizing, a truth that stripped away the comforting illusion of a simple narrative.

Elara felt a wave of nausea, the weight of newly acquired knowledge pressing down on her. The idealized image of her parents, meticulously constructed over years of grief and longing, was shattered. They were not perfect, not flawless. They were human, flawed and vulnerable, just like her. And this realization, while painful, was also strangely liberating. It allowed her to release the burden of impossible expectations, the weight of their idealized image that she had carried for so long.

As they walked back toward the familiar world, Elara found herself grappling with the implications of what she had learned. The encounter with the otherworldly entity had offered answers, but not the neat, packaged solutions she had hoped for. Instead, it had laid bare the complexities of existence, the interwoven threads of fate and free will, the cyclical nature of life and death. The knowledge resonated within her, not as a set of instructions, but as a profound sense of acceptance.

The silence between Elara and Lyra was not uncomfortable, but rather a shared space for contemplation. They didn't need words to understand the depth of their mutual experience. Lyra's presence was a constant reassurance, a silent affirmation of their bond, a testament to the strength they had discovered in their shared journey. They walked hand in hand, the path back seeming shorter, the weight of their burden lighter.

Returning to the physical world, Elara felt the shift in her perception. The colors seemed more vivid, the sounds sharper, the emotions more intense. She was no longer shielded from the raw reality of life, but she was no longer overwhelmed by it either. She had learned to embrace the complexities, the contradictions, the pain.

Days turned into weeks, and Elara found herself gradually integrating the new knowledge into her life. She spoke to Lyra about her discoveries, sharing her newfound understanding of her parents, their love, and their failings. Lyra listened patiently, offering solace and encouragement, her wisdom grounding Elara's turbulent emotions. They delved into the nuances of the ethereal realm, exploring the implications of their experience and its impact on their lives.

One evening, as the sun dipped below the horizon, painting the sky in hues of orange and purple, Elara found herself drawn to her parents' old house. It had remained untouched since their passing, a silent monument to their loss. Entering the house, she was greeted by the thick dust and the lingering scent of old memories. Each object, each photograph, each piece of furniture, seemed to whisper stories of a life lived, a love shared, and a loss endured.

She spent hours sifting through her parents' belongings, rediscovering forgotten treasures, and piecing together the fragments of their past. She found old journals, filled with her mother's poetic musings and her father's meticulous notes on his work. She found photographs, some familiar, others entirely new, each revealing a glimpse into their lives, their joys, and their struggles. She found letters, expressing their hopes, their dreams, and their deepest fears. It was a poignant journey through time, a tapestry woven with threads of love, loss, and the relentless passage of time.

Through this journey, she saw the depth of her parents' love, a love that transcended the fleeting conflicts and misunderstandings. She saw the vulnerability beneath their stoic exteriors, the struggles they had silently endured. She saw their flaws, their imperfections, and she understood that this was what made them human, what made their love so profound.

The house was more than just a building; it was a repository of memories, a sanctuary of love. In revisiting this space, Elara felt a sense of peace, a quiet understanding that permeated her being. It wasn't a closure, not in the traditional sense, but a profound acceptance, an integration of the past into the present, a recognition that grief was a part of life, a part of who she was.

Her journey into the ethereal realm had not erased her pain, but it had transformed it. It had given it context, depth, and meaning. It had allowed her to see her parents' lives not as a narrative of tragedy, but as a story of love, resilience, and the enduring power of the human spirit.

As she prepared to leave the house, Elara took one last look around, a quiet gratitude filling her heart. The house remained a testament to their loss, but now, it was also a symbol of healing, a reminder of the enduring power of love, a testament to the enduring strength of the human spirit, and an acknowledgement of the beautiful, messy, and ultimately human lives her parents had lived.

Leaving the house, Elara walked toward the setting sun, the lingering warmth on her skin a comforting embrace. The world felt different now, not without sadness, but with a newfound appreciation for life's complexities, its bittersweet beauty, and the enduring strength of the human heart. She carried the weight of her grief, but it no longer crushed her. It was a part of her, interwoven with her memories, her love, her life. She was no longer defined by her loss, but by her resilience, her strength, and her profound understanding of the intricate tapestry of existence. The journey had been difficult, harrowing at times, but it had led her to a place of quiet peace, a place where she could finally begin to heal and embrace a new dawn.

The unanswered questions remained, but they no longer held the same power; they were simply part of the journey, a testament to the unyielding mysteries of life itself, mysteries that she now faced not with fear, but with a quiet, unwavering acceptance.

The weeks that followed were a blur of quiet introspection and gradual healing. Elara found solace not in answers, but in the process of understanding. The ethereal realm hadn't provided a neatly packaged explanation for her parents' death, but it had offered something far more valuable: a perspective shift. It had allowed her to see beyond the singular event of the accident, to perceive the intricate web of circumstances, choices, and unforeseen occurrences that had culminated in that tragic moment. It was a chaotic tapestry woven from human frailty, unforeseen events, and the relentless march of time.

She began to understand that grief wasn't a linear process, a neat progression from sorrow to acceptance. It was a swirling vortex, a chaotic dance of emotions that ebbed and flowed, sometimes overwhelming, sometimes receding into a quiet hum beneath the surface of daily life.

There were days when the pain was a suffocating weight, a constant reminder of her loss. And then there were days when a fragile sense of peace settled over her, a quiet acceptance of the immutable nature of life and death.

Lyra remained her steadfast anchor throughout this turbulent journey. Their bond, forged in shared grief and strengthened by their otherworldly experience, deepened with each passing day. They spoke little of the ethereal realm, but their unspoken understanding transcended words. They shared quiet moments, long walks under the twilight sky, and silent evenings spent side-by-side, their presence a comforting balm against the relentless ache in Elara's heart.

Elara delved deeper into her parents' lives, meticulously piecing together the fragments of their past. She spent countless hours in the local library, poring over old newspapers, researching family history, and slowly unraveling the threads of their story. She discovered details she had never known – her father's youthful dreams of becoming a musician, her mother's hidden talent for painting, their shared passion for traveling, and the quiet struggles they faced throughout their marriage. It wasn't a perfect story, devoid of conflict or hardship. Instead, it was a deeply human narrative, a testament to the enduring strength of love in the face of adversity.

She learned of her father's struggles with self-doubt, his quiet battles with depression, and the unspoken pressures he bore as the sole provider for their family. She discovered her mother's quiet resilience, her unwavering support for her husband, and the sacrifices she made to nurture their dreams. She unearthed the subtle cracks in their seemingly perfect façade, the moments of conflict and misunderstanding that were a natural part of any long-term relationship.

This newfound understanding didn't diminish her grief; instead, it enriched it, gave it context, and transformed it from a raw, agonizing wound into a complex tapestry of emotions. She understood that her parents were not perfect beings, immune to the trials and tribulations of life. They were flawed, vulnerable human beings, and their love, in all its complexity and imperfection, was all the more profound for it.

The wisdom she gained wasn't a set of answers, but a recognition of the inherent mystery of existence. She learned to accept the unanswered questions, the unresolved uncertainties, the inherent ambiguity of life itself. The ethereal experience had shown her the vastness of the universe, the infinite possibilities, and the humbling realization of humanity's place within it.

She understood that life was a paradox, a complex interplay of light and shadow, joy and sorrow, love and loss. It was a journey filled with both profound beauty and unimaginable pain. And it was within this very paradox that she found a deeper appreciation for the preciousness of life, a more profound understanding of the enduring power of love.

One evening, as the stars blazed across the inky canvas of the night sky, Elara sat by Lyra's side, sharing her discoveries. Lyra, a beacon of unwavering support, listened intently, offering insightful observations and gentle words of encouragement. Their shared journey had transformed them, binding them together in a bond that transcended the ordinary.

Elara realized that the ethereal realm hadn't provided answers to her questions, but it had given her the tools to find her own answers, her own understanding. It had instilled in her a sense of profound acceptance, a quiet understanding that life's greatest mysteries often remain unsolved, that the very nature of existence is a tapestry of unanswered questions.

The understanding she had achieved wasn't a triumph over grief, but a profound integration of it into her life. It was a recognition that grief wasn't a linear process, a neat progression towards closure. It was a complex, ever-evolving entity that shifted and changed, sometimes appearing as a suffocating blanket of sorrow, other times receding into a quiet ache beneath the surface of her daily existence. And she learned to live with that ache, to carry it with her as a testament to the love she had shared and the lives she had lost.

Through her journey, Elara discovered that wisdom wasn't about finding definitive answers, but about embracing the journey of seeking them. It was about accepting the complexities of life, its inherent uncertainties, and the inevitable pain that accompanies existence. It was about finding beauty in the darkness, discovering strength in vulnerability, and accepting the unyielding mysteries of the universe.

The ethereal grove, a place of otherworldly beauty and unsettling truths, had become a symbol of her transformation. It had served not as a sanctuary from grief, but as a crucible where she forged a deeper understanding of herself, her parents, and the nature of reality. The knowledge she acquired wasn't a set of neat solutions, but a kaleidoscope of perceptions that enriched her understanding of life and death, love and loss, and the profound, inexplicable beauty of existence.

Her journey, fraught with pain and introspection, led her not to a definitive ending, but to a profound beginning. It was a beginning of self-discovery, a journey of embracing the unknown, and a testament to the resilience of the human spirit in the face of unimaginable loss. The mysteries remained, but they no longer held the same power. They were now part of her story, a reminder of the enigmatic nature of life and a testament to the enduring strength of the human heart, capable of both immense joy and profound sorrow. Elara carried her grief, not as a burden, but as a part of her intricate and beautiful tapestry of life. The world, once a bleak landscape defined by loss, was now revealed as a vibrant, complex place, full of both light and shadow, and she was ready to step into it, her heart both wounded and whole.

Chapter Fourteen Whispers from Beyond

The quiet hum of acceptance that had settled over Elara began to crack. The peace she'd found, fragile as a newly hatched butterfly, felt threatened by a burgeoning need – a need to connect, to reach out, to touch the living world with the changed lens of her experience. The ethereal realm had shown her the interwoven nature of existence, the delicate threads linking the living and the dead, but she felt a desperate yearning to bridge that gap, to communicate, however faintly, with those she'd left behind.

Her first attempt was clumsy, almost childish. She tried to leave messages, subtle hints, in the places her friends frequented. A single white feather on Liam's favorite bench in the park, a half-finished line from her mother's favorite poem scrawled on a napkin at the coffee shop Sarah often visited. These were desperate, almost frantic attempts at contact, fuelled by a deep-seated loneliness that gnawed at the edges of her newfound peace. They were subtle clues, hoping that those attuned to her would notice, that they would sense the whisper of her presence.

The results were, predictably, nothing. Liam probably thought the feather was a random act of nature. Sarah likely tossed the napkin into the recycling bin without a second thought. Elara found herself wrestling with the limitations of her newfound understanding. The ethereal realm had demonstrated the intricate tapestry of life, death, and the in-between, but it hadn't provided a clear manual for communicating across its boundaries.

Disappointment, sharp and bitter, washed over her. The silence of the living world felt deafening, a stark contrast to the vibrant, if unsettling, whispers she'd heard in the grove. She'd expected some sort of reaction, a ripple in the mundane, a sign that her attempts were reaching someone, anyone. The lack of response only amplified her feeling of isolation, a chilling reminder of her liminal state, neither fully alive nor fully dead, but existing in a frustratingly ambiguous space between.

Lyra, ever perceptive, sensed Elara's growing despair. "You can't force connection, Elara," she said one evening, her voice soft, laced with empathy. "You're trying to impose the language of the ethereal realm on the living world.

It's like trying to speak a forgotten tongue to someone who only understands the modern vernacular."

Her words struck a chord. Elara realized she'd been approaching this all wrong. She hadn't been communicating; she'd been broadcasting. She hadn't been building bridges; she'd been throwing stones hoping for a response. She needed a new approach, a more subtle, nuanced way to reach those she yearned to connect with.

She started small, focusing on individual relationships. With Liam, she began leaving small, thoughtful gifts – a book he'd mentioned wanting to read, a carefully chosen piece of music he'd admired. These were simple gestures, devoid of any overt attempt at communication from "beyond," but infused with a genuine desire for connection. It wasn't about making her presence known; it was about expressing her continued care, her enduring friendship, even from her altered perspective.

With Sarah, she channeled her creative energy, writing heartfelt poems and sending them anonymously, a silent offering of her feelings, her continued presence in their shared world. The poems were cryptic, ethereal, hinting at shared memories and unspoken sentiments, but stopping short of any explicit claim of otherworldly origins.

The transformation wasn't immediate, but subtle shifts began to occur. Liam, initially baffled by the unexpected gifts, responded with his own tokens of friendship – a shared song on his playlist, a casual invitation to his band's upcoming performance. Sarah, deeply touched by the anonymously delivered poems, shared them with a poetry circle, unknowingly broadcasting Elara's words to a wider audience, unknowingly opening a circuit for shared emotion.

Elara's interactions with her extended family took on a different approach. She started subtly influencing events, guiding decisions in ways that resonated with her parents' values, and creating ripples of positive change within the family dynamic. She prompted her aunt to finally pursue her dream of writing a novel, nudging her uncle towards reconciliation with his estranged brother.

These interventions were subtle, indirect, manifesting as inspired thoughts and intuitive decisions rather than overt pronouncements of her existence beyond the veil.

It was a slow and painstaking process, requiring immense patience and a willingness to relinquish control. She learned to observe, to subtly guide, to plant seeds of change that would slowly blossom into new growth. She was no longer reaching out with frantic pleas; she was engaging in a gentle dance with the living world, weaving her influence into the fabric of daily life.

The most profound change came from within Elara herself. Her interactions with the living weren't just about reaching out; they were about letting go. The need to prove her continued existence, to offer explanations, faded as she focused on sharing the love and wisdom she'd gained through her ordeal.

One evening, she found herself sitting by the old oak tree in the ethereal grove, no longer feeling the urgency of communicating with the living. The whispers of the grove were still present, but their urgency had abated, replaced by a serene acceptance of her place in the interconnectedness of existence. She'd discovered that communication wasn't about breaking through barriers, but about transcending them, flowing into the currents of life itself, a gentle force shaping reality in subtle and meaningful ways.

She understood now that the most powerful communication wasn't vocal, nor was it through obvious signs. It was the lingering fragrance of a cherished memory, a shared understanding in a fleeting glance, an unexplainable feeling of guidance in a moment of doubt. It was the silent language of the heart, spoken not in words, but in feelings, actions, and the intangible threads that bind the living and the dead in an eternal embrace. Her journey to connect with the living wasn't about proving her existence on the other side, but accepting and sharing the love that had endured and changed her forever, forever intertwining her essence with the world she'd left behind, a faint echo of her voice present in the ripple effects of kindness and love, a silent whisper felt, but never heard.

The pain of loss still lingered, a constant reminder of her parents' absence, but it was no longer a suffocating weight. It was a quiet ache, a poignant reminder of the love she had shared, woven into the tapestry of her life, a tapestry now rich with new hues, colors born from loss, but vibrant with renewed understanding and a profound sense of connection. Elara carried her grief, not as a burden, but as a testament to the enduring strength of love, a love that whispered in the quiet moments, resonated in the subtle changes, and found expression in the gentle dance between life and what lay beyond. The whispers from beyond, once a yearning cry, had transformed into a silent song, a gentle melody resonating in the hearts of those she loved, a symphony of love played on the strings of memory, hope, and an enduring connection that even death couldn't erase.

The shift in Elara's approach wasn't merely a tactical change; it was a profound internal metamorphosis. She'd initially sought validation, a desperate need to prove her continued existence to the living. This desire stemmed from a deep-seated fear – the fear of being forgotten, of becoming a ghost not only in the physical world but also in the memories of those she cherished. Now, that fear began to recede, replaced by a quiet acceptance of her altered state and a deeper understanding of the nature of connection itself.

Her interactions with Liam took on a new dimension. He was still the same kind and sensitive soul she knew, yet his life had moved forward, subtly reshaped by the passage of time and the weight of her absence. Elara found herself acting as a silent guardian, guiding him through moments of doubt, subtly influencing his decisions without ever revealing her hand. For example, when Liam faced a crucial crossroads in his music career - a tempting but potentially risky offer from a major record label - Elara found herself subtly nudging him towards a more fulfilling path, one that aligned with his genuine artistic aspirations rather than the allure of commercial success. This wasn't about controlling his choices but about subtly enhancing his intuition, allowing his inner wisdom to shine through. She did this through shared dreams, through a heightened sense of intuition that came to him unbidden, almost as if a whisper on the wind.

These subtle interventions were not manipulative; they were acts of love, born out of her continued connection and her unwavering support for his well-being. They were the embodiment of her enduring friendship, a silent conversation conducted not through words but through shared experiences, subtle hints, and an unwavering presence in his life, felt rather than seen.

Sarah, too, benefited from Elara's watchful presence. Sarah, ever the creative soul, was struggling with writer's block, a crippling inertia that threatened to derail her burgeoning career. Elara, understanding the depths of Sarah's creative passion, found ways to subtly inspire her, to reignite the flames of her artistic spirit. She didn't offer direct solutions or critique, but instead nurtured Sarah's innate creativity, channeling her own ethereal perspective to help Sarah break through her creative block.

This came in the form of seemingly random encounters – a conversation overheard in a coffee shop, a book discovered on a library shelf, a piece of music that inexplicably resonated with Sarah's inner world. These were subtle yet powerful nudges, glimpses of inspiration that helped Sarah find her creative voice once more. The poems Sarah received anonymously continued, though now they were infused with a deeper sense of understanding, a shared journey of grief and resilience, helping Sarah navigate her own emotional landscape. The poems became not just messages from an unknown source, but touchstones for self-discovery, silent allies in the process of healing and creative renewal.

Elara's interaction with her extended family was a more complex undertaking. The loss of her parents had created rifts and unspoken tensions within the family, unresolved conflicts that had festered for years. Elara, from her unique vantage point, could see the interconnectedness of these familial threads, the intricate patterns of love, resentment, and unresolved grief.

Her role here wasn't to solve these problems directly but to subtly encourage reconciliation, to facilitate communication, and to nudge her family members toward understanding and forgiveness.

She guided her aunt, a woman burdened by self-doubt, to finally pursue her lifelong dream of writing a novel, whispering encouragement through shared dreams, subtle coincidences, and unexpected opportunities. She prompted her uncle, a man consumed by bitterness and anger, to reach out to his estranged brother, fostering a reconciliation that healed old wounds and restored a sense of family unity. These interventions were not acts of overt control but gentle suggestions, subtle shifts in perspective, fostering positive change through the ripples of inspiration.

These actions weren't about proving her presence but about subtly shaping the lives of those she loved, guiding them toward paths of healing, growth, and happiness. It was a quiet, gentle influence, a silent affirmation of her enduring love and support, a manifestation of her continued presence in their lives, albeit in a form unseen yet felt.

The most significant aspect of Elara's journey was her transformation. She no longer yearned for acknowledgment or validation. The desperate need to prove her existence had given way to a quiet acceptance of her position in the grand tapestry of life and death. Her focus shifted from demonstrating her presence to nurturing the lives of those she left behind, a silent guardian angel guiding her loved ones towards a brighter future.

This wasn't about power or control, but about unconditional love, a selfless desire to protect and guide those she held dear. It was a profound demonstration of the enduring strength of human connection, a love that transcended the boundaries of life and death, expressed not in words but in deeds, in the subtle shifts of fate, and in the gentle guidance offered from beyond the veil.

The whispers from beyond were no longer frantic pleas but quiet affirmations, gentle nudges towards healing and understanding. They were reminders of her enduring love, a silent presence felt in shared moments, in unexpected opportunities, and in the gentle guidance that led her loved ones towards a path of peace and reconciliation.

The pain of loss still resonated within Elara, but it no longer defined her. Her grief was now interwoven with a profound sense of purpose, a renewed understanding of life's fragility, and an unwavering commitment to cherishing the memories and relationships that shaped her life, both past and present.

She had found a new way to express her love, a unique form of connection that transcended the limitations of the physical world, finding its expression in the gentle ripples of kindness, the subtle shifts of destiny, and the enduring power of love's silent whisper.

Her journey had been a testament to the power of love, a love that not only survived death but evolved into something even more profound – a silent guardianship, a gentle guidance, an invisible presence felt in the hearts of those she left behind. The whispers from beyond had become a silent song, a melody of love, a constant affirmation of her enduring bond with the living, a love that whispered in the gentle breeze, danced in the sunlight, and resonated in the quiet moments of shared understanding.

The once-bitter sting of loss had been transformed into a bittersweet symphony, a song played on the strings of memory, hope, and a connection so profound that even death could not erase it. Elara's journey demonstrated that the most enduring communication often came not from grand pronouncements, but from the quiet language of the heart – the silent language of love, expressed in gentle guidance, subtle shifts in circumstance, and the profound comfort of a presence felt but unseen. Her whispered messages, once a desperate plea, had evolved into a loving embrace that stretched beyond the veil, a testament to the enduring strength of a bond that even death couldn't break. It was a love that found its voice not in a shout, but in a whisper, a soft melody carried on the wind, resonating in the hearts of those she loved, a quiet song of enduring connection.

The final sunset painted the sky in hues of amethyst and rose, a fitting backdrop to the culmination of Elara's journey. Her influence, once a desperate cry for recognition, had subtly woven itself into the fabric of her loved ones' lives, a silent tapestry of guidance and inspiration. Liam, his music career now flourishing, played a new song, one that resonated with a depth and understanding that surpassed even his own comprehension. The melody was infused with a quiet strength, a subtle grace that hinted at the unseen hand that had guided his artistic vision. He didn’t know it was Elara, but a profound sense of peace settled upon him as he played, a feeling of being gently guided on his path.

The song became an anthem of resilience, echoing Elara's own transformation from a spirit yearning for validation to a silent guardian, her love a constant companion on his journey.

Sarah's novel, finally completed, was a testament to the power of quiet inspiration. It was a story brimming with vivid imagery, sharp prose and a deep emotional resonance, a reflection of the subtle nudges Elara had provided. The writer’s block that had once threatened to extinguish her creative flame was a distant memory, replaced by a confident flow of words and a renewed belief in her abilities. The anonymously received poems had ceased, their purpose fulfilled; they had served as a bridge to her own creative wellspring, leading her to an understanding of her own strength and the beauty within her own voice. She felt a deep sense of gratitude, though she couldn't quite pinpoint the source of her inspiration.

Elara's family, once fractured by grief and unresolved conflicts, experienced a gradual healing. Her aunt, emboldened by a series of fortunate encounters and seemingly coincidental opportunities, finished her manuscript, finally publishing her cherished novel. The book was a beautiful, poignant tale of resilience, resonating with readers across the world, and becoming a testament to the power of pursuing one's dreams. Her uncle, previously consumed by bitterness, reconnected with his estranged brother, their reunion marked by a profound sense of forgiveness and renewed kinship. They rebuilt their relationship, their bond strengthened by a shared understanding and the healing power of time. These events weren't grand gestures, but subtle shifts in circumstance, gentle ripples of change orchestrated by Elara's quiet influence. Each family member experienced a personal renaissance, their lives blossoming in unforeseen ways, guided by an unseen hand.

But Elara's influence extended far beyond her immediate circle. Her presence rippled outward, touching the lives of strangers in unexpected ways.

A young musician, struggling with self-doubt, found inspiration in Liam's music, a song that mirrored his own internal struggles and offered a pathway towards self-acceptance. A young writer, grappling with the pressures of the publishing world, discovered Sarah's novel, finding within its pages a reflection of her own experiences, renewing her passion for storytelling and creating a community among her peers. It was a network of mutual influence, a ripple effect of inspiration emanating from Elara's gentle guidance and creating change in the world, one person at a time.

These acts, though subtle, were profoundly impactful. They weren't about control or manipulation but about fostering growth, inspiring creativity, and facilitating reconciliation. They were the embodiment of Elara's enduring love, her spirit reaching out to touch the lives she had left behind, weaving a legacy of kindness, resilience, and hope. The world felt a little brighter, a little kinder, because of her quiet presence, a subtle change in the atmosphere, a shift in energy.

Lyra, Elara's counterpart, her journey interwoven with Elara's, left her own unique imprint on the world. Her influence was perhaps more overtly artistic.
Her paintings, previously shrouded in darkness and despair, blossomed with vibrant colours and breathtaking beauty, reflecting her own transformation and newfound serenity. The art galleries that initially hesitated, now eagerly sought her work, captivated by its unique blend of ethereal beauty and raw emotion. The exhibitions became platforms for emotional release for others, her art resonating with a universality of experience that transcended the personal. Lyra's work became a symbol of healing and hope, connecting people through shared experiences of loss and renewal, sparking important conversations and creating a sense of community among art lovers.

Lyra's influence extended beyond the canvas. She initiated workshops, sharing her journey and her artistic techniques, empowering others to express their emotions through art. These workshops, once intended as therapeutic practices for herself, became beacons of hope for others.

They became places of healing and self-discovery, providing a safe space for participants to explore their creativity, find their voice, and create a sense of community. The shared experiences fostered lasting bonds, forging friendships and networks of support that extended beyond the confines of the workshops.

Lyra's legacy was a vibrant tapestry of artistic expression, a collection of artworks which spoke of resilience and transformation. Her impact on the art world was significant; her unique style redefined artistic boundaries, her pieces becoming iconic representations of profound emotions. Her legacy was not just her artwork itself, but its ability to empower others to express their feelings and find solace through creation. Her workshops became legacies in their own right, shaping the lives of many and inspiring a new wave of artistic expression. It was a legacy of sharing, empowering, and connecting people through the universal language of art.

Together, Elara and Lyra, though existing in different realms, crafted a shared legacy of quiet influence, a testament to the enduring power of love, resilience, and the profound impact a single life can have on those left behind.

Their whispers from beyond were not merely echoes of loss, but a symphony of quiet strength, a message of hope and healing carried on the wind, resonating in the hearts and minds of countless individuals, creating a positive change in the world, an enduring legacy of love that transcended life and death itself.

Their story echoed in the lives they touched, a testament to the indelible mark left by a love that defied mortality. The quiet strength, the subtle guidance, the gentle nudges – these became the echoes of their presence, reminders of a love that knew no bounds, a bond that death could not sever. The whispered messages, once desperate pleas, evolved into a loving embrace, a legacy carried on the wind, a constant, comforting presence in the lives of those they loved.

Their journey transcended grief, transforming it into a testament to the enduring power of connection, a love that lived on, not in memory alone, but in the lives it had so profoundly touched, shaping the future and leaving a legacy of enduring hope. Their story served as a profound reminder that even in loss, love endures, finding new ways to express itself, to connect, to inspire, and to leave its unique and lasting mark upon the world.

Their story was a whisper of hope, carried on the breeze, a quiet testament to the enduring power of love.

The shimmering veil that separated Elara from the world of the living felt less like a barrier and more like a softly rippling curtain. She could see the lives she had touched, the subtle shifts in fortunes, the blossoming of creativity, all playing out like a delicately orchestrated symphony. It wasn't the grand gestures of a celestial being, but rather the gentle nudges, the whispered encouragement, the subtle shifts in circumstance that brought about profound change. And in watching, in witnessing the unfolding ripple effect of her influence, Elara found a profound sense of purpose, a fulfillment she hadn't anticipated in the afterlife.

It wasn't the validation she had craved in life; it was something far deeper, far more meaningful: a sense of belonging, a connection to the living world that transcended the limitations of mortality.

She observed Liam, his music evolving, growing in depth and resonance. Each note was a testament to his resilience, a reflection of his healing journey, subtly guided by her unseen hand.
She didn't manipulate his creative process; rather, she provided a gentle push, a whisper of inspiration at the right moment, helping him navigate the complexities of his emotions, transforming his pain into art. The songs, filled with a quiet strength, resonated not only with him, but with countless others who had experienced similar struggles. His music became a beacon of hope, a testament to the power of overcoming adversity, an anthem of resilience that carried her message of healing to the world.

Sarah's novel, a story woven with threads of quiet inspiration, also unfolded before Elara's gaze. She watched as Sarah's creative block shattered, replaced by a powerful flow of words.

The anonymously received poems, now a distant memory, had served as a catalyst, a bridge to her own creative voice. Elara hadn't written those poems with the intention of becoming a literary muse, but rather as a way to connect, to offer support, to plant a seed of belief in Sarah's talent. The novel itself, a poignant and powerful story of resilience, became a source of comfort and inspiration for countless readers, each page carrying Elara's message of hope and perseverance.

The healing within her own family was perhaps the most rewarding aspect of her afterlife journey. She witnessed her aunt's success, the culmination of years of dedication and hard work, spurred on by seemingly coincidental opportunities that Elara had subtly orchestrated. The published novel, a beautiful testament to her talent, resonated with readers worldwide, becoming a symbol of hope and the pursuit of dreams. Her uncle's reconciliation with his estranged brother was another testament to her influence; the subtle nudges, the opportune meetings, the gentle whispers in their hearts, all contributed to the healing of a fractured bond, a reunion filled with forgiveness and renewed kinship.

Elara's influence extended beyond her immediate circle, a ripple effect spreading outwards, touching lives in unexpected ways. A struggling musician, deeply resonating with Liam's music, found the courage to pursue his dreams despite his self-doubt. A writer, overwhelmed by the pressures of the publishing world, found solace and inspiration in Sarah's novel, reigniting her passion and connecting her to a supportive community.
These weren't grand interventions but subtle shifts, gentle nudges, small acts of kindness that collectively created a profound impact. It was a testament to the power of quiet influence, a ripple effect of positive change emanating from her presence.

These acts of subtle guidance, far from being acts of manipulation or control, felt deeply fulfilling. They were expressions of her enduring love, her spirit reaching out to nurture and support the lives she cherished. Her presence had become a silent guardian angel, a beacon of hope in the lives of others. The world felt a little brighter, a little kinder, imbued with a subtle shift in energy, a gentle grace emanating from her quiet influence.

Lyra, her counterpart, her journey inextricably intertwined with Elara's, was also making her unique mark on the world. Elara watched as Lyra's paintings, once cloaked in darkness, blossomed with vibrant colors and breathtaking beauty. The galleries that once hesitated now eagerly sought her work, captivated by its raw emotion and ethereal beauty.
The exhibitions weren't just displays of artistic skill; they became platforms for catharsis, for shared experiences of loss and renewal, connecting people through the universality of emotion.

Lyra's workshops, initially conceived as a personal therapeutic practice, blossomed into beacons of hope for others. They offered a safe space for self-expression, a place where participants could explore their emotions through art, finding solace and connection with others who shared similar experiences. The workshops fostered a sense of community, a network of support that transcended the confines of the art studio, forging lasting friendships and connections.

Elara observed the evolution of Lyra's legacy – a vibrant tapestry of artistic expression, a collection of artworks that spoke volumes about resilience and transformation. Her influence extended beyond the canvas, shaping the lives of countless individuals, inspiring a new wave of artistic expression and creating a network of mutual support. Her art became a symbol of healing, a testament to the power of self-expression and the ability to find beauty in the midst of pain.

In the afterlife, Elara and Lyra's journeys were intertwined, their legacies interwoven, a shared testament to the enduring power of love, resilience, and the profound impact of a life lived with purpose. Their whispers from beyond were not echoes of loss, but a symphony of quiet strength, a message of hope and healing carried on the wind. They had found a profound sense of purpose in their afterlife, their influence a gentle current weaving through the fabric of the living world, leaving an enduring legacy of love, connection, and inspiration.

It wasn't the validation they craved in life, but something far deeper, far more meaningful: a profound sense of belonging, a connection that transcended mortality, a legacy of love that extended beyond the boundaries of life and death itself. Their journey, once defined by loss and grief, had been transformed into a testament to the enduring power of love, a symphony of quiet strength, a message of hope and healing carried on the wind, resonating in the hearts and minds of countless individuals.

Their whispers from beyond continued to shape the world, leaving an enduring legacy of inspiration and resilience, a gentle reminder that even in the face of loss, love endures, finding new ways to express itself, to connect, to inspire, and to leave an indelible mark on the world.

Their story was not merely a whisper of hope, but a powerful anthem of resilience, carried on the wind, a testament to the enduring power of a love that defied mortality itself. Their journey served as a poignant reminder that even in loss, love transforms, finds new paths to express itself, and leaves behind a legacy of enduring hope that touches countless lives.

And in that shared legacy, Elara and Lyra finally found the peace and fulfillment they had sought throughout their lives, their love a constant, comforting presence in the lives they had touched, a whisper of hope carried on the breeze, a testament to the enduring power of love that transcended the boundaries of life and death.

The shimmering threads of connection, Elara realized, were the most potent force in the afterlife. It wasn't just the grand gestures, the dramatic shifts in fate, but the subtle, almost imperceptible ways in which individuals touched one another's lives. She saw the quiet strength of a friendship formed over shared grief, a bond forged in the crucible of loss, blossoming into a source of enduring support and comfort.

It was a testament to the resilience of the human spirit, a reminder that even in the darkest of times, connection offered a lifeline, a beacon of hope in the vast expanse of loneliness.

Liam, for instance, had always been a solitary figure, his music a reflection of his introspective nature. But in the wake of his loss, he'd found solace in an unexpected place – a small online community of fellow musicians, each grappling with their own unique struggles. Elara witnessed the slow, tentative development of friendships, the sharing of vulnerabilities, the mutual support that blossomed in the digital space. They weren't physically together, but their connection was palpable, a virtual embrace that offered warmth and understanding. The music they created together, a collaborative symphony born out of shared pain, became a powerful testament to the healing power of collective experience. It was a testament to the human need for connection, a yearning for belonging that transcended physical proximity.

Sarah's journey echoed a similar theme. While her novel explored themes of isolation and loneliness, the process of writing itself became a bridge to connection. The feedback from her early readers, the online discussions, the collaborative critique sessions – these interactions shaped her work, enriching its depth and resonance.
The connection wasn't merely about receiving praise or validation; it was about sharing her story, connecting with others who resonated with her experiences, and finding solace in shared vulnerability. The writing community, initially a source of intimidation, transformed into a supportive network, a warm embrace in a sometimes cold and competitive world. Her book, in turn, became a vehicle for connection, fostering empathy and understanding among its readers.

Elara observed the ripple effect of these connections, the subtle shifts in the lives of those who were touched by the work of Liam and Sarah. A shy teenager, overwhelmed by anxiety, found solace in Liam's music, connecting with the raw emotion and vulnerability expressed in the lyrics. A grieving widow, struggling to cope with her loss, discovered a sense of community and shared experience in

Sarah's poignant narrative. These weren't grand acts of intervention, but subtle touches, gentle nudges that reminded people they weren't alone in their struggles. It was a testament to the power of shared experience, the unifying force of human connection that could bridge the chasms of grief and isolation.

Even within Elara's own family, the importance of connection was undeniable. Her aunt, once isolated by her relentless pursuit of success, found renewed purpose and fulfillment in mentoring younger writers, sharing her knowledge and experience. The connections she forged with her mentees weren't simply professional collaborations; they blossomed into genuine friendships, offering a sense of community and belonging. Her uncle, initially resistant to reconciliation, was eventually drawn back to his brother through a series of carefully orchestrated encounters, a chain of events that underscored the potency of shared history and the enduring power of family bonds. The carefully orchestrated encounters, seemingly random yet perfectly timed, facilitated the healing of a long-standing rift, bringing forgiveness and renewed kinship.

Lyra's journey mirrored Elara's in its emphasis on connection. Her art became a conduit for shared experience, a platform for vulnerability and empathy. Her workshops weren't merely art classes; they were spaces for healing, for self-discovery, for the creation of meaningful relationships.
The participants, initially strangers, bonded over shared vulnerabilities, creating a supportive community that extended beyond the walls of the studio. Their shared experiences of loss and grief became the foundation for an enduring network of support, a testament to the healing power of collective experience and the profound importance of human connection.

Lyra's art itself served as a bridge to understanding, transcending linguistic and cultural barriers. The raw emotion conveyed through her brushstrokes resonated with audiences worldwide, creating a sense of shared humanity, a testament to the universal language of art.

The exhibitions themselves became spaces for connection, fostering dialogue and empathy among visitors from diverse backgrounds.

The vibrant colors and textures of her work didn't simply depict a visual reality; they evoked deep emotions, fostering connections between viewer and artist, viewer and viewer.

Elara watched as Lyra's work transformed not only her own life, but also the lives of those who engaged with it. A young woman struggling with body image issues found solace and empowerment in Lyra's depiction of the female form, her art challenging conventional beauty standards and celebrating the diversity of human experience. A man grappling with his own grief found a sense of peace and validation in Lyra's portrayal of loss and renewal, her paintings a mirror reflecting his own inner turmoil. These connections were profound and lasting, transforming lives and fostering a sense of shared humanity.

The significance of these connections extended beyond the individual level. Elara witnessed how the healing process within her family and the blossoming of Liam and Sarah's careers had created a wider ripple effect, touching countless lives. The acts of kindness, the shared experiences, the support offered – these were the building blocks of a more compassionate and connected world.

The importance of connection wasn't just a human experience; it was a fundamental aspect of the universe itself. Elara realized that the very fabric of existence was woven with threads of interconnectedness, a complex tapestry of relationships that bound all living things. The afterlife, she discovered, was not an escape from this interconnectedness, but a deepening of it, a heightened awareness of the profound influence each individual had on another.

The whispers from beyond weren't simply messages of solace or guidance; they were echoes of connection, reminders of the enduring bonds that tied individuals together, across lifetimes and across the veil of mortality.

The love, the empathy, the shared experiences – these were the enduring legacies, the whispers that resonated across time and space, leaving an indelible mark on the world. They were proof that even in the face of death, the human spirit could find solace and meaning in the enduring power of connection, a testament to the deep-seated human need for belonging and the transformative power of human relationships.
Even in the vastness of the afterlife, the most powerful force was the subtle, yet profound impact of human connection, the enduring legacy of shared experiences, the ripple effect of love and empathy rippling through generations.

Elara and Lyra's influence wasn't about grand gestures of power or control, but about fostering the quiet, everyday connections that made life meaningful. They were the unseen threads that bound individuals together, the gentle nudges that guided people toward healing and self-discovery.

Their legacy wasn't simply about their own individual accomplishments; it was about the network of relationships they had nurtured, the bonds they had strengthened, the lives they had touched. This network, extending far beyond their physical presence, was a testament to the enduring power of human connection, a living testament to the strength found in shared experiences and mutual support.

Their whispers continued to resonate, a symphony of shared connection, echoing across time and space, leaving an indelible mark on the tapestry of human existence.

Chapter Fifteen Final Time to Rest

The iridescent veil of the afterlife shimmered around Elara, a gentle, ghostly curtain that separated her from the world of the living, yet simultaneously connected her to it in ways she couldn't have imagined. She felt a profound sense of peace, a stillness that settled deep within her soul. It wasn't the absence of emotion, but a transcendence of it—a serene acceptance of what was, and what would be. This wasn't an ending, but a transformation, a shifting of perspectives. The frantic energy that had once characterized her existence was replaced by a calm, unwavering certainty. There was a profound understanding, a knowing that permeated her being - her journey, and Lyra's, wasn't over, but had simply shifted form.

Lyra, beside her, mirrored this serenity. Her hands, once restless with the creative urge, now rested gently in her lap. Her eyes, which had once burned with a passionate intensity, now held a soft, knowing light.

There was a quiet strength emanating from her, a radiant aura of acceptance that radiated outward, touching everyone within its embrace. They sat together on a precipice overlooking a breathtaking expanse of celestial light, a landscape of shimmering stars and nebulae that stretched to infinity. The view was breathtaking, yet they found themselves drawn inward, to the quiet contentment that blossomed between them.

Their acceptance wasn't a passive resignation, but an active embrace of their new reality. It was a conscious choice, a deliberate relinquishing of the earthly anxieties and attachments that had once held them captive. The grief, the loss, the relentless pursuit of earthly validation – these were fading echoes, remnants of a past life that had shaped them, but no longer defined them. They had earned their rest, their peace, and they embraced it fully, without reservation or regret.

The whispers of the afterlife—the subtle echoes of connection—continued to surround them. They were no longer the frantic calls for attention that had initially overwhelmed them, but gentle, soothing melodies, a soft hum that resonated with the deepest parts of their souls. These whispers carried the echoes of lives touched, of hearts healed, of bonds strengthened. They spoke of the ripple effect of their actions, the profound impact they had on the world of the living, even in their absence.

Elara thought of Liam, his music echoing across the digital landscape, offering solace to countless souls. His melodies, born from grief and loss, had become beacons of hope, transforming the lives of strangers. The quiet strength of his music, the vulnerability expressed through his art, resonated with those who felt lost and alone. He had found purpose, meaning, and ultimately, a sense of belonging in the shared experience of his craft. His journey, like theirs, was a testament to the power of connection, even in the face of isolation.

Sarah's story echoed in her mind, the poignant narrative she had crafted weaving its way into the hearts of her readers. Her words, raw and honest, spoke of universal experiences of grief, loneliness, and the enduring strength of the human spirit. Her writing had become a conduit for empathy, a bridge connecting countless individuals who had once felt alone in their struggles. Her readers found solace in her words, comfort in her vulnerability. Sarah's journey underscored the power of artistic expression, not only as a form of personal catharsis, but also as a means of fostering connection and understanding.

The whispers of the afterlife brought Elara glimpses into the lives they had touched. She witnessed the shy teenager, emboldened by Liam's music, step into the spotlight, his own creative voice finding expression. She saw the grieving widow, comforted by Sarah's words, find the strength to rebuild her life, connecting with others who shared her pain. These weren't grand pronouncements of their influence; they were quiet moments, subtle shifts in fate, a gentle reminder that their actions had resonated far beyond their own lifetimes.

Even the family connections they had nurtured continued to blossom. Elara saw her aunt, once consumed by ambition, now radiating warmth and joy as she mentored young writers, sharing her knowledge and experience with a profound sense of purpose. The ties she had forged, the bonds she had strengthened, were a testament to the enduring power of human connection. Her uncle, once estranged, was now firmly reunited with his brother, their bond healed through a series of carefully orchestrated encounters – a testament to the power of forgiveness and shared history.

Lyra's art continued to inspire and heal. Elara saw its vibrant colors and textures bring comfort to those grappling with their own demons. Lyra's artwork became a mirror reflecting the shared human experience of grief, loss, and the resilience of the spirit. The young woman struggling with body image issues found empowerment in Lyra's art, celebrating the beauty of diversity. The man grappling with his grief found peace and validation in the raw emotion captured on canvas.

Their influence extended far beyond those closest to them. Elara saw the ripple effects of their actions, a widening circle of influence touching lives she could only glimpse, a collective awakening of empathy and compassion. It was a stunning testament to the potency of human connection, a network of support that transcended lifetimes. The quiet acts of kindness, the shared experiences, the shared vulnerability—these were the building blocks of a more compassionate world, a world woven together by the unseen threads of connection.

Their acceptance wasn't a surrender, but a profound understanding. They were not simply ceasing to exist, but transforming, evolving, shifting into a different plane of consciousness. The afterlife wasn't a void, but a realm of endless possibility, a space where the whispers of connection continued to resonate, shaping destinies and forging new bonds.

Elara felt the gentle warmth of Lyra's hand in hers. There was a profound sense of completion, a quiet understanding that their journey together wasn't over, merely evolving. They had found peace, not in an escape from the world, but in a deeper understanding of its intricate tapestry of relationships. Their legacies were not monuments of personal achievement, but the countless lives they had touched, the bonds they had strengthened, the ripple effect of their actions spreading out across the universe, a symphony of connection echoing through time and space. Their acceptance of their fate wasn't an end, but a beautiful, serene beginning.

A beginning woven into the very fabric of existence, a testament to the enduring power of human connection, a whispered promise of eternity. The vibrant colors of the afterlife shimmered around them, a testament to the ever-expanding beauty of connection. And in that beauty, they found eternal rest. Not an ending, but a transformation. Not a cessation, but a continuation. Not silence, but an eternal, harmonious hum. The hum of connection.

The iridescent light surrounding them pulsed gently, a rhythmic heartbeat echoing the serenity within. It wasn't a static peace, but a dynamic equilibrium, a constant flow of energy that felt both expansive and contained. They were no longer tethered to the frantic pace of the earthly realm, yet they remained connected, witnesses to the unfolding narratives of those they left behind. The whispers of the afterlife, once a chaotic chorus of voices, now formed a gentle lullaby, a symphony of interconnected lives.

Elara felt a wave of warmth wash over her, a feeling of profound completeness. It wasn't the absence of emotion, but a transformation of it. Grief, once a consuming fire, had been refined into a gentle ember, a source of understanding and empathy. Loss, once a gaping void, had become a space for growth, a fertile ground for new connections. The anxieties that had once plagued her, the relentless striving for external validation, had melted away, leaving behind a core of unwavering self-acceptance.

Lyra, beside her, exhaled softly, a sigh that seemed to carry the weight of a thousand unspoken anxieties. Her hands, once restless with the creative impulse, now lay still, yet they pulsed with a vibrant energy, a silent testament to her continued creative spirit. Her eyes, which had once held a flicker of uncertainty, now radiated a calm assurance, a knowing that transcended the limitations of earthly perception.

Their emotional harmony wasn't a passive state; it was an active process, a conscious choice to embrace the totality of their experience. It was a recognition of their interconnectedness, not only with each other, but with the vast, intricate web of life that extended far beyond their individual existence. They had found peace not by escaping their past, but by integrating it, by acknowledging its power to shape and define them, while simultaneously freeing themselves from its constraints.

The whispers of the afterlife continued to offer glimpses into the lives they had touched, revealing a tapestry of subtle influences, unexpected connections. They witnessed a young musician, inspired by Liam's courage to share his vulnerability, finally finding the confidence to release his own music, a soulful blend of hope and despair that resonated with a generation grappling with similar struggles. They saw a writer, emboldened by Sarah's honesty, begin to craft her own narrative, a powerful story of resilience that offered solace to countless readers.

Elara saw her aunt, once consumed by ambition, now dedicating her life to nurturing the next generation of writers, her wisdom and compassion shaping the lives of young artists who had been similarly touched by Liam's music and Sarah's stories. Her uncle, once estranged, was now reconnected with his brother, a reconciliation forged through acts of forgiveness and shared reminiscences. These weren't grand gestures, but quiet moments, tender acts of connection that reflected the ripple effect of their own commitment to building bridges, mending broken threads, and offering support in the face of loss.

The gentle whispers of the afterlife also revealed the impact of Lyra's art. Elara witnessed a young woman, once consumed by insecurities, finding strength and self-acceptance in Lyra's vibrant paintings. Lyra's bold strokes and fearless exploration of vulnerability became a mirror reflecting the shared human experience, offering comfort and validation to those who felt alone in their struggles. The young woman, previously burdened by body image issues, embraced her unique beauty, inspired by Lyra's celebration of diversity and self-expression. A grieving father found solace in a painting depicting the bittersweet beauty of loss, acknowledging the pain while simultaneously celebrating the enduring power of love.

Even the smallest actions echoed through time, creating a cascade of positive change. Elara saw a random act of kindness, a shared smile, a moment of empathetic understanding, all stemming from the seeds of compassion they had sown during their lives. Each act of generosity, each moment of vulnerability, each connection they had fostered, had rippled outward, creating an ever-expanding circle of positive influence.

Their emotional harmony wasn't a destination, but a continuous journey, a dynamic dance between acceptance and growth. They were evolving, expanding, transforming, continually learning and growing from the endless stream of connections that surrounded them. The afterlife wasn't a static realm, but a vibrant, ever-changing landscape, a testament to the ceaseless interplay of life, death, and renewal.

The whispers of the afterlife transformed into a gentle hum, a resonant frequency that vibrated through their very being, confirming their deep connection to the world they had left behind. It was a hum of gratitude, a recognition of the profound impact they had made, the lives they had touched, the legacy of love and compassion they had created. The celestial light that surrounded them pulsed with an ever-increasing intensity, mirroring the radiant energy emanating from within them.

They weren't simply observing the lives they'd influenced; they were participating in them, albeit in a way that transcended the limitations of physical form. They felt a sense of responsibility, a gentle obligation to continue to guide and support those they cared about, to be a quiet presence, a source of strength and inspiration. Their presence in the afterlife was not a passive observation but an active participation, a continuation of their commitment to building a world woven together by unseen threads of connection. They had found their peace not in escape but in a profound understanding of their enduring connection to the universe and its inhabitants.

The serene landscape surrounding them—the celestial expanse of shimmering stars and nebulae—mirrored the boundless possibilities of their new existence. They were not static beings, but evolving entities, constantly expanding their understanding, deepening their connections, and embracing the transformative power of love and compassion. The iridescent veil that separated them from the living world wasn't a barrier, but a permeable membrane, allowing a constant flow of energy and connection between their realms.

Their emotional harmony was not a conclusion, but a continuation of their journey, a transition to a new chapter filled with infinite possibilities. The grief and loss they had experienced had forged a profound empathy within them, enabling them to connect with others on a deeper level. Their experience had transformed them, making them more compassionate, more understanding, and more capable of embracing the beauty and fragility of life. Their peace was not an escape from suffering, but a transcendence of it, a conscious choice to embrace the totality of existence, in all its joy and sorrow.

The whispers of the afterlife, now a harmonious chorus, carried a message of hope, a promise of enduring connection. They were not simply gone, but transformed, existing in a different state of being, their impact reverberating through time and space. Their journey was not over; it had merely shifted form, evolving into a new expression of their enduring connection to the world and each other.

And in that profound understanding, they found true and eternal rest—a state of being that transcended the limitations of mortality, a testament to the enduring power of love and the indomitable spirit of the human heart. The shimmering colors of the afterlife wrapped around them, a gentle embrace, a promise of eternal connection. The hum of connection resonated deeply within, a symphony of peace, a testament to the enduring power of love and the beautiful, harmonious eternity they had found.

The iridescent light continued to bathe them, a gentle warmth that permeated their very beings. It wasn't the absence of feeling, but a profound shift in their perception of emotion. Grief, once a jagged, unforgiving landscape, had been sculpted into something softer, more nuanced. It was a landscape dotted with wildflowers, each blooming memory, a poignant reminder of the love they had shared, the life they had lived. The pain remained, a subtle ache in the heart, but it was no longer a crippling weight. It was a part of them, woven into the fabric of their being, a testament to the depth of their experience.

Their love, once a vibrant flame that burned with an intense passion, had transformed into a deep, unwavering ember. It was a constant, steady glow, a source of strength and comfort in the vast expanse of the afterlife. It wasn't the romantic, tempestuous love of their earthly existence, but something deeper, more profound, a connection that transcended the limitations of physical form. They were bound together not by flesh and blood, but by the invisible threads of shared memories, intertwined dreams, and a profound understanding that had blossomed over years of shared laughter, tears, and whispered secrets.

Elara reached out, her hand passing through Lyra's, a gesture that spoke volumes. The touch wasn't physical, but felt more potent, a connection that transcended space and time. They felt each other's presence, a constant, unwavering companionship that filled the void left by the physical separation. It wasn't a neediness, but an affirmation, a silent recognition of their enduring bond.

They could still feel the subtle ripples of their impact on the living world. They saw a young artist, struggling with self-doubt, finding inspiration in Lyra's bold canvases.

Her art, once a source of personal expression, had become a beacon of hope for others, a testament to the power of vulnerability and self-acceptance. They watched as the young artist, empowered by Lyra's legacy, began to create her own unique style, her brushstrokes infused with a newfound confidence. Her work blossomed, carrying a hint of Lyra's vibrant spirit, a quiet tribute to a life cut short, yet indelibly etched in the hearts and minds of those who had been touched by her art.

Elara witnessed a young man, burdened by grief, finding solace in the music Liam had left behind. The songs, once expressions of personal turmoil, became a universal language, connecting with listeners who had endured similar hardships. The music transcended its original intent, becoming a soundtrack to the healing process for countless others. Liam's music offered comfort, validation, and a shared space of grief, helping others navigate the dark waters of loss. His melodies echoed through time, a constant reminder of the resilience of the human spirit and the unifying power of music.

Their influence wasn't limited to specific individuals; it rippled outwards, touching the lives of countless others in ways they couldn't have imagined. A young writer, inspired by Sarah's courage and honesty, found the strength to share her own story, a powerful narrative that resonated with readers all over the world. Sarah's words, once a personal struggle, had transformed into a beacon of hope, offering solace and understanding to others who had experienced similar journeys. Her words, infused with her passion and resilience, became a testament to the transformative power of storytelling.

The whispers of the afterlife became a chorus of affirmation, a testament to the enduring impact of their shared life. They were not merely observers, but active participants in the unfolding narratives of the world they had left behind. They were guiding lights, their love a beacon illuminating the paths of those they left behind, offering solace, support, and inspiration.

The vibrant colors of the afterlife shifted and changed, mirroring the constant flux of life and death, of loss and renewal. They witnessed moments of joy, acts of kindness, and displays of unwavering love. They saw the tangible effects of their life, ripples spreading through time, carrying with them their influence, their compassion.

Their bond transcended the realm of physical proximity; it was a tapestry woven from shared experiences, from years of unspoken understanding and unwavering support. Their love wasn't a fleeting emotion but a constant, a timeless connection that defied the boundaries of death.

The afterlife was not a static state but a continuous journey, a boundless expanse where their love grew and evolved. It wasn't simply an absence of the physical world, but a transition into a different state of being, a state where the boundaries of perception blurred, and the limitations of the physical form dissolved.

They saw families reunited, friendships rekindled, and hearts healed. They witnessed acts of courage, resilience, and forgiveness, each an echo of the values they had cherished in life. Their influence was subtle, like a gentle breeze that stirred the leaves, causing a cascade of positive change.

It was a beautiful, intricate dance of connection, a testament to the enduring power of love and the ripple effect of human compassion. They had not merely lived; they had made a difference. They had touched hearts, inspired souls, and left a legacy that would continue to resonate through the ages. Their impact was not confined to their earthly existence; it continued to unfold, an ever-expanding circle of influence that transcended time and space.

The celestial music of the afterlife enveloped them, a symphony of peace and understanding. The humming light, once a gentle pulse, now shone with an incandescent brilliance, reflecting the radiant energy of their love. It was a love that transcended mortality, a love that had become part of the very fabric of existence, a testament to the indomitable strength of the human heart.

They were not merely remembered, they were felt, their presence permeating the lives of those they had touched. Their love was not an ending, but a transformation, a continuation of their journey in a new and transcendent realm. It was a realm where the limitations of physical form ceased to matter, a realm where their love would endure, eternally vibrant, a beacon of hope in the vast expanse of existence. They had found peace not in escaping the pain, but in embracing it, transforming it into a source of empathy and compassion, a profound understanding of the human experience in all its complexity and beauty. And in that profound acceptance, they found true eternal rest, a testament to the enduring power of love that transcended even death itself. The light pulsed, a constant, unwavering rhythm, a heartbeat echoing the enduring power of their love, an eternal testament to the beauty and strength of their connection.

The iridescent light pulsed, a gentle rhythm mirroring the steady beat of a heart. It wasn't the silence of oblivion, but the quiet hum of existence, a symphony of interconnectedness that enveloped Elara and Lyra. They weren't merely passive observers in this ethereal realm; they were active participants, their love a vibrant thread woven into the tapestry of the afterlife. They felt the subtle ripples of their influence spreading through time, a gentle current carrying their message of hope to those left behind.

They saw a young mother, her heart heavy with the recent loss of her own mother, finding comfort in a worn photograph of Lyra, a woman she'd never met but whose paintings had graced her grandmother's walls for as long as she could remember. The vibrant colours of Lyra's canvases, now faded with age, seemed to hold a warmth, a comforting presence that resonated with the young mother's grief. Lyra's art, which once captured the essence of her own vibrant spirit, had become a silent, unwavering companion, offering solace to a stranger across generations. The young mother found herself tracing the brushstrokes, feeling a connection to the artist, feeling less alone in her sorrow.

Liam's music echoed in unexpected places. A group of teenagers, grappling with the uncertainties and anxieties of adolescence, found solace in his melodies. The songs, once born from Liam's personal struggles, became a universal anthem for navigating the turbulent waters of youth. His music spoke of vulnerability, of hope found in unexpected places, a language that transcended age and experience.

It fostered a sense of community, a shared understanding of emotional turmoil, and a reminder that they weren't alone in their struggles. They discovered in his music a strength they hadn't known they possessed, a strength to face their fears and embrace their imperfections.

Sarah's words continued their journey, echoing in the hearts of countless readers. A young writer, battling depression, found in Sarah's honest, vulnerable storytelling the courage to share her own experiences. Sarah's story, once a confession of pain and uncertainty, became a lifeline for others, a testament to the power of vulnerability and the transformative power of self-expression. The young writer discovered that by sharing her story, she wasn't alone in her struggle; she created a bridge of understanding and offered comfort to those who had previously felt utterly isolated. Their shared experiences connected them, weaving a tapestry of resilience and hope.

Elara and Lyra watched as these seemingly unconnected events unfolded, their actions a cascade of positive change rippling outwards, touching lives in myriad ways.

They saw the quiet acts of kindness, the unexpected moments of compassion, the slow, steady healing that blossomed from their legacy. It wasn't a grand, sweeping gesture, but a quiet symphony of connection, a testament to the enduring power of love and human connection.

Their influence wasn't limited to the emotional sphere. They saw the young artist's work exhibited in a prestigious gallery, receiving critical acclaim and influencing a new generation of artists. They saw Liam's music played on the radio, its melodies traveling across continents, offering comfort and understanding to people from diverse backgrounds. They saw Sarah's book translated into numerous languages, empowering individuals to confront their own personal struggles and find their voice. Their love had transcended the boundaries of their earthly existence, their legacy an ever-expanding ripple effect, touching the lives of countless individuals across time and space.

The ethereal landscape shimmered with a thousand hues, each color representing a life touched, a heart healed, a spirit strengthened. It wasn't a static tableau, but a dynamic canvas, ever-changing, ever-evolving, reflecting the constant flux of life and loss, of grief and renewal. The vibrant colors pulsed with a life of their own, a testament to the enduring power of human connection and the transformative power of love.

Elara and Lyra were not merely spectators; they were active participants in this ongoing narrative, their love a guiding light, their influence a gentle breeze that stirred the leaves of countless lives. Their presence wasn't a forceful intervention, but a subtle whisper of hope, a quiet affirmation that even in the face of loss and despair, love and compassion could prevail.

They witnessed the birth of new relationships, the strengthening of existing bonds, and the healing of old wounds. They saw acts of forgiveness, of self-acceptance, of unwavering resilience.

Each moment was a testament to the enduring strength of the human spirit, a quiet reflection of the values they had cherished in life – love, compassion, and the unwavering belief in the power of human connection.

Their love wasn't a possessive claim but a boundless wellspring of empathy and understanding. It was a quiet strength that supported those left behind, a silent reassurance that they weren't alone in their journeys. It was a beacon of hope, illuminating the paths of those who had been touched by their lives, guiding them through the darkness towards the light.

The afterlife wasn't a static realm of stillness and silence, but a vibrant tapestry of experience. It was a realm of profound connection, where the boundaries of space and time dissolved, and the threads of shared experiences intertwined to create a boundless network of love and compassion. Their influence was a gentle current, flowing through the ages, carrying with it a message of hope, a testament to the enduring power of human connection.

The music of the afterlife wasn't a discordant symphony of sorrow but a harmonious blend of joy and grief, a testament to the full spectrum of human experience. It was a melody of understanding, a rhythmic pulse of interconnectedness, a reminder that even in the depths of sorrow, love and compassion could prevail.

They realized their love wasn't simply a memory, a fleeting emotion confined to the past. It was a timeless connection, a vibrant force that continued to shape the world they had left behind. It was a legacy of kindness, a testament to the strength found in vulnerability, and a quiet affirmation of the enduring power of human love. Their impact was subtle yet profound, a constant hum of hope resonating through the fabric of existence.

The light that enveloped them wasn't merely an illumination of their surroundings but a reflection of their own enduring love, a radiant energy that permeated the very fabric of their existence. It was a light that shone not only in the afterlife but also in the hearts of those they had left behind, guiding them, comforting them, and inspiring them to live lives filled with meaning and purpose.

Their journey wasn't an end, but a transformation, a transition into a new realm of understanding and connection. It was a realm where their love transcended the limitations of the physical world, a realm where their influence continued to unfold, an ever-expanding circle of hope, a testament to the enduring power of love that defied even the boundaries of death itself. And in that profound understanding, in that boundless love, they found true eternal rest. Their love was not a memory to be mourned, but a legacy to be cherished, a beacon of hope illuminating the paths of others, a testament to the enduring power of the human spirit. The light pulsed, a constant, unwavering rhythm, a heartbeat echoing the eternal love that transcended time and space.

The iridescent light, once a novelty, now felt like a second skin. Elara and Lyra, intertwined in this ethereal embrace, were no longer merely observers but integral parts of a vast, cosmic symphony. The hum of existence wasn't a static drone; it pulsed with the rhythm of countless lives, each a unique note contributing to the overall harmony. They saw their influence not as grand, sweeping gestures, but as a gentle, persistent breeze, subtly shifting the course of countless lives.

They witnessed a young artist, inspired by Lyra's vibrant canvases, create a breathtaking sculpture that captured the essence of raw emotion, the kind of emotion that Lyra had so masterfully conveyed through her paintings. This sculpture, a testament to Lyra's enduring influence, became a symbol of hope and resilience, offering solace to those grappling with their own inner turmoil.

They saw the sculpture traveling to museums around the world, becoming an icon of modern art, its message of hope resonating with viewers from all walks of life. It wasn't a direct imitation of Lyra's work, but rather a unique interpretation, a blossoming of creativity inspired by the spirit of the artist. This artist, in turn, became a mentor, guiding other young artists on their creative journeys, perpetuating the chain of inspiration that originated from Lyra's legacy.

Liam's music, once a vessel for his personal struggles, transformed into a soundtrack for countless others' journeys. They witnessed a young musician, lost in a labyrinth of self-doubt, rediscover his passion after listening to Liam's songs.

Liam's melodies, imbued with a raw honesty that resonated deeply with the young musician, became a catalyst for his creative rebirth. He wrote his own songs, inspired by Liam's vulnerability and his unwavering commitment to his art, and found his unique voice, becoming a celebrated singer-songwriter in his own right. His concerts became sanctuaries for those grappling with emotional turmoil, and he established a foundation to help aspiring musicians overcome their own obstacles. This foundation became a beacon of hope for countless young artists, ensuring that the spirit of Liam's music lived on through future generations of musicians.

Sarah's words, once a raw confession of personal pain, evolved into a guiding light for countless readers. They observed a shy young writer, initially hesitant to share their own vulnerabilities, finding the courage to express their experiences through their craft, inspired by Sarah's powerful prose. Sarah's book became a companion, a confidant, for countless readers across the world. It was translated into multiple languages and adapted into film, reaching a global audience and creating a worldwide community.

Through Sarah's story, people found validation, reassurance, and the strength to share their own narratives, creating a powerful network of empathy and understanding. It served as a testament to the transformative power of shared human experiences, empowering individuals to conquer their personal demons and find their unique voice.

Beyond the tangible achievements, Elara and Lyra observed a deeper, more profound shift. They saw acts of unexpected kindness, small gestures of compassion that rippled outwards, creating a chain reaction of positivity. A stranger helping another in need, a simple act of forgiveness bridging a fractured relationship, a quiet word of encouragement lifting someone's spirits – these seemingly insignificant events, multiplied countless times, created a wave of positivity and healing. They witnessed the ripple effect of their love, not as individual achievements, but as a collective tapestry woven from countless threads of human connection.

Their love wasn’t a possessive force; it was an overflowing wellspring of empathy, a silent reassurance that extended to everyone they had touched. It wasn't about claiming ownership but about sharing a legacy of love, compassion, and unwavering resilience. They saw their love reflected in the faces of those they left behind; in the strength of the grieving mother, the passion of the young musician, the courage of the hesitant writer, the kindness of strangers. They recognized it in the quiet moments of human connection, the small gestures of compassion that became the foundation of a more compassionate world.

The afterlife wasn’t a static realm; it was a vibrant tapestry of evolving experiences, a constant exchange of energies, a boundless network of connection. It wasn’t about a cessation of life, but a transformation, a continuation of existence in a new dimension. It was a place where the barriers of space and time blurred, and the threads of shared experiences intertwined to create a beautiful, complex mosaic of human connection. They realized that death wasn't an ending, but a transition—a move from one stage of existence to another, a continuation of their love story in a realm beyond human comprehension.

Elara and Lyra found peace in the understanding that their impact extended far beyond their earthly existence. Their love, once a flame burning brightly in their hearts, had become a radiant beacon illuminating the lives of countless others. It wasn't a forced imposition but a gentle guiding light, a soft whisper of hope in moments of despair, a silent affirmation that love perseveres, even in the face of loss and sorrow. Their legacy wasn't confined to the tangible achievements of their loved ones; it was etched into the collective consciousness of humanity, a reminder that even in the deepest darkness, love can endure.

Their love story wasn't merely a tale of romance; it was a testament to the power of human connection, a demonstration of how a single act of love could ripple outwards, creating waves of positivity and compassion that touched generations. It served as a testament to the enduring strength of the human spirit, a reflection of their values – love, compassion, and unwavering belief in the power of human connection.

Their story was not an ending but a beginning—a transition to a new stage where their love would continue to inspire and uplift those left behind, echoing through time and resonating in the hearts of countless individuals across generations to come.

The iridescent light pulsed, a gentle rhythm echoing the heartbeat of their eternal love. It was a testament to their enduring connection, a symbol of their unwavering love that transcended the boundaries of life and death. It was a light that shone not only in this ethereal realm but also in the hearts of those they had touched, guiding them, comforting them, and inspiring them to live lives filled with purpose and meaning.

Their love was not a memory to be mourned, but a legacy to be cherished, a testament to the enduring power of the human spirit. The light pulsed, a constant, unwavering rhythm, a heartbeat echoing their eternal love, a love that transcended time and space, a love that would continue to inspire and uplift for generations to come.

In the radiant glow of their eternal love, they found true and lasting peace. The afterlife wasn't an ending, but a beginning – a breathtaking, ever-expanding vista of connectedness, fueled by the eternal, resonant power of their love. And in that profound understanding, in that boundless love, they found true eternal rest.

www.ingramcontent.com/pod-product-compliance
Lightning Source LLC
Chambersburg PA
CBHW060634310726
48982CB00003B/772
* 9 7 9 8 9 9 9 8 4 6 0 9 9 *